The Bone Witcher of Knob Mountain

Intuitive Investigations, Book One

BECKI WILLIS

ISBN: 978-1-947686-36-6

CONTENTS

1

Willow Alexander didn't consider herself particularly superstitious.

But even a non-believer such as herself knew that when the door opened at exactly thirty-three minutes past three on the third day of March—3-3, 3:33—trouble was brewing.

The old man didn't look like the typical troublemaker. A few decades ago, perhaps, but not now, and not in his current state. Dried mud and motor oil had settled into the creases of his rumpled clothes, and the smell of a wood fire clouded the air around him. His shock of white hair escaped in all directions, bringing to mind Albert Einstein. The difference was in the eyes. This man's were a rheumy blue, their color and vitality fading with each passing year. If not for the prick of apprehension dancing along her skull, Willow might feel sorry for him.

The air had a sudden chill to it. Intuition told her that a storm had followed him in.

Willow glanced at the other woman in the room. If Everleigh felt the change, she didn't let it show. Her smile was as friendly and effervescent as always. "Welcome to Intuitive Investigations. How can we help you today, sir?"

Her friendly demeanor was the perfect buffer for first-time clients. Approaching a private detective agency could be daunting for most people, but her smile helped put them at ease.

Without preamble, the old man blurted, "I know who killed them boys."

With a sharp intake of breath, Willow pushed away from her desk and approached the raggedy old man. "I'm Willow Alexander." She extended her hand with what passed as a smile. "And you are?"

The hand he offered was stiff from arthritis, and marred from age and hard work. Willow was surprised to feel the strength in his grip. "Gus McMurray."

"It's a pleasure to meet you, Mr. McMurray." She motioned to the other woman. "This is Everleigh, my daughter and one of my partners. Why don't we have a seat and discuss your situation."

"I ain't got a situation. I got answers to a twenty-five-year-old mystery, and I aim to get it off my chest, once and for all!" Gus McMurray punctuated the bold claim by banging his fist on the edge of Everleigh's desk.

"I understand that, Mr. McMurray, but we really need more information than that in order to help you."

Exasperated, the older gentleman threw his arms out to his sides. "What more is there to say? Those boys went missing in the hills twenty odd years ago, they're dead, and I know exactly who killed them!"

Willow had no doubt as to his sincerity. It was his mental acuity she questioned. "I'd really like to hear more. Please, let's step into the next room so we can talk privately."

"I done spilled the beans in front of her," he said, hitching his thumb toward Everleigh.

"I meant from anyone who might come in from the street. Everleigh will be joining us, of course."

Willow led the way into the adjoining conference room.

The older man was hesitant to follow. Undaunted, Everleigh took his arm and started chatting as she gently led him forward. "Do you like coffee, Mr. McMurray? Please tell me you'll join me for a cup. We have a new machine, and I just love using it! It makes regular coffee, of course, but if you like lattes or cappuccinos, I can whip up one in just a jiffy. Just say the word."

A bit confused by the little whirlwind beside him, he managed a stuttered, "Uh, I reckon just a normal coffee. I don't even know what them other things are."

She flashed him another bright smile. "No problem! You have a seat right here, and I'll grab our coffees." She thoughtfully led him to the chair with the highest seat, guessing that his joints didn't move as easily as they once had.

The room was designed to feel more like a living room/dining room than a place of business. A small leather settee and several armchairs created an intimate conversation area, all upholstered in warm beiges, browns, and blues. Behind them was an antique dining room set that doubled as the conference table. Everything about the room was warm, inviting, and meant to put clients at ease.

"Tell us a little bit about yourself," Willow encouraged while they settled into their seats. "Where do you live? I don't believe we've ever met before."

"Not far from the border, 'bout twenty miles into the hills." He offered a backward nod of his head to indicate the direction.

Perched so close to the Missouri-Arkansas line, *Intuitive Investigations* was licensed in both states. Their cases often crisscrossed between the two.

"If you don't mind me asking, how did you hear about us?"

The keen old gentleman knew what Willow was doing. "Look." His manner was straight forward. "There's no need to chatter. I've been keeping this secret bottled up inside me for too long now, and it's ready to bust plumb out of my soul!"

"Why *have* you kept this bottled up for so many years, Mr. McMurray?"

A fine bead of sweat formed on the old man's forehead. He pulled a handkerchief from the pocket of his overalls, ran it across his face, and stuffed it back in its place. "Fear, I reckon. Or stupidity. But my days are numbered now, and I don't want to meet my maker with this burden weighing down my heart. It's time to tell the truth. Those young 'uns deserve as much."

There was no need for Willow to pretend she didn't know what boys he meant. Their disappearance had been the biggest mystery to rock the hills since the gruesome murder of Ella Barham in 1912.

Everleigh returned with three cups of steaming coffee balanced on a tray. Placing it on the coffee table, she narrowed her eyes and murmured, "Three college boys from the city were here to film a small-time documentary on the legend of the Flaming Woman, but they never returned home. Right?"

"Right," Willow confirmed. "It was after that teenage horror movie came out, the one about the witch in the woods. The boys used the premise to make their own version based on local legend."

"That's the movie I rented for a slumber party, and you made us turn off halfway into it!" Everleigh accused.

Her mother sniffed. "It had filthy language, a ridiculous premise, and was hardly suitable for preteens."

Gus McMurray wasn't interested in hearing their squabble. The horror he experienced was far worse, because it had been real.

Stopping her rant abruptly, Willow's tone was contrite. "I apologize, Mr. McMurray. We didn't mean to get side-tracked, but I do believe that was the catalyst for those boys being here. But their bodies were never found. There's no proof there was a crime committed, or that they didn't make it out of the mountains alive."

He countered with, "There's no proof they did, neither."

"Can you tell us why you believe the boys are dead?"

"I told you. I *know* they're dead because I know

who killed them!"

They were getting nowhere, and Willow's patience was thin. "And who would that be, sir? Who do you think killed those boys?"

"I don't think," he repeated stubbornly. "I know!"

"Have you gone to the sheriff with this information?"

It wasn't a trick question, but the old man's entire countenance changed. He slid a nervous glance toward the door. His bushy brows bunched together, creating the illusion of a hairy caterpillar crawling across his forehead. "Goin' to the sheriff would be a mistake."

"I don't understand, Mr. McMurray," Willow said with a sigh. "You say a crime was committed, but that you can't go to the sheriff. What is it you think we can do that he can't?"

"You can help me find the proof."

"Proof?" Everleigh all but squeaked. "I thought *you* had the proof."

"Not 'xactly," he admitted. "I ain't wrong, but I ain't got all the proof I need to prove it, neither. That's why I want to hire you ladies. You've earned yourself a reputation of getting results, and results is what I need."

"That's our goal, Mr. McMurray," Willow assured him as her voice gentled. "But we didn't earn that reputation by going into a situation unprepared. That's why you need to start from the beginning and tell us everything you know."

Gus rubbed his fingers across his forehead, concentrating on where and how to begin.

"Near 'bout twenty-five years ago, I was out trappin' in the woods when I heard a ruckus. I followed the sound and saw two of them boys up near Kinney Knob, arguing with an older fella. The third boy was peeking out from around a bush, filming the whole thing. Next thing I know, there's a scuffle, and one of them boys goes flying off the ridge." Gus shook his white head in sorrow. His disbelief was palatable, even after all these years. "The second boy fought back, but the man pulled out a knife. He used it on that poor boy, then pushed him over the edge, same as his friend."

Everleigh's blue eyes filled with empathy.

Willow managed a whispered sentence. "He pushed them over the side of the ridge? But... that's at least a thirty-foot drop! Onto more rock, no less. What did you do?"

His chin dropped to his chest. "It's what I didn't do that haunts me," he mumbled. It took him a moment to collect himself. When Gus finally lifted his head, his eyes were clouded as he stared into the past.

"Everyone knew them boys were there to make a film. At first, I reckoned the fight was part of it. There'd be a safety net over the edge to catch the boys when they fell."

"When did you realize that wasn't part of the film?" Willow asked softly.

"When the man pulled the knife. Even that could have been part of it, I reckoned, even if the blood looked real. Then the third boy cried out. The first two hollered when they went over, but I figured that, too, was all for show. But that third boy..." Gus pulled his hand over his face. "It was like a wounded animal. I heard a mama panther screech like that one time when her baby was killed by a poacher. The sound sent chills all through my body."

He needed another moment before continuing. "The man whirled around and saw the boy cowering there by the bush. Quick as a wink, the boy pushed his camera under a clump of leaves and old branches."

Both women sat at the edges of their seats, knowing, yet dreading, the outcome of his story. It was like watching a terrible accident unfolding before their eyes. They knew what was coming, but they were unable to do anything about it. It was too horrible to see. Too painful to imagine. Yet still they watched.

"And then?" Everleigh breathed.

"There was another ruckus. The man was yelling, wanting to know how much the boy saw. The boy lied, but it was no use. The man punched him hard, knocking him to the ground. He didn't even bother with the knife. He just kept on, beatin' and beatin' and beatin'. I ain't never seen a man so angry."

"He didn't know you were there?" Willow guessed.

Swallowing hard, Gus shook his head. "I might could have saved that boy, but I was a coward. While he was beating that boy to a pulp, I slipped back into the woods. The last thing I saw was the man kicking the boy's body over the side of Kinney Ridge."

Silence thrummed throughout the room. It took a moment for them all to catch their breaths.

"Not a minute goes by," Gus said in a broken

voice, "that I don't regret my cowardly ways."

It would do no good to condemn the old man. What was done was done, and his grief was plain to see. "How did you get away?" Willow asked.

"I grabbed the camera and hid there until dark. Didn't go down until I was sure the man was long gone."

"You got the camera?" Everleigh asked excitedly, impressed he had thought to grab it.

"Snatched it on my way out. Took it home with me but didn't know what to do with it."

"You could have started by taking it to the sheriff," Willow pointed out.

"Told you," he insisted stubbornly, "I couldn't do that. I had my family to think of, and I was no match for money and power. No one would've believed an old mountain boy like me."

She chose to overlook his foolhardy notion for the moment. "Do you still have the camera?"

He squirmed in his seat. "Not 'xactly."

"So, you hid the only proof you had, and now you've lost it?"

"I haven't 'xactly lost it. I just don't know where it is."

Everleigh cocked her head to one side, sending red curls tumbling. "Did you somehow misplace the camera?"

"You might say that. You see, I hid it, but it ain't there no more."

"What do you think happened to it?"

"My boy cleaned out the shed a few weeks back. I reckon he may have sold it like he did most of the other stuff." He mumbled something about no respect for history and tradition.

"Have you asked him?" Willow wanted to know.

"Can't, at least for now. He went off on one of them retreats." He waved his weathered hand by his temple, snorting with disapproval. "Supposed to give him clarity and cleanse his soul, or some other such nonsense."

"When will he be back?"

"With Gideon, you never know. He disappeared for almost a year without nary a word. If we hadn't just buried my Delta, it would have plumb killed her."

Willow couldn't imagine not seeing her own daughter for that long. Her voice softened as she said, "I take it you don't want to wait for him to return so that you can ask him."

Gus McMurray pushed a hand through his spiky white hair. That explained the Einstein look he sported. "Don't have time for that," he answered in a gruff voice.

Not unsympathetically, Willow stood her ground. "I'm still not sure how you think we can help."

"I can't go runnin' around, checking out every pawn shop and resale store on either side of the state line! I want to hire you to find that movie camera, then you can help me prove who killed them boys."

"Mr. McMurray—"

He stopped her before she could say anything more. "Would you really deny a dying man?" he challenged. His rheumy eyes bore into hers.

Willow shifted uncomfortably in her seat. A sense of danger danced in the air, pricking at her skin.

She sent Everleigh a questioning look, wondering if she felt the same foreboding.

Concern warred with sympathy in the younger woman's sapphire-blue eyes. After the slightest hesitation, Everleigh offered a subtle nod.

Willow trusted her daughter's instincts. "I'm still not sure how much we'll be able to help you, Mr. McMurray, but yes. We'll take your case."

Relief flooded his face. "I 'preciate this, ladies. You don't know how burdened I've been all these years, holding in a dark secret like this. It's high time it saw the light of day."

Willow nodded. "We'll need to draw up a contract and have you sign it."

"I reckon you'll be needing some money, too." He struggled to his feet so he could dig into the front pocket of his overalls.

"Yes, but we'll need to discuss your budget and—"

He cut her off as he handed her a wad of bills. Along with the musky notes of old paper, Willow detected a whiff of coffee. She guessed his piggy bank came in the form of an old coffee can. "Should be a thousand dollars there," he told her. "That should get you started."

"Yes, but—"

Gus McMurray interrupted her again. "I've done had my truck parked outside long enough. Come around tomorrow morning, and I'll sign your papers and take you to the place it all happened. Show you the cupboard, too, where the camera was last time I saw it."

He gave them no time to respond. Once his

joints warmed up, he walked with surprising speed and agility. He was halfway to the front door by the time the women thought to follow.

"We don't even know where you live," Everleigh protested.

"Near the top of Scrimshaw Ridge. Turn right off Carter Loop, cross Carter Springs, and you'll see a log house to the right. That ain't me. Turn at the next mailbox and follow the road up to the house. Can't see it from the road, but it's there." He turned back as he opened the door. "My Delta got a notion to paint the front door bright red. I hated it at the time, but I've become right fond of it through the years." The memory roughened his voice more than it already was. He looked at the younger woman. "It won't be nothing fancy, but I'll put a pot of coffee on when you come."

Everleigh lightly touched his arm and smiled. "That sounds lovely, Mr. Murray. We'll see you in the morning."

The women watched as Gus McMurray paused on the sidewalk, glancing up and down the street before climbing into his two-toned brown and tan truck. It was a classic holdover from the 70s.

"Did you see that?" Everleigh murmured. "I wonder who he's afraid will see him here."

"I don't know. But that man is definitely afraid of something."

"Or someone."

"You touched his arm," Willow pointed out.

"It didn't help. It all felt jumbled."

Willow studied the busy street on the other side of the window. "Do you think he's mentally stable? Maybe his feelings are jumbled together because his mind is, too. His memory of the events could be off."

"I don't think so. He was so adamant about the details."

Willow continued to study the town beyond their window. As the workday wound down, patrons made a last-minute dash into businesses. Traffic ticked up a beat. Soon, the streetlights would flicker on, beginning on the east end of the street and working their way west. At precisely 4:32, Mrs. Helm across the street would flip the sign on her door to *Closed*, signaling that *The Book Store* was no longer accepting customers. Despite the hours stenciled on the glass, the old woman adhered to a strict twenty-eight-minute early start, early close. Not twenty-five. Not thirty. Always twenty-eight.

It was just one of the many quirks about the town of Border. Their pharmacy still had a soda fountain, where the owners served ice cream delights and richly blended sodas in frosted glass dishes. Parking meters still dotted the street, the old-fashioned kind, accepting coins and parking stickers only, with no option for credit cards. Some citizens pushed for free downtown parking like there was at the shopping center out by the highway, but the meters' proceeds went toward the Main Street Project Fund.

Tucked among the mom-and-pop businesses stood a pizza shop bearing the logo of a national brand. With the post office situated next door, letters and packages often held the faint hint of pepperoni. The benches spaced along the sidewalks were where husbands waited patiently for wives to shop, and where Bobby Ray Neyland and Tully Brown visited every Monday morning. It was a known fact that a 'secret' poker game took place in the back room of the barber shop every other Tuesday night.

Slow in coming, Willow's reply held caution. "I'm inclined to agree with you. I believe he's telling us the truth," she said. "At least, his version of the truth. His memories could have become skewered over the years, or maybe he prefers his version over reality."

"Do you think he's protecting someone?"

"Not necessarily. I just don't think he's telling us the whole truth." Her eyes narrowed. "He's holding something back."

"I know that look on your face," Everleigh said. "You sense something, don't you?"

There was no denying the fact that her skin still prickled. No denying the shadows edging in on the street.

Still gazing out the window, Willow whispered, "Danger. I sense danger."

2

KARNIE

People called her the Old Mountain Witch. Her name was Karnie—no one was certain if it was her first or last name—and her age was indeterminable; even Karnie had lost track of the years.

She lived on the side of Knob Mountain in a log cabin as weathered as she was. The cabin was so old, it could have sprouted from the rocky soil alongside the oak and hickory saplings. The trees were mature now, towering over the little structure and cradling it within their protective arms.

Built by her ancestors, the cabin looked much the same today as it had a hundred years ago. No power lines stretched overhead. No phone lines hung from pole to pole. No blacktop road squiggled its way over the boulders and bushes, connecting her to the outside world. Just two simple ruts marked the way to her humble abode.

Two stone chimneys still defined the roofline. Sometime in the early 30s, the cabin was upgraded with a wood-burning stove in the kitchen. Even now, most any time of day, any time of year, smoke wafted from at least one of the three to mingle with the fresh mountain air. There was still a tin-roofed porch running the length of the cabin. It still had the same set of stone steps, although the mortar had been patched over time. It was the same with the chinking between the logs. Every so often, the current occupant of the cabin had to reseal or replace it, but the structure remained sound. It seemed time marched on, yet the cabin stayed the same.

Karnie was fine with things staying the same. She liked the consistency of the familiar. Sound footing was important in life, and the old ways—the tried-and-true methods her parents had used, and their parents before them, and their parents before them—were better than these new-fangled notions folks had nowadays. Her way of thinking hadn't failed her yet.

She was completely self-reliant here on her mountain. She had fresh water, a fine vegetable garden, wild fruits and nuts, more wood than she could burn in a lifetime (which was admittedly growing shorter with each passing day), fish in the nearby creek, wild game she could harvest, and all the creature comforts she needed. Best of all, she knew how to use the plentiful herbs, plants, and trees that grew around her. She knew which charms and chants made the natural products more potent, and she could dig into the rich earth to find a variety of resources. Roots. Water sources. Even buried bones.

Karnie wasn't just known as the Mountain Witch. Some used the term douser because she could witch for water. Others called her the Bone Witcher, because she could find old bones, no matter how deep they lay beneath the soil.

That was her mission today. She was witching for bones. She needed the bones of three different animals to make a powerful poultice for Merv Ridley. His bones were weak and brittle from age, and with his latest fall, he had broken his arm. His wife was worried it would be a hip next time, so she asked Karnie to make him a charm to strengthen his bones.

Karnie headed out from the cabin, careful to latch the door. She didn't want what heat she had accumulated overnight to escape through a half-latched door. She was dressed much the way she always was, in faded blue jeans, layered shirts, and boots. Today she had on her fur-lined, rubber-soled ones. It could be treacherous on some of the boulders, and there was still a definite nip in the air, the kind that always seemed to settle in her feet. Once her feet got cold, she was cold all over.

For added warmth, she wore her plaid coat, also lined with a furry fleece. She could always shove it into her backpack if she got too warm. She had her walking stick and her divining rods, and a nice warm cap on her head. She was all set and ready to go.

The short hike was easy. For a woman who had walked all her life, traversing these hills was still doable. She knew the day would come when the peaks would become too high, the declines too steep, the rocks too shifty for her to navigate them safely. But until that day came, she was determined to live life the way she always had.

Consistency, after all, was important.

Karnie didn't have many neighbors here on the mountain, and that suited her just fine. There were the Buseys down the mountains a way. They had newfangled things like electricity and a telephone, and even one of those things they called a cell. Her own granddaddy had spent too much time in a jail cell for bootlegging, and it had soured her on anything that shared the ill-begotten name.

The Buseys were good to her, trading store-bought items for fresh milk and eggs, and for the medical advice she doled out. The family hadn't been blessed with good looks or good fortune—they had even been shorted in the good sense department, Karnie reckoned—but they had good hearts. One of the boys, in particular, was good to check on her every few days. Elroy did the more difficult chores around the house, things her old body struggled with these days, and he drove her to the places she couldn't walk.

The Mustons lived just over Speckback Creek. Unlike most people in these parts, they hadn't always lived here. They had chosen to move to the mountain on purpose, and what's more, they had chosen to live off the grid. They depended on nature and their own energy sources to provide for them, much like Karnie did. They often used a generator to operate some appliances, so in the summer, when it was too hot to fire up her own wood stove, Karnie traded a special charm or medical advice for a loaf of freshly baked bread.

The Busey and Muston families were the only neighbors Karnie liked, and the only ones she associated with. If that made her a veritable hermit, so be it. And if being a hermit who lived in an old log cabin by herself and practiced witching made folks afraid of her, then so be that, too. Karnie was just fine with folks being afraid of her.

She reckoned it helped that she lived on Knob Mountain. Every so often, a group of daredevils decided to test the fates, but tales of the Flaming Woman kept most folks away. It made a bone witcher sound even more ominous.

Like most legends, the truth behind the Flaming Woman was a far sight less exciting than the rumors. Karnie knew the real facts behind the outrageous tale, even though no one wanted to hear such a sad story.

Back during prohibition, the Hoke family lived up here. Farming the rocky soil took hard labor and a good dose of luck, and even then it didn't pay enough to keep a family of eight from starving to death. In hard times like those, the only surefire way to feed a family was to supply liquor to those who could afford it.

The Hokes' still was high up on Kinney Knob, tucked between a nice grove of trees and the mouth of Bentwood Cave. By day, the men tended the livestock and the corn patches, and by night, they turned the corn into moonshine. Some said their still produced some of the finest corn liquor in Northern Arkansas.

With fame like that, word had gotten back to the much-feared 'revenuers.' Moonshiners and bootleggers everywhere saw the revenue agency as the enemy, hellbent on destroying their stills and, thereby, destroying their very way of life. Revenuers were to be avoided at all costs.

One night, Freida Hoke got word that the enemy was headed up to Kinney Knob. She had to get there first and warn Elias, or else they would arrest him and dismantle her family's still. They might take the boys, too, and then who would take care of the farm? She had her hands full managing the vegetable gardens, the endless household chores, and the three young 'uns still underfoot. Without the menfolk and the still, they would all surely die of starvation.

The night was black, hiding Freida's hurried scramble up the mountain. She took a seldom-used path to avoid being followed. It cost her precious time, but few people knew the trail existed.

Unbeknown to Freida, the overcast night hid the revenuers' approach by way of a different path. By the time she reached the knob, it was too late. The government men had already pulled their guns.

"Elias Hoke! This is the Internal Revenue Service. You, sir, are operating an illegal still and are instructed to step away immediately," the lead agent said. His words were clear and distinct in the darkness.

"The hell I will!" her Elias had said. Pride swelled in Freida's chest when she heard how strong and brave he sounded.

"Then you leave us no choice but to arrest you, Mr. Hoke." Five agents stepped from the shadows. As the first man took his handcuffs out, he instructed the others to dismantle the still. "Destroy it," he said.

Gilbert, the middle son, grabbed his shotgun and pointed it at the approaching men.

"Back up," he warned. "I ain't afraid to shoot

you. No one's messin' with this still. I'll kill ever one of you before I let you put a hand on it."

"Gil—" Elias protested. "Put your gun down."

"Listen to your pa," the leader said.

His eyes wild, Gilbert pumped his gun.

One of the younger agents, overeager and ready to put this hillbilly in his place, put a finger on the trigger of his own gun. He didn't mean to pull it, he later sobbed, but it just happened. The gun went off. A bright red blossom stained the front of Gilbert Hoke's overalls.

Freida screamed when the gun went off. Elias flew into action, beating the agent with his fists, as havoc broke out on the mountainside. Henry, the oldest son, grabbed his fallen brother's shotgun and took down two of the agents before a third man's bullets found him.

Freida held back, weeping as two of her sons lay dead, and her husband fought for his life. Only their youngest son—sweet, simple-minded Junior— stayed calm among the melee. He steadfastly tended to the still. He kept mumbling to himself, the only way he knew to tune out the world and protect himself from things he didn't understand.

Junior added another log to the fire and stirred the red-hot flames ever hotter. He was oblivious to his father's frantic fight just a few feet away, and to the direct punch he took in the face. Another punch sent Elias reeling, and he stumbled into the fire.

The red-hot fire that jumped onto his pants leg and climbed greedily upward.

Frightened and confused, Junior jerked backward. His foot caught one leg of the still, and it toppled with a deafening *boom*! The still burst into flames, fueled by its own contents. Each effusion was a chain reaction of the last.

Somewhere among the roiling explosions, the boy's screams of agony broke through.

Freida rushed forward, desperate to reach her son. She knew her Elias was gone, but there was still hope for Junior, if only she could reach him...

The flames spread outward, gobbling up the space between her and her sweet boy. She couldn't give up, not even at the ghastly sight of him, already nothing more than a charred version of his former self. She fought to reach him, until the flames caught the hem of her own skirt.

Panicked, frantic with horror, and reeling from the shock of losing all her menfolk, Freida did the worst thing possible. She ran.

As she raced away from the horrific scene, the flames followed. They rode on her skirt, on her heels, and on her back. They scrambled to get ahead of her, crawling over her hair and racing down the front of her apron. They overtook her toes and turned upward again, until they consumed her entire body.

And still she ran.

She ran until she reached the edge of Kinney Knob, then she was sailing over the edge, into the dark abyss below.

It was a horrific sight within itself. A flaming woman, driven over the edge of sanity.

There were only two people who lived to tell the tale of what happened that night: the young agent who started the horror to begin with, and Karnie's Uncle Ham.

She heard the agent later took his own life.

And her uncle—a bootlegger for the Hokes, there to restock for another run—never forgot the horror he saw that night, or the haunting sounds that he heard. He talked about it until his dying day, but no one other than his family would listen. The legend had already taken hold, a story about a flaming woman who walked along the edge of Kinney Knob.

The legend tagged onto another one, an unproved claim that Bentwood Cave held treasure. There were some who claimed that outlaws—it variated between the Bald Knobbers and Jesse James, depending on who told the tale—had hidden a stash of gold in the cave. They were caught before retrieving it, and the story was that the Flaming Woman haunted the ridge to protect their stash, should they ever return for it in the afterlife.

On the darkness of nights, folks claimed to see red embers glowing atop Kinney Knob. 'Proof,' they said, that the Flaming Woman was real.

Only the most foolish believed the story, but that was fine by Karnie. It kept outsiders off her mountain.

Dismissing the legends from her mind, Karnie took the copper rods from her backpack and went to work divining, or witching, for animal bones.

There had been some good that came from the Hoke explosion. Once the fires were out, the bodies removed, and the leftover embers cooled, Uncle Ham had gone back to the site. He salvaged what he could of the copper, including two slender rods he fashioned into divining rods.

The very rods Karnie used today.

3

"As curious as I am," Everleigh admitted, "I really think Landee should be the one to go with you to see Mr. McMurray. She knows the hills and back roads so much better than either of us."

Her words took both of her companions by surprise.

"You're certain you don't mind?" her grandmother asked.

Ireland Garrett—Landee to her granddaughter—had grown up in the hills, so far back, she claimed her daddy had to pump in sunlight. She hadn't lived there in over fifty years, but Ireland knew the hills as well as she knew any old, cherished friend.

"I get lost just going to Aunt Purdy's," Everleigh insisted. "You're the most logical choice."

"You're sure you'll be okay here by yourself?" Willow asked worriedly.

"Seriously, Mom? Half the time, I'm always here by myself. Why are you suddenly so worried about it?"

Willow looked out the window. The mid-morning sun hung bright and cheerful in the sky. No clouds were in sight. Yet she swore she saw shadows hovering close to the ground.

"I have that feeling again." Her voice sounded uneasy. "There's trouble headed our way."

"You know what I always say." Ireland waved a manicured finger to make her point. "Don't wait for trouble to come to you. Meet it head-on, on your own terms."

"Easier said than done. I'm not sure where it's coming from."

Her daughter offered her opinion. "My guess would be Mr. McMurray."

"He may be the cause of the trouble," Willow agreed, "but not the danger. I can't say who or what's causing it, but it's there."

"I suggest we start with this new client and go from there." Ireland retrieved her handbag from a desk drawer and gracefully looped it over her wrist. With its designer label, the bright red leather perfectly matched her shoes and lipstick. "Ready?" She smiled brightly.

Willow looked at her daughter. "Everleigh, do you have the contract?"

"Right here." She produced a manila folder with papers inside.

"Thank you. We'll be back"— she paused to shrug— "whenever."

"No problem. Just keep me posted." They were already down the hallway when Everleigh leaned over her desk and called, "Be. Careful!"

"Always, darling," Ireland assured her

granddaughter, tossing a laugh over her shoulder.

Their retreating footsteps echoed along the wooden floors. It was an old brick building, stretching deeper than it did wide. Once upon a time, it had been dark and dreary in the far-back corners, but when Willow acquired the building through her divorce, she added plenty of lights. The stylish fixtures along the hallway offered ambient lighting, while the bulbs overhead brightened the way.

The moment they stepped outside, a gust of cold air blew sharp against their faces. Willow wished it were strong enough to blow coming troubles away.

"We'll go in my car," her mother insisted. "I know the roads better, so it makes sense that I drive." She unlocked the doors of a sporty Mercedes-Benz and slid behind the wheel.

Willow had been dismayed the first time she saw her mother's new ride. This was hardly the car of a great-grandmother. How would all their family fit inside? There were only four of them, but the backseat was small and cramped. She had to wonder what Landee was thinking when she bought such a car.

It still rankled Willow to think about it. Nonetheless, the left-over ire was a nice distraction from comparing the buttery-soft leather of the sports car to the cloth seats of her Toyota Corolla. Though faithful and still rolling along, her Corolla paled in comparison to this.

She had to admit that the sports car hugged the curves of the road like a caress. The tires sped along on the pavement, climbing the rugged hills with ease. Willow decided to sit back and enjoy the ride while her mother navigated the way to Scrimshaw Ridge.

As she stared out the window at the fleeting scenery—Landee had never adhered to the posted speed limit signs—Willow thought about her unease from the day before, spurred into action when their door opened at 3:33. She still maintained that she wasn't superstitious, but she *was* cautious.

Willow knew that around here, superstitions were embedded in the rocky soil the same as the roots of a stubborn scrub oak. Tales of omens and signs were passed down from generation to generation, along with their antidotes. Some required a healing ritual, while others called for less drastic measures. Herbs, plant-based potions, and faith were the favored means of warding off ills and evil, although some used spells, charms, and protective objects.

She knew that suspicion, particularly of outsiders, had a way of settling low in the hollers. Strangers often had to prove themselves before being accepted here. It began with the famed outlaws who hid out in these parts and spilled over to the 'revenuers' who tried to stop their stills and homemade liquor. Even though it was the twenty-first century now, some of that distrust still lingered.

Up here, secrets could hide their shame within the dark crannies of eroded rock and earth. Mankind's worst transgressions could bury deep in area caves.

One thing Willow admired most about the locals was their undying perseverance. Bolstered by their most cherished traditions and those that came before them, they still clung to their faith.

Their folklore danced on the breeze, lifting spirits and stirring imaginations. Tales of larger-than-life heroes—and outlaws—rose with the first strands of morning sunlight. The heroes spun hope and fanciful dreams for those who believed. The outlaws added excitement and romanticism to their everyday lives. And at night, when the moon climbed its way over the ridges, it glowed with the glory of days gone by, and with the promise of days yet to come.

The very foundation of mountain living came from old beliefs, old wisdom, and old superstitions. Willow knew to never take their way of life for granted. If not for the stories and the sense of pride they invoked, their history would be lost. The newer generation would never know who their people were and how they came to be.

Gus McMurray was one of those old-timers. She had seen a treasure trove of knowledge in his weakening eyes. A thousand stories, not just the one he told them. Whether that story was based on truth or delusion was still to be seen.

"What were those directions?" Ireland asked. "We're nearly to Scrimshaw Ridge."

"Turn right off Carter Loop, cross Carter Springs, and look for a log house on the right. His is the next mailbox."

The sports car slowed as the road wound its path up the mountain. Sharp curves and steep drops required Ireland's full attention. Through the trees and rocky earth, Willow saw patches of blue sky overhead, and deep ravines below.

"There's Carter Loop." She pointed.

With a steep drop on their right, there was

only one option on which way to turn. They waited for an oncoming motorhome to pass before crossing the other lane. Willow cringed at the thought of maneuvering one of those oversized monstrosities up the mountain. Going down, she suspected, would be even worse.

The narrow road marked as Carter Loop backtracked their progress for a way, climbing and dipping, delivering them deeper into the wooded hillside. The first right was at least a mile in. The road turned to gravel, twisting like a drunken tornado, ever climbing, before crossing a wooden bridge. Willow assumed that the water below was Carter Springs. After a hairpin curve and one last ridge, the ground leveled out.

A spectacular, upscale log home stood among the spindly pines, dispelling the popular but misguided notion that only backwood hicks lived up here. Floor-to-ceiling windows, two stone chimneys, and three staggered levels pushed the house well into the million-dollar range.

The next mailbox was a quarter mile away. Trees crowded around the rocky path. Their limbs hung low, turning the tunnel effect into one of a protective hug. Gus was right. The house couldn't be seen from the road.

What appeared to have started with a small log cabin—the old kind, unlike his neighbors'—and had sprouted wings over the years. One side was clapboard, once painted white and sporting a fading red door. The other wing was older and starting to sag, as if the weight of its asbestos siding was too much to bear.

"Let's hope he's more forthcoming today than he was yesterday." Willow's words sounded doubtful.

"Mountain folks tend to play things close to the chest." Ireland shot her daughter a reproachful glance. "You should know this."

"I do. But I can always wish."

Ireland pulled up beside Gus' truck and killed the motor. Both women sat for a moment, surveying the house and the area around it.

"Chimney, but no smoke," Willow noted.

"No dog, which strikes me as odd. You normally see dogs in these parts."

Willow nodded. "They make for dual purpose companion/alarm system."

Eyes scanning the property, Ireland further observed, "Standard well shed and decrepit barn. Rundown barbed-wire fences along the tree line. Typical of old farms like this."

"Not much else to see," Willow mused. She placed a hand on the door handle. "Shall we?"

"Let's." Opening her door, Ireland gracefully swung her legs over the sill. Willow's movements weren't as smooth, partly because there wasn't enough room in the sports car for her long legs.

That was what she told herself, anyway.

They paused for another moment beside the safety of the car. Something in the stillness of the morning had both of their senses on high alert.

Suspecting that Gus McMurray didn't have central air and heat, Willow found it even more surprising that the chimney stood idle. The higher the altitude, the lower the temperature. "I don't like the air up here," she murmured.

No breeze rustled the trees around them, but bad energy found a way to swirl in the air.

"I feel it, too. Let's get this over with," her mother said.

Ireland squared her shoulders as she followed Willow to the red door. Judging from the way the end of the porch sagged in front of the log walls, they assumed the original entrance was no longer used.

Noticing a dark blotch on the boards of the old porch, Willow sniffed the air for hints of spilled chemicals. Gus wouldn't be the first person to carelessly keep fuel so close to the house. The stain itself didn't give off hints of pending danger, but something did.

A newer porch fronted the clapboard addition, where two rocking chairs and a small table resided. Peanut shells scattered around the chair nearest the door, and a few of the husks floated in a nearby water bowl.

"Dog bowl, but no dog," she noted.

"Maybe it's inside with Gus."

They were about to find out. Willow knocked firmly on the red door.

A few moments ticked by with no sounds of response from the other side. She knocked again, this time more firmly.

"Mr. McMurray?" she called. "It's Willow Alexander. I'm here with my other partner, Ireland Garrett. We had an appointment to meet you here this morning."

Another minute ticked by. "Either they're both deaf, or no one's inside," Ireland commented. "You said his son cleaned out the shed, but maybe we should check it out for ourselves."

The shed wasn't far from the house. All they found inside was the well pump and a few tools used to repair it.

"Maybe the barn?" Willow suggested.

Like most barns of its era, the overall frame and trusses were solid, but many of the side boards had turned loose from their nails. Slipping through every missing or broken board, sunlight spilled into the damp darkness of the dimly lit interior.

Once their eyes adjusted, the women could see the jumbled mess before them.

"Wow. It looks like a bomb went off in here," Willow said with a low whistle.

The shelves lining the walls had been trashed. Boxes were tossed carelessly aside, their contents emptied onto the dirt. Buckets, cans, and old bottles were either overturned or flung to the floor.

With a dainty finger to her nose, her mother agreed. "Maybe a horse or a mule got loose and tore the place up. I certainly smell the lingering odor of one."

"Along with moldy hay, diesel, and half-dozen other offensive smells. But the ground isn't trampled like a horse or mule would do," Willow argued. She pointed to the middle of the dirt floor. "All I see are shoe prints. The kind that goes on two-legged creatures, not four."

"From the looks of all that's left, I'd say his son didn't get around to cleaning the barn out. Not with this much stuff still left," Ireland murmured.

"Maybe. It doesn't look like much of value. The better tools must have been in the well shed."

"So, maybe Mr. McMurray searched the barn one last time for the recorder."

Willow twisted her lips. "If that's the case, he was definitely frustrated. This place is a wreck."

"Mr. McMurray?" Ireland called. "Are you in here? This is Ireland Garrett. Maybe you know me better as Irie Perkins? We came to meet with you, just like you asked."

Willow looked sharply at her mother. "You know him? You never mentioned that."

"I don't, really. But most people in these parts know the family name. And my hill family still calls me Irie, you know." She looked none too pleased over that fact.

"Maybe he can't hear us."

They took turns calling his name as they cautiously moved further inside. There were more shelves in the back, lined up in rows, and a small tack room.

"You look behind those shelves," Willow suggested. "I'll check the tack room."

A bare bulb hung from the rafters over the shelves to offer a modicum of light, but the tack room was dim and poorly lit. Willow used the flashlight feature on her phone to look into the shadowy interior.

"Mr. McMur—" Willow broke off in dismay as she saw the crumpled body on the floor. The dark stain beneath their client didn't bode well.

She crouched near him on bended knees, careful not to disturb the scene. She put two fingers against his wrist, searching for a pulse. "Oh, Mr. McMurray," she murmured in distress. "What happened here?"

Her mother's voice drifted from the main part of the barn. "I got nothing. What about you?"

"I think you should come in here," Willow called back. As an afterthought, she added, "But don't touch anything!"

"What is it? Did you find something?"

"You could say that." When her mother appeared in the doorway. Willow stood to face her. She moved aside so that she had a better view. "I found his body."

Ireland's eyes darted toward the prone heap on the floor, and then back at her daughter. "Is he—?"

Willow answered in a flat voice, "Yes. He's dead. I think he was murdered."

4

"Murdered?" Ireland squeaked. Using the flashlight on her own phone, she saw blood pooled beneath him. She lowered her voice to whisper, "Do you think the killer is still here?"

"No. His body is already cold, and the blood is dried." Her forehead creased in thought. "This doesn't make sense. The killer was searching for something, and my money is on the recorder. How did they know about it? And why hadn't they looked before?"

"From what you said, he was definitely burdened by keeping such a huge secret all these years. Maybe he finally broke."

"You think he confessed to the wrong person?"

"It's possible."

Practically set in. "We need to take pictures. We need to document what we found and when we found it."

Ireland looked down at the crumpled body on the ground. "And I suppose we should call the sheriff. This is suddenly a murder investigation."

When she started to dial 911, Willow put a

hand out to stop her. "Not just yet. Once Mathers gets involved, we'll be completely shut out. I think we owe it to Gus to find that missing recorder."

It wouldn't be the first time *Intuitive Investigations* butted heads with Sheriff Lew Mathers. The hardline official considered private investigators a thorn in his side and an overall menace to law enforcement, if not society itself.

"Right. He may threaten to throw us in jail for interfering with a police investigation. It seems to be one of his favorite mantras."

"Let's take a few pictures of the inside of the barn first. Then we'll take a peek at the house."

They split up to snap their pictures before heading to the house.

The stillness of the morning felt heavy and oppressive. Negative energy was the only thing that stirred.

"I still don't like the feel in the air," Willow muttered.

"Is it any wonder? Just a few hours ago, a man was murdered here."

By mutual accord, they didn't speak again as they retraced their steps to the house. It was, in part, out of respect for Gus' body still lying in the barn, but part was out of caution. He had been killed hours ago, but was the killer still on the premises? In the house, perhaps?

Willow pulled the gun from her hidden holster and kept it close to her side. Ireland did the same with the Ruger LPC 380 tucked into her bra holster.

This time when they approached the house, they did so quietly. Instead of knocking, Willow used the doorknob.

Unlocked, the faded red door swung easily open.

Neither woman was surprised to see the ransacked room that greeted them. Couch cushions gaped open, slashed and missing half their stuffing. The remnants lay on the floor like low-hanging clouds. The sole bookcase in the room was overturned, its contents now buried beneath. The living room was sparsely furnished, but anything that could have hidden a video camera had been searched, trashed, and carelessly discarded.

Hearing no movement and sensing no activity inside, the women moved through the house the best they could amid the mess.

The latest addition to the old cabin consisted of only three rooms: the living room, what appeared to be the master bedroom, and a somewhat modern bath. The story in those rooms was the same. Thoroughly searched and destroyed.

The original log structure housed the kitchen and a casual dining area. What had probably once been a bedroom had been transformed into a formal dining room. It wasn't difficult to imagine Delta's pride in the polished dining table and the glass-fronted china cabinet. Willow's senses tuned into the late woman's joy decorating room and knew she would be heartbroken to see it now. Most of the dishes were broken and discarded on the floor by what appeared to be a sweep of the arm.

A rudimentary bath and a pantry—again, what was possibly once a bedroom—completed the house's origins. Each addition flowed into the other without benefit of a hallway. *It probably made the thieves' jobs easier*, Willow thought bitterly.

The far side of the house, with its uneven floors and saggy ceilings, told the same sad story. One of the two bedrooms had been converted into a den, of sorts—Gideon's, perhaps—with a bathroom separating them. All were wrecked. The thieves left no stone unturned, it would seem. Unable to find what they were looking for, it appeared their frustration had given way to anger. That part of the house had the most damage. Even the walls had holes in them.

"It makes sense, I guess," Willow said. "The side with the red door looks newer. This was probably where Gus and his family were living when the boys' murders occurred."

"Suggesting the killer knew Gus well enough to know his house," her mother surmised.

"It certainly looks that way. Why don't you call 9-1-1, and I'll call Everleigh and tell her we'll be delayed."

It was another thirty minutes before three patrol cars and an ambulance pulled into the overgrown lane, lights ablaze and sirens blaring.

A pickup truck with 'Chief of Police, Border County' emblazoned on its side skidded to a stop, and Sheriff Lew Mathers crawled out. He took one look at the women and threw his cowboy hat into the dirt.

"I should have known it was you two!" he said in disgust. "Why is it every time there's trouble, your family isn't far behind!" It was an accusation, not a question.

"Every time?" Willow asked coolly. "Isn't that a

bit of an exaggeration?"

"It happens way too often!" He bellowed as he reached down to scoop up his hat and cram it onto his head. In an effort to disguise his hair loss, the poor excuse of a comb-over did little to hide the shiny spot on top of his head.

"Where's the body?"

"In the barn. Small room at the back."

"Stay here. I'll need to take both your statements. And we don't need you underfoot while we do our preliminary investigation."

It didn't take long for the team to confirm Gus' death, but it took a while for the sheriff and one of his deputies to return. Obviously, he wasn't worried about keeping the women longer than necessary.

"You'll need to answer some questions, ladies." His tone was stern.

"Why, of course, Sheriff," Ireland purred. "We have nothing to hide."

At that, he grunted.

"One other thing you should know," Willow added. "The house was trashed, as well."

He muttered an oath and ordered his deputy to check it out. He then turned back to the ladies with an angry expression on his face. "How do you know that? And why were you two up here to begin with?"

"We had an appointment with Mr. Murray. We knocked, but he didn't answer. The door was open." She didn't offer the order of how things transpired.

The sheriff's voice was scornful. "And you just let yourself in."

"Like I said, he was expecting us. He could have been in the back or didn't hear us. We called for him several times before stepping inside." It wasn't a lie. They called his name repeatedly before finding his lifeless body in the barn.

"What was the appointment about?"

Willow lifted her chin. "I'm not at liberty to answer that question."

"Not at liberty?" the sheriff hooted. His voice turned thunderous. "Not at liberty! Who do you think you are, young lady? I asked you a question, and by God, you'll answer!"

"It was a private matter, Sheriff Mathers, and frankly, none of your business." Willow's tone was cold.

"I'm making it my business. Tell me why you had an appointment."

Ireland stepped in to answer. "Mr. McMurray hired us for a private matter. Like my daughter said, we aren't at liberty to divulge the nature of the case."

"The case? The case! You aren't police detectives!" Spittle flew from the corners of his mouth. "*WE* are the only ones investigating this case!"

Ireland made a show of wiping imaginary saliva from her shirt collar. "The murder investigation, perhaps," she agreed. "We were here on a different matter."

"Which was? And don't give me that malarkey about not being at liberty to answer a direct question by an officer of the law. I can arrest you for obstruction of justice!" Mathers shook an angry finger at the women.

Willow sighed, looking bored. "Don't you ever get tired of making that same threat every time you see us?"

"Not when you're interfering with an official investigation."

"Sheriff, Mr. McMurray hired us to investigate a private matter for him. We have a strict policy of client-investigator confidentially."

"Your client is dead, Mrs. Alexander," he said coldly, "so that policy no longer applies."

"Of course it does. Integrity doesn't end with the last breath of life."

In response, the sheriff practically growled. "You'll need to wait here while I see what Deputy Galvez found."

Watching him storm off toward the house, Ireland let out a breath of resignation. "Do you get the feeling he'll deliberately keep us waiting for as long as possible?"

"I wouldn't expect anything less from him."

Making themselves comfortable, the two women took seats in the nearby rocking chairs. When the sheriff eventually came out of the house, he belittled them for their casual demeanor.

"Have you no respect? A man's dead body lies fifty feet away, and you two are just making yourselves at home on his front porch!"

Without comment, Ireland called attention to the deputy resting on a stump in the front yard. Her gaze spoke volumes.

"Boggs!" the sheriff called in a sharp voice. "Get up here and make yourself useful!"

The young deputy jogged their way.

"Take the lady to the car and get her statement," his boss instructed, nodding toward Ireland. "I'll interview this one here on the porch." His implied insult was clear. He didn't consider Willow in the same category as her mother.

Not that it was anything new. While Ireland was dainty and graceful, Willow was tall and awkward. She tried hiding it by dressing in chic, professional attire, but there was no taming her unruly dark curls. The best she could do was wear them short and messy, like it was a deliberate style. She hadn't given into vanity yet by covering those pesky gray strands that appeared with increasing regularity. She figured she had earned every one of them, particularly over these last five years. Her hips were wider than she wished they were, but her body was still slender, and she was slowly starting to get comfortable in her own skin.

Willow spent years being the good wife, entertaining Marcus' business associates, and throwing parties for people she really didn't care for. In a way, the divorce had given a different sort of freedom than simply release from her wedding vows. She now had the freedom to speak her mind.

She clearly lacked her mother's tact. When Mathers lowered himself into the chair beside her, Willow launched a pointed barb. "If you prefer, we could stand."

He merely glared at her in response and flipped open his notebook.

"What time did you arrive?"

"A few minutes before nine. We left the office close to eight, but as you know it takes a while to get here."

"The 9-1-1 call didn't come in until 9:28." His eyes bore into hers.

"As I said, we knocked several times and repeatedly called his name before going inside." She silently added *the barn*. They went inside the barn first.

"Again, why the thirty-minute delay?"

"We were giving him time to answer the door before going any further. He wasn't inside the wrecked house, so the most logical place was the barn. It took a while to work our way to the back, where we eventually found his body."

When he still looked suspicious of the timing, Willow motioned to their remote location. "Cell service isn't the best up here. It took several tries before we got a signal." That part was entirely true.

"Hmm. Did you check his body for a pulse?"

"Yes. But it only took one look at all the blood and the color of his skin to know it was too late."

"Did you move the body in any way?"

"I'm a trained investigator, Sheriff," she said pointedly. "I knew not to move the body unless there was a chance of saving him. And yes, I was careful not to disturb any surrounding evidence."

He asked a dozen more questions, many of them repeatedly. Deputy Boggs had finished interviewing Ireland long before that. Hauling himself to his feet, the sheriff told Willow, "You're free to go. For now. But don't assume this is over."

Willow flashed a humorless smile. "Of course not."

Joining her mother in the car, Willow noticed Detective Boggs still gazing at the car in adoration. "He didn't drool on the seats, did he?"

"Almost!" Ireland laughed. "Ready?"

"And then some." She snapped on her seatbelt as her mother put the car in reverse.

"How did it go?"

"He tried his best to trip me up," Willow reported, "but I was careful not to lie, while also not telling the entire truth. He asked why it took thirty minutes for us to call in the body."

Ireland's blue eyes were wide and deceptively innocent. "We were giving him ample time to answer the door, obviously. I'm sure neither of us specified exactly when we let ourselves into the house, and when we searched the barn."

"Obviously."

They were both quiet for a moment while they worked through scenarios in their own minds.

"Do you think it's a coincidence that Gus came by the agency yesterday and was almost immediately murdered?" Ireland asked.

"Not at all. You didn't see him yesterday. He was worried that his truck had been parked out front too long. He looked around the street almost frantically, afraid he had been seen."

"Meaning it would probably be someone local he was afraid of."

"More than likely. Although, a lot of people do come from the outlying areas to take care of business and do their shopping," Willow pointed out.

"Which doesn't narrow it down very much."

"No, it doesn't."

"Now what?"

"We go back to the office, brainstorm with Everleigh, and see if we come up with any solid leads."

The youngest member of the team was understandably upset to hear the news. They had just met the man yesterday, and now he had been murdered.

"How was he killed?" Everleigh asked as they gathered around the conference table. Willow and Ireland had paper and pen in their hands, while the younger woman opted for her laptop.

"We didn't want to disturb the body, but I saw a bloody hay fork nearby. I think he was stabbed," Willow replied.

"How awful!"

"From the condition of his body, I'm assuming it happened last night, after he left our office."

"So, someone *did* see him!" Everleigh said with a slight gasp. "I just thought he was being paranoid."

"Can you imagine living like that for all these years? Always looking over your shoulder, afraid someone will discover your secret?"

"No wonder he wanted to get it off his chest before he died," Ireland tsked.

"There must have been more than just his age to make him think his days were numbered," Willow surmised.

Everleigh nodded. "I'll do some digging and see what I can find."

"While you're at it, try to find out where his son is," Ireland suggested. "Maybe he has some insight into what happened way back then. Hopefully, he can at least tell us what happened to the camcorder."

"I've already gone through Gideon McMurray's social media accounts."

"Find anything?" Ireland asked.

Everleigh pulled up a window on her computer. "Only that his interests are all over the place, and his attention span is worse than Laura Beth's when she was three! He's been a member of a dozen special interest groups. Everything from saving sea life, forests, and wildlife preservation, to banning red meat in school cafeterias. Then he does a complete 180 and is fighting for unrestricted hunting laws and more research on the dangers of substituting tofu and plant-based alternatives in lieu of real meat."

"It does sound like he's all over the place," Willow agreed.

"I think it's more like he's easily influenced by the company he keeps and the current woman he's seeing." She turned the screen so that the others could see it. "Elana Selman was a very avid sea life advocate. She's posted several photos of herself protesting and marching for awareness. Some of the protests grew rowdy and landed her in jail a couple of times." She opened another tab. "In this post, you can see the overzealous Sheri Daniels, who once chained herself to a tree to stop the logging company from cutting the forest."

"At least she's passionate about the cause," Ireland offered in the girl's defense.

"She swallowed the key. They had to cut the tree down to free her from the chains and rush her to the hospital, where she wound up having a three-hour surgery. She later protested outside the hospital, saying they had taken hasty and undue action."

Everleigh clicked the next tab. "See the blue-haired girl screaming into the camera? Here she is again when they booked her into jail. She took protesting a little too far and sneaked into the school cafeteria, where she proceeded to dump all trays of meatloaf and spaghetti onto the floor."

"He certainly has questionable tastes in girlfriends," murmured Willow. "And the others?"

Another tab, another social media page. "This is Mandy Hernandez and Gideon, all decked out in their hunting gear. And this is Marianna, protesting alternatives to red meat while enjoying her own *very* rare steak."

"Put that away," her grandmother said, using her hand to shield her view of the screen. "I'd call that raw, not rare."

"Any other girlfriends you can find?" Willow asked.

Everleigh nodded. "Meet the two latest, although I'm not sure if either relationship is current. Sharika, the yoga instructor, and Moon, a free spirit who leans toward the dramatic. Sharika is a lifestyle coach who encourages healthy choices, self-awareness, and betterment of the inner soul. Moon is a self-proclaimed expert on natural and spiritual healing, and the medicinal benefits of marijuana."

Ireland censured her with a single look. "You know our people come from a long line of natural healing. Don't mock your heritage."

"I meant no disrespect, Landee. But this is New Age stuff, not methods that go back hundreds of years. Some of theirs include animal sacrifice and… and worse."

Willow looked concerned. "Worse?"

"Not exactly burning at the stake, but close enough to be highly disturbing."

Appalled, Ireland shuddered and said, "I certainly hope the boy had the good sense to break up with her!"

"That boy," her granddaughter said in a dry tone, "is ten years older than me and capable of making his own choices in life, rather than following other people's lead like a blind, helpless sheep."

Willow looked thoughtful. "Is there anything in there about him going to a retreat of some kind? Gus said it was one to 'give him clarity and cleanse his soul.' That sounds like something Moon would encourage."

"As a matter of fact, Moon has been a guest speaker at several spa events, retreats, mental health rallies, and the like. She hasn't been shy about tooting her own horn. If she were speaking at the retreat, I'm sure she would have advertised the event."

"What if she attended as a guest?"

"Maybe. But again, it seems like she's the kind to want to be the star of the show, not just in the audience."

"Maybe he met someone new at one of her rallies, and the two of them went on this retreat together," Ireland suggested.

"I think the only way we'll find out is to contact these two latest women, particularly Moon." Everleigh twisted the laptop around, tapped on a few keys, and sat back with a satisfied smile. "Done. I've requested more information about her speaking schedule, and someone will reach out to us soon."

"It's a start, at any rate." Willow said, trying to look encouraged. In truth, they didn't have much.

"We have an ace up our sleeves, you know," Everleigh pointed out. "The sheriff probably thinks this is a random burglary gone bad, but he doesn't know about the recorder. That's something that only we're privy too."

"Us, and the killer," Willow muttered glumly.

"Don't be a buzzkill. It's something in our favor, and it seems to me that for now, it's all we've got." Everleigh had inherited her upbeat, bubbly personality from her grandmother.

"Not necessarily," Ireland disagreed. "I can talk to Aunt Purdy. We're overdue a visit anyway. Maybe she's familiar with Moon. Better yet, maybe she knows of some such retreat."

Everleigh nodded. "They've become increasingly popular in recent years. Spas, lodges, and massage therapists often host them. For a generous fee, of course."

"It must have been, if Gideon needed to go through his father's things and sell them off." Ireland was clearly not happy with such a choice.

"If you can find an address, I'll talk to the yoga instructor," Willow volunteered.

"If?" Her daughter sounded insulted.

"Okay, *when* you find the address."

5

There were two Border Counties that, ironically, bordered one another. One lay within the geographical boundaries of southern Missouri. The other stretched across the northern edges of Arkansas.

In Border County, Arkansas, Lew Mathers was convinced he knew everything there was about being a lawman. It was in his blood. His own father had been the sheriff, like his father had been before him, and his had been before that. As a fourth-generation sheriff and keeper of the peace, Mathers claimed he had either seen or heard it all. It didn't matter to him that much of that came by way of his ancestors, who handed down their accumulative knowledge through oral history and fireside tales. Nor did it matter to him that back in the day, lawmen relied on their gut instincts and the presumed honesty of the public, rather than forensic evidence and scientific facts.

"This," he told his deputies just one day later in their morning briefing, "is clearly a burglary gone bad. Someone broke into the McMurray home looking for valuables and anything they could pawn. They were probably hoping that someone McMurray's age would have a medicine cabinet full of pills and some coffee cans stashed around the place, full of money. After they were done with the house, they moved to the barn. There's always some money to be had selling off metal and old tools. They came upon the homeowner in surprise and killed him on the spot. A needless crime by some drug addict, cut and dried."

Damien Boggs risked the sheriff's ire and raised his hand. "Are you sure about that, sir? It seems to me—"

"Oh, it seems to you, huh? Tell me, Deputy, how long have you been a lawman?"

"I graduated from the academy thirteen months ago, sir."

"And I've been an officer of the law for twenty-six years, over twenty of those as the sheriff. That means I've been doing this for..." He tried doing the math in his head.

"For over three hundred months, sir," Terri Garcia supplied.

"Thank you, Garcia." Sheriff Mathers stared down his challenger. "For over three *hundred* months, Boggs, to your thirteen. So, tell me. Who do you think has the most experience in solving crimes and getting to the root of the problem?"

"You, sir."

"That's right. And I've seen enough of these kinds of cases to determine that someone broke in with the intention of burglarizing the premises, where he unintentionally encountered McMurray, which took both men by surprise. In a panic, the burglar used a weapon he found there in the barn to kill his unfortunate victim." Mathers crossed his arms over his chest, confident of his assessment of the situation. "Other than Deputy Boggs, does that scenario seem logical to anyone else in the room?" He peered out at his other deputies, daring any one of them to challenge his expertise.

No one was brave enough to defy him, although Sam Binger's murmured agreement was lackluster.

"Binger?" the sheriff asked sharply. "You agree with Boggs?"

"Deputy Boggs didn't express an opinion, sir, so I can't agree or disagree."

"Oh, well, in that case…" Mathers sneered in sarcasm. "Very well, Boggs. After thirteen months out of the academy, what is your esteemed opinion of this case?"

"I didn't disagree with your assessment, Sheriff. I merely wondered if it was too soon to make a judgment call. We haven't had time to do a thorough investigation. Very few fingerprints were taken at the scene, and the results of the autopsy haven't come back yet."

Mather's face turned an angry red. "I don't know how they did things down in Little Rock, but here in Border County, there's hardly enough budget to pay your salary, much less have an autopsy and fingerprint analysis done! Unless you're volunteering to forgo your paycheck for the next three months, I'm willing to save the taxpayers a slew of money and determine that McMurray was stabbed to death— numerous times, I might add—by a pitchfork."

Damien cocked his head to one side, not fully understanding the sheriff's comments. "Won't we need that print analysis done in order to apprehend the subject, sir? Or subjects, as the case may be?"

"So now you think there was more than one perpetrator?"

"It's always a possibility, sir."

"Boggs, you are coming very close to having your paycheck become completely nonexistent! Do I make myself clear, young man? We will rely on the same tried and true methods my father used and all the lawmen that came before him. We'll find potential witnesses if they're to be found, ask if they saw or heard anything unusual on the day in question, and follow up on any leads we may find. No fancy and expensive tests and analysis. Just good old-fashioned legwork." He glared at the younger man. "I will ask again. Is that clear, Deputy Boggs?"

"Absolutely, sir."

"With that in mind, since you seem so gung-ho on the case, I'm assigning you to canvasing the neighborhood."

"It's a remote area, sir. What do you consider the neighborhood?"

Mather's smile was one smirk away from malicious. "The entire mountain."

The sheriff was in a foul mood. All he needed was some greenhorn deputy messing up this case. Fresh out of the academy and still wet behind the ears, Boggs had no idea what it took to be a true lawman. Especially up here in the hills, where things were done in the traditional manner.

Mathers nursed his whiskey glass. "What does he know about our heritage, anyway?" he grumbled to himself.

"What's that, Tully?" Odell Oliver asked. "Need another card?" He was the official dealer of their Tuesday night poker games.

His barber shop, his rules.

"What? Naw. Naw, I'm good." Clearly distracted, Mathers looked down at his cards. The whiskey was more appealing than this hand, even though it wasn't half bad. His heart wasn't into playing cards tonight, but he hadn't backed out. It was, after all, tradition.

Ned Jessup laid his hand down with the word, "Call," when Mathers' phone rang. He took one look at the caller ID, pushed his poker chips to the middle of the table, and muttered something about having to answer. He didn't pick up until he was to the door.

"Took you long enough to answer!" the caller complained.

"I was in a meeting," Mathers replied.

"Not my problem. But I'll tell you what *is* my problem. I heard one of your deputies was up here on the mountain today, asking a bunch of nosy questions."

"What of it?" Mathers asked.

"I don't need undue attention called to this project. You're the sheriff. Do something about that deputy!" the man on the other end demanded.

"I can't exactly do that. A man was murdered yesterday. The matter calls for a certain amount of investigation."

"Then do it somewhere else!"

"I can't exactly move a murder scene, you know. Gus McMurray was killed on his property. I say it's a robbery gone bad. Gus came in on the robbery and got himself killed. But I got a new deputy who could stir up a real stink if we don't go through the motions of a proper investigation. It won't take him more than a day or so to question folks who live up there. Unless they report seeing a vehicle or the crime being committed, there won't be much else to look into. This will all blow over by the end of the week."

"End of the week?" the man yelled. "It had better not take that long, Mathers! I want this matter cleared up in no less than two days. You have until Wednesday afternoon to call off your deputy."

"What if he makes a complaint to the state police? Then they'd be crawling over the mountain. Did you ever think of that?" Mathers jeered.

"No, because I thought you had control of your men. Obviously, I was wrong."

"You're not wrong. I am in control of my men," the sheriff insisted. "But I have the public to answer to, and the fact is that a man was murdered. Let me do my job. Lack of evidence will prove the old man was in the wrong place at the wrong time. Simple as that."

"There's nothing simple about this, Mathers! Sending a deputy up here is a complication we don't need."

"I assure you; it will be over by Friday."

"No." The caller's voice was cold and flat. "It will be over by Wednesday. Do you hear me,

Mathers? Wednesday by five o'clock."

The line went dead before the sheriff had a chance to reply.

6

The Mercedes took the mountain curves with graceful ease, gliding over the dips and climbs like a thoroughbred running through rolling pastures.

It was the perfect day for a drive. Bright and sunny. Completely opposite from the storm brewing within its driver.

Ireland rolled her shoulders to dispel the tension gathering there. She was headed back to the mountains. Back to the place she called home.

Back to the memories.

The journey was always bittersweet.

She wasn't ashamed of her upbringing. But hers was a different generation. The mindset was different back then, particularly in the hills and hollers. The march of 'modern progress' hadn't yet made its way to Dalton Holler. That wouldn't come for a few decades yet.

There were still places, however, tucked deep within the hills, that clung to the old ways of life. Many lived off the grid. Not because they had to, which had been the case with Ireland's family, but because they *chose* to. They reasoned that if it had been good enough for their ancestors, it was good enough for them. Others had a deep distrust of the government, while still others simply didn't know a different way of life.

Outsiders assumed their lack of modern civilization equated to lack of intelligence, but Ireland knew that nothing could be further from the truth. The forgotten mountain people, as the media often dubbed them, may not have been educated in computer skills and political science, but they were fluent in something much more important: life skills. They didn't rely on calculators and Google search engines to give them answers. They used common sense to solve problems. Nature and experience were their best teachers.

These mountaineers Ireland admired and proudly claimed as her people. Her blood relatives had caused the tension in her shoulders and the bruise on her heart. Oddly enough, the pain hadn't subsided in fifty years.

Shaking the memories loose, she concentrated on the one bright spot she could look forward to. Aunt Purdy. Less than a decade may have separated them chronologically, but genetically, Purdy was her mother's sister. She was also the best friend and confidante Ireland had ever had.

The higher the altitude climbed, the better Ireland's spirits kept pace. She had the top down so that she could soak in the full essence of her roots. Two of her favorite things in the world were the taste of fresh air and the earthy scent of the soil. Even the boulders had a scent of their own.

She didn't worry that the wind would destroy her carefully crafted hair. *That* Ireland, the one who was known for her style and her poise, stayed behind in Harrison. Up here, she was Irie.

Gone were the high heels and stylish blazers. Here, she wore blue jeans and simple blouses. She even kept a pair of sensible boots tucked into the back corner of her closet, reserved solely for visits like today. Without the hairspray and careful arrangement, her hair was playing tag with the wind. If Ireland had been here, she would have been horrified, but Irie didn't even care.

She didn't think of one version of herself as being fake, the other authentic. She was both versions. The two women living inside her existed in very different worlds. They led their own lives, each independent of the other.

Irie had been raised in the wild before suddenly being 'set free' into captivity. That was the way she had viewed the city at first, with its trappings of vanity and riches. Society could be a bitch.

Ireland learned that lesson early on, so she had adapted to it while staying true to herself and her values. She played the perfect hostess but never once envied the snobs she entertained. She enjoyed the luxuries her new world provided, but she never worshiped them.

Life in the mountains gave Irie her roots and her all-important core values. Life in the city gave Ireland a future.

Different women, different worlds. Different men they each had loved.

The car topped one last hill, curved to the right, and headed into the little holler Irie knew as 'home.' It was considered a holler because it nestled between two ridges, but in truth, it still enjoyed impressive heights. Irie knew she could follow the narrow road running through Gibler's Pass and have a magnificent view of the valley below.

Bittersweet was definitely the right word for the emotions that washed through her every time she visited. Some of her memories of this place were bitter. Others were painfully sweet.

She slowed as the little cabin came into sight. What was once her grandparents' homeplace now had a large roadside sign that read 'Aunt Purdy's Gifts from Nature.' A smaller sign below promised 'Herbal Remedies, Teas, Soaps, Quilts, Crafts, and More!'

It was almost closing time, and only a few customers remained. Ireland's timing had been deliberate. She didn't want to share her aunt with anyone else.

Ireland opened the door and had a brief moment to look around before her aunt spotted her. The store looked great. It was an authentic Ozark cabin with scrubbed pine floors and log walls. It was so different from the house Ireland remembered, yet so very much the same. Goosebumps crawled over her skin every time she stepped inside.

She was never quite certain if they were the good kind or the bad kind.

"Ireland!" her aunt shrieked in delight. She said a quick word with her customer and rushed over to engulf Ireland in a heartwarming hug.

Purdy was the only one in the family who

called Ireland by her birth name, but maybe it was because she was the one who had named her.

Normally, the local mid-wife went to the expectant mother's home to deliver the child, but Rebecca had been visiting her family when her water broke. She had given birth here in this very cabin. It wasn't the first delivery eight-year-old Purdy had assisted her mother with, but it was definitely the most magical. While the other children were shooed from the cabin, Purdy stayed to help.

She could have sworn that baby came out sprinkled with stardust. She loved her at first sight. And when she had her chance to hold her little niece, she looked up at her sister in hushed wonder. "Oh, Becca. She's the most beautiful baby I've ever seen! She looks just like one of those Irish fairies in that book you have. Her hair is so soft and so blond." She had giggled when one of the still-damp curls wrapped around her finger. "Look at that little mouth. And her curious blue eyes. She looks… magical! Like she belongs in an Ireland castle. Maybe she's a fairy!" Her own eyes had been filled with imagination. "That's what we should name her!"

"Fairy?" Rebecca asked in amusement. "You want me to name my baby Fairy?"

"Not Fairy. Ireland! You always dreamed about going there to see the castles. Now you could have your very own Ireland, right here in Arkansas!"

And so, Ireland it was, and the baby was all the more special to Purdy because she had been the one to name her. It forged a bond between the two females that not even time, a family feud, marriages, or children had come between.

"Why didn't you tell me you were coming?" Purdy asked now in rebuke. "I would have gotten the guest room ready for you."

"I can make my own bed, thank you very much. Go on," she said, shooing her away. "Go back to your customers. You know I love to browse around and see what you've added since the last time I was here."

"Have a look at that shelf yonder." Already turning away, Purdy pointed in the direction of the old living area. If there was a dollar left to be had, Purdy would find it.

Ireland skirted around a rack holding handmade aprons and potholders, and another shelf that held an array of homemade jellies, jams, and pickled garden delights. She pushed away the watery image floating in the edges of her mind. She saw a faded green couch with her grandfather sitting there, reading an out-of-date newspaper; the paper held old news by the time it arrived in their mailbox. He chewed on a wad of tobacco and spat the juice into an old tin cup reserved solely for that purpose. There was never a television in the Granger cabin, just the radio her grandparents listened to faithfully.

Threatening tears blurred the already watery image. In the time it took to blink them away, Ireland had reached the suggested shelf.

The free-standing unit displayed a new line of herbal soaps, lotions, and rubbing oils. Ireland picked up random offerings and sniffed. She didn't need labels to identify the ingredients and their uses. Honey and ginger for coughs. Lavender for calming. Elderberry for immune support. She was familiar with them all. Helping herself to the sample, Ireland rubbed magnesium lotion into her hands. She was loathe to admit it, but arthritis was slowly stealing mobility from her joints.

"You ready?"

Ireland turned around to see her aunt locking the front door and turning the OPEN sign over to read CLOSED. She hadn't realized the store was already empty, and it was time to go.

"Don't you need to close the register?" She motioned toward the modern cash register sitting on an antique counter. The counter came from the old general store that was once the centerpiece of Dalton Holler.

"I'll come in a few minutes early tomorrow and take care of it. I'd rather visit with my Irish fairy." Her eyes sparkled mischievously.

Purdy led the way to the back door of the cabin. Ireland stepped onto the porch, enjoying the view as her aunt locked the door behind them. It was as beautiful as ever up here.

When Purdy turned the old cabin into her place of business, she had made an addition to the porch, a T that tied the cabin to the barn behind it. The covered walk had always reminded Ireland of a bridge, in part because of the small ditch it crossed.

The barn itself was a relic from the past. Weathered walls, a combination of hand-hewed logs and old planks. The roof was made of tin and had the obligatory weathervane on its peak. This one was missing the W, and the rooster cocked to one side.

It could have been one of a thousand similar barns in the area, except for the lock holding the massive front doors together. No crossbar. No pin and hasp. No padlock. This one had an electronic keypad lock.

Purdy punched in a sequence of numbers, and a green light shone. One door swung inward, revealing a wide corridor with walls made of new metal siding in pristine white. Overhead lights came on to illuminate the space when the door closed behind them. The walls separated the outer shell of the old barn from the newly constructed home built within it.

Despite its untraditional location, her house was bedecked in traditional white siding with a front door painted in black. It wasn't some James Dean spy house, nor was it one of the popular barndominium style that was taking the real estate market by storm. This home was in a class all its own, exactly like its owner.

"Come on in." Purdy used a short code to open the inner door. "Make yourself comfy."

Ireland knew where the switches were to fill the room with light. She flipped one up on her way to the sofa.

She sank into the welcoming cushions with a sigh. The butter-soft leather reminded her of the seats in her sports car. Willow didn't understand, but there came a time in life when a woman deserved to selfishly pamper herself.

"If I'd known you were coming, I would have put something in the crockpot," Purdy apologized. "Looks like we're stuck with left-overs. Of course, I could cook something…" They both knew it was a lame offer.

"I'm fine with raiding your refrigerator. A can

of soup works, too."

There was no such thing as DoorDash or takeout in the Holler. And neither of the women mentioned going out to eat, considering the nearest café was almost an hour away.

"Why don't you see if there's anything that appeals to you in the fridge?" Purdy suggested. "I'm going to change into something more comfortable."

Purdy had a uniform, of sorts, that she wore at the store. The customers expected to see a 'typical' mountain woman dressed in plain clothes that could have come from another generation. That usually meant dressing more like the Amish, but Purdy believed in giving the customers exactly what they wanted. Her uniform consisted primarily of black or dark-colored skirts, sensible shoes, hair in a neat bun, and simple cotton blouses. No frills, no stylish blazers, and no makeup.

She emerged from the bedroom looking like a different woman. Her silver hair hung loose from its bun to cascade down her back, the mane still full and shiny. She had traded the drab skirt for a pair of silk lounge pants in vivid blue, top to match, and a brightly patterned kimono-style wrap.

"Ah, much better," she announced with a contented sigh. She joined Ireland in the open-concept kitchen. "Finding anything in there suitable to eat?"

Ireland bumped the refrigerator door with one hip, her hands filled with an assortment of fresh vegetables. "Soup and salad. I've already chopped the lettuce and kale. Now for the garnish." She indicated the pile in her hand.

"Did you find the shredded chicken in there?"

"Already on the counter."

They worked together comfortably, each chopping the array of add-ins for their salad.

After a few minutes of idle chitchat, Aunt Purdy slyly asked, "Any new interesting cases at that investigation business of yours?" She sensed there was more to her niece's visit than simply catching up.

"Actually, there is. Do you remember Gus McMurray?"

"Of course. He and Delta have been in these parts for years."

"*Had.* Gus was killed yesterday morning."

"Oh, no! I hadn't heard. How?"

"He was murdered."

"Murdered? *Murdered?*" she repeated incredulously. "That's awful! Who on earth would want to kill Gus? Is that the case you're working? I can't believe Lew Mathers is letting you anywhere near this one!"

"Mathers didn't hire us. Gus did."

Now the wrinkles on her forehead had wrinkles. "I don't follow. He knew he was going to be murdered?"

"Not exactly, although I do think he was afraid of that."

"You'd better start at the beginning. I'm thoroughly confused."

"I know you remember when those three college boys disappeared in the mountains." Ireland didn't pose it as a question.

"Of course. I still hear people talking about it."

"Gus came to the office day before yesterday,

claiming he knew what happened to the boys. He said they had been killed, he knew who had done it, and he could show us where their bodies were disposed."

Purdy looked dazed. "That's… that's amazing. Who did he say did it?"

"He didn't. All he would say is he couldn't go to the sheriff, not then and not now, because the killer was a prominent member in the community. He couldn't put his family in danger. But now, Delta's gone, Gideon is off doing whatever it is Gideon does, and apparently, Gus wasn't in good health. He wanted to get this dark secret off his conscience. We were supposed to meet him at his house yesterday morning and he would take us to the murder site. Instead, when Willow and I got there, we found him lying in his own blood." A shudder rattled through her thin shoulders. "It was gruesome."

"You and Willow found him? You poor dears!" Careful to avoid the knives in their hands, Purdy gave her niece a comforting side hug.

"We decided that for Gus' sake, we had to honor his wishes and reveal the killer."

"How will you do that if you don't have a name, much less proof? They searched for their bodies for a good year or more. Occasionally, explorers still try to find their remains, though it's doubtful such exists after all this time."

"Gus said he had proof. *Had* being the operative word." Ireland tossed her pile of vegetables into the salad bowl. Purdy had finished chopping the tomatoes and mushrooms and was now heating a can of soup.

"What did he say happened to it?"

As Ireland relayed the story Gus told, they fixed their plates, poured soup into mugs, and took a seat at the table.

"Did you look for the video camera? Maybe Gideon left it behind."

"That's what we had hoped. Apparently, the killer believed he still had it, and probably killed for it. Either before or after the murder, someone had ransacked the house and barn."

"You don't think it was a simple robbery? Maybe Gus came in on them, and they panicked."

Ireland shrugged. "That's always possible, of course. And I'm sure that's what Sheriff Mathers will dismiss it as. But what if it wasn't so simple? I wasn't there when Gus came in, but the girls said he was paranoid about being seen at our office. He believed he wasn't safe but was determined to get this off his chest."

"That does sound suspicious," Purdy agreed. "What can I do to help you?"

"Is there anything about Gus or Gideon you can think of that would be useful? I vaguely knew Gus, but I don't recall him being hard to get along with. Did he have any enemies that you know of?"

Finished eating, Purdy suggested. "Why don't I clean up in here while you move your car around and bring in your bag? I'll think about your questions, and we can discuss in on the couch over a bottle of wine and a nice fire."

It didn't take much to persuade Ireland or to persuade her into changing clothes similar to her aunt's. Hers were in more sedate colors, but just as silky and comfortable.

"Come up with anything?" Ireland asked, sinking back into the welcoming cocoon of the leather cushions.

Purdy handed her a long-stemmed glass filled with wine. "I've been racking my brain but haven't come up with much. I do know that some logging company was after Gus to sell them his land. He refused, so possibly that's something?"

"It could be. I'll have Everleigh check it out. What about Gideon? I don't believe I ever knew him."

"Gideon is a different story. That boy was born with trouble on his mind. Discipline issues at school, at home, and at every job he ever had. He took a few college classes right after high school, but they didn't last any longer than his attention span. There was talk that he was the one to tell those college boys about the legend of the Flaming Woman."

Ireland was thoughtful. "Interesting. What other trouble has he been in?"

"Minor skirmishes with the law now and then. I'm not sure of all the details, but I hear the rumors. Rumors also have it that he's involved in some New Age concept that leans heavily into being a cult."

"A cult?" Just the word was disturbing. "Does this cult have retreats, by chance?"

"I think I've heard something about that. A farmer over on Finn's Ridge came across a group of people with tents trespassing on his property not long ago."

"Do you remember hearing anyone mentioning the name Moon? First name, not last."

"That doesn't sound familiar, but I think the farmer's name is Harp. You might find him and ask."

"It's worth a shot," Ireland agreed. "Is there anything else you can think of that could help?"

"Not really. After he lost Delta, Gus didn't get out much."

Ireland thought of a new angle. "Do you happen to know the people in the big log house before Gus' drive?"

"As a matter of fact, I do. Their last name is Homer, and the wife is a customer of mine. She's very likable; the husband, not so much. He's some bigwig within his own company. Comes from money, and it shows. He came with her to the store once. He was on the phone almost the entire time, barking out orders and thoroughly chewing out the unfortunate person on the other end. He abruptly said they were leaving, and that was that. He made her leave her half-filled basket there on the counter."

"I dislike him already. Is there anything else you can tell me about him?"

"Not really. I do know their place backs up to the edge of Gus', if that's of any help."

"Really?" Ireland perked up. "Can you ask them if they've seen any unusual vehicles going in and out of Gus'? I know the sheriff's department will have asked them the same thing, but maybe they'll open up more to you."

"Conveniently enough, Carolyn Homer had me mix up a special powder for her headaches. She's supposed to come in next week to pick it up, but I suppose I could make a friendly gesture and deliver it to her." Her mischievous smile took years off her aging face.

"That would be great. We don't have a lot of

leads so far, so anything you find is better than nothing."

"You know I love being in the thick of things! The few times I've helped you in the past have been a lot of fun."

"Remember, Auntie," Ireland cautioned, touching her arm. "Those were minor investigations. You need to be extra careful this time. We're dealing with murder."

7

Like two teenage girls at a slumber party, the women stayed up late into the night. They talked and giggled and polished off the rest of the wine.

Despite the late hour last night, old habits had them up early the next morning.

It wasn't until after their first cups of coffee that Purdy asked the question Ireland had been dreading.

"Are you going to see them?" she asked quietly.

Ireland squirmed in her seat. "I haven't decided."

"It's been a while, you know," her aunt said in soft rebuke.

"I know. But visiting brings up so many old feelings. Feelings of resentment, and of hurt."

"Surely there are plenty of good feelings in there, too. I know you have some happy memories of your childhood."

"It wasn't my childhood that was the problem. It was my coming to age years." Her voice still held traces of that pain.

"Irie, sooner or later you have to come to terms with your past."

Whenever Purdy called her that name, Ireland knew they had subtly shifted from best friends to aunt/niece. It was only natural that, as her aunt, Purdy could see both sides of the age-old pull between mother and child.

"I'm seventy-two. Why rush things now?" Ireland quipped.

"This is no laughing matter, as you well know. Rebecca is twenty years your senior. Her days are numbered now. Make amends before it's too late. Your father's already in the ground. Your brothers aren't getting any younger, either, you know." She placed her hand on Ireland's arm and gently squeezed. "Isn't it time, my sweet Ireland, to let it all go?"

She jerked her arm away. "Your special influence doesn't work on me."

Purdy looked appropriately chastised. "You can't blame me for trying."

"If I didn't love you so much, I could," Ireland said, turning the tables and touching her aunt's hand.

Purdy laughed. "I know what you're doing, and it won't work on me, either." She took Ireland's hand so that their fingers intertwined, neither influencing the other. "Let's agree to disagree—again—and not ruin this beautiful morning."

Some people called their innate ability witchcraft. Some called it magic. Others called it foolishness, simply the power of suggestion. Still others, particularly here in the mountains, saw it as the gift it was. 'The touch' wasn't just for healing. For

Ireland and her aunt, the gift of persuasion by touch came with heavy responsibility. It couldn't be used for evil or wrongdoing. It couldn't be used for personal gain. The touch was meant to help soften the hearts of others, so that they could resolve old grievances and find peace within themselves.

It was seldom as easy as merely influencing their emotions. Most often, it was used to encourage some action on their part. Now, for instance, Purdy tried compelling Ireland into visiting her family. Ireland tried encouraging her aunt not to overstep her bounds.

Neither were successful.

When Purdy changed into her work uniform, Ireland dressed in her own sort of uniform. She thought of it as her 'Irie uniform.' Going back in time was a job of a completely different caliber. She slipped on the same jeans and boots as the day before, put on a fresh long-sleeved shirt, and resisted the urge to fix her hair.

She stopped in the log cabin to hug her aunt goodbye, grabbed a treat for Laura Beth, and proceeded to her car. After some debate, she turned left. Higher into the mountains. Back to her old home.

In the end, she didn't pull down the familiar gravel road. Cell service was sketchy here, but she was up high enough to receive a text message.

Heard back from Sharika and Moon! Everleigh announced.

It offered just the excuse Ireland needed to delay the inevitable. Eventually, she would have to see her family again. She had missed her father's funeral—her sister's too—but she didn't want to miss the opportunity to tell her Mama goodbye, if only to whisper 'I'm sorry' to her casket.

She was far too old to feel like an errant child, but it didn't stop the sense of relief that washed over her. She had dodged the bullet for another day.

On my way, she typed.

Driving back to the office, Ireland mulled over the sparse information Purdy had to share. She had been in the business long enough to know that often the smallest of threads managed to unravel the whole case. She'd share what she discovered with the girls. Together, they might weave a plausible theory from the meager threads.

Ireland smiled, thinking of the unlikely hodge-podge that made up *Intuitive Investigations*.

When Willow's husband traded her in for a newer model, his new lady love convinced him to be ruthless in the divorce settlement. The newly formed couple was awarded the four-bedroom house in Springfield; Willow had to settle for the aged building in downtown Border. He convinced the judge that the funds heavily invested in lucrative stocks and bonds and the bulk of their bank accounts were part of the inheritance he acquired prior to their marriage. He was generous enough to grant Willow the funds in their household and savings accounts. It hadn't been much.

Back when Willow first suspected her husband of cheating, she had recruited Ireland to help gather evidence against him. At the time, they laughed about their sleuthing abilities, until the full impact of their findings hit Willow. Hard. Realizing she had no husband, limited work skills, limited funds, and a building she couldn't sell, she needed a way to provide for herself.

Everleigh suggested the prospect of becoming a private investigator. It seemed ludicrous at first, but the more Willow thought about it, the more intriguing the possibility. Ireland, widowed and always up for a challenge, offered to take the course with her. She even offered to loan her daughter the money to start her own agency. When Willow stubbornly refused the loan, Ireland did the next best thing; she became her partner.

Soon, Everleigh quit her boring desk job and joined them as a third partner. Her father had always been more generous with her than he had been with his former wife, which meant he unwittingly helped fund their venture, a fact the partners often laughed about.

Together, the trio used their intellect and innate abilities to build a successful investigation agency.

Ireland wasn't the only one to possess special skills. As an empath, Everleigh used her version of the touch to feel what others were feeling. She didn't simply *understand* their motivations and personal convictions. She *felt* them. And when she touched Gus McMurray's arm, she had felt the jumbled tangle of his emotions. It had taken her a day to decipher the genuine remorse in his heart.

Willow's talent didn't involve the touch, but it was every bit as insightful. She wasn't a seer. She couldn't predict the future. But she 'had the knowing' as old-timers called it. She could *sense* what was and what was yet to come. She had incredible intuition, hence the name of their agency. If Willow felt danger surrounding their late client, they all knew there was danger afoot. His murder was proof of her uncanny accuracy.

Their unique talents were part of a strange phenomenon among Ireland's maternal people.

For generations now, during her twentieth year, a daughter who possessed 'the gift' gave birth to a girl child of her own. That child would also possess a unique gift. And when the daughter turned twenty, she, too would give birth to a gifted girl child.

Ireland had often wondered about the curious trait. Centuries ago, had someone cast a spell on one of her female ancestors? Was there a charm involved? A sprinkling of water, thawed from the first winter's snow? Were magical words whispered at midnight neath a full moon, or chanted while holding a three-pronged branch over glowing embers? The hills were full of such stories, passed from one generation to the next, steeped within folk legend and conjecture, and seasoned with whimsy.

The origin of her family's peculiar trait was uncertain, but there was no doubting the fact that each of the daughters born during their mothers' twentieth year possessed a special gift. Sometimes, a mother had more than one child with the gift, as her grandmother had done in the case of her mother and Aunt Purdy.

At ninety-two, Rebecca had the gift of healing. She had been midwife to generations of mountain families, and still practiced faith healing when needed. Ireland, with her gift of touch, was seventy-two, and at fifty-two-years old, Willow had the knowing. Everleigh was thirty-two and a gifted empath. At the tender age of just under twelve, Laura Beth's gift was still unclear, but it would soon become obvious, and at the age of twenty, she, too, would pass the phenomenon down to her daughter.

Ireland's coffee was already brewing when she arrived at the office. Sometimes the Family Circle tracking app was intrusive, but in times like these, it paid off. Everleigh knew just when to start her coffee.

After taking a moment to neatly hang her coat and shuck the head scarf (she was Ireland now and couldn't be seen driving through town with hair like this!) Ireland joined her daughter and granddaughter in the conference room.

"What did you find out?" Ireland asked once they were seated.

Everleigh was happy to report her findings. "I tracked down Sharika, and she's agreed to talk to us. She and Gideon didn't part on the best of terms. He started attending meetings that encouraged a lifestyle she didn't support. Sharika said it was bad for her chakra, and she didn't need such a strong source of negative energy in her life."

Ireland nodded. "That jives with what Purdy told me. She's heard rumors that Gideon was involved in some New Age movement that leans heavily toward being a cult. She wasn't aware of any retreats, but not long ago, a farmer over on Finn's Ridge came across campers trespassing on his property."

"Did she know the farmer's name?" Willow asked as she jotted the information in her notebook.

"All she said was Harp."

"Okay. At least that's something." Willow didn't look as hopeful as the words sounded. "I'll drop by and see the yoga instructor. Maybe I can get a sense of what happened between her and Gus. What about this Moon? What did she have to say?"

"Well, it was a generic response," Everleigh admitted, "but it did provide useful information. Moon offers, among other things, a Lunar Immersion Experience. It's a three-week retreat that culminates with a full moon. It promises, and I quote, *spiritual accord with the universe and a deeper, more fulfilling understanding of our true purpose in life*." She read the words from her screen. "*Earth friendly accommodations and all-natural food and supplements are included in this life-altering experience*."

Ireland made a sound of disapproval. "What do you want to bet those all-natural supplements can be rolled and smoked?"

"Or eaten as gummies," Willow agreed. "Does is happen to say what this amazing experience will cost?"

Everleigh smirked. "Apparently, you can't put a price tag on such a mind-blowing, life-altering event. Each package is *specifically curated for individual needs, assuring that each attendee achieves the one-on-one coaching he or she deserves*."

"In other words, they milk you for every penny they can get," Ireland said with disdain. "The more emotional baggage you have, the more profit they make."

Willow agreed. "I'll bet that questionnaire is a mile long. They'll capitalize on every negative thought and emotion they can find."

"This could be a steppingstone to joining a cult," Everleigh speculated.

"It may not be a typical cult, per se, but it does sound like a potentially dangerous culture. Not everyone uses the art of persuasion for good." She gave Ireland a nod of appreciation.

"How very true," her mother murmured.

"No offense," Everleigh continued, "but I think I'd be a more believable candidate for the retreat. It's assumed that the younger you are, the easier you are to manipulate. I may not meet their target demographics, but between all of us, I come the closest."

"While thirty-two is hardly middle age, they've clearly never met my very headstrong daughter," Willow pointed out.

"Why, thank you for the compliment," she replied with a cheeky grin.

Ireland felt compelled to defend her granddaughter. "She gets it from you."

"And according to Aunt Purdy, I get it from you," Willow shot back.

"Now that we have the thinly veiled insults out of the way," Everleigh interrupted, "let's get back to business. Landee, did Aunt Purdy have anything else helpful to say?"

"She mentioned Gideon had a few run-ins with the law in the past, but nothing major that she was aware of. Oh, and she heard rumors that he knew those boys from his brief stint in college, and that he was the one to tell them about the legend of the Flaming Woman."

"I wonder if that was noted in the original

police files," Willow murmured.

"It's doubtful. The boys could have heard about it anywhere. That's why it's called a legend." Ireland recalled one other detail. "Oh, she also told me that there was a logging company pressuring Gus to sell his land."

"Do you know which one?"

"No, but I assured her that Everleigh could find that out." She nodded toward her granddaughter, who was already tapping on her keyboard.

"It looks like two companies are vying for that entire mountaintop," Everleigh said triumphantly. "One of them, Brushy Creek Logging, buys the rights to cut hard timber, but Mulfred Logging wants rights, deed, the whole shebang."

"She said Gus flatly refused."

"That could be something," Willow considered. "An argument may have gotten heated, and tempers flared."

Her mother whistled lowly. "That was some temper. And a lot of blood."

"Everleigh, can you get their numbers?" Ireland asked. "Maybe one of us can check them out."

"Already sent." Simultaneously, their phones binged with an incoming text message. "Since I'm waiting for more information from Moon, I'll do the honors of talking to them."

Willow looked down at her notes on the case. "If neither woman knows Gideon's current whereabouts, I don't think we should wait to look for the camcorder. Knowing where he sold it would be a huge help, but who knows how long it will take to find him? We'll have to look for it on our own."

"You make that sound so easy," her daughter grumbled, rolling her eyes. "How do you propose we go about finding it? Search the entire countryside?"

With a winced smile, Willow admitted, "Something like that."

"You have *got* to be kidding!"

"Just hear me out. We could split up and visit the different pawn shops and resale stores around us. Second-hand shops, antique stores, that sort of thing. He could have taken it anywhere, but the bigger towns would be my first bet. We could start with Branson and Harrison and branch out from there if we have to."

"You do realize that'll be like looking for a needle in a haystack."

"Yes, but if neither woman can put us in touch with him, it may be our only hope. We need to cover all bases, and the sooner we get started, the sooner we should have answers. I'll pay Sharika a visit today. When did you say Moon's next meeting is?"

"They aren't very forthcoming with the details. You don't get the date or location until after you've paid the deposit."

"Deposit? You have to pay a deposit to attend a meeting?" her mother asked incredulously.

"Did I forget to mention that earlier? Apparently it's to weed out false actors who wish to do their organization harm."

"AKA, the police," Ireland predicted. "How much is it?"

"It's a three-hundred-dollar deposit, fully refundable or can be applied to the purchase of an experience."

"Obviously, you can't use the company card or check. Write it from your personal account, and the company will reimburse you."

Everleigh smirked. "It really is best that I go," she said smugly. "No one writes checks anymore."

8

Willow parked outside the *Build a Body Fitness and Lifestyle Center*. When the mall closed down a few years ago, the space was converted into a huge shared-space facility. On one end was the gym and fitness center. An aquatic center stood in the middle. People could take swimming lessons, water therapy or aerobics, practice for competitions, and, during select times, swim purely for enjoyment. On the weekends, the pool catered to the youth. Despite the chilly temperatures outside, the heated indoor pool made the space warm and muggy.

On the far end of the massive space, past the giggling teenagers and the excited children scurrying toward the steam-fogged doors, were the lifestyle rooms. One room, with its optional doorway opening to the backside of the mall, was reserved for AA meetings, weight loss classes, and such gatherings that appreciated discretion. The other rooms faced the open corridors. Among them was a space designated for art lessons, with others for karate and ballet. Another space boasted a fully equipped kitchen for cooking classes, and another was a specialized learning center.

Willow headed toward the door with fancy lettering that spelled out 'Restore Your Soul.' A yoga class was wrapping up, and she didn't want to interrupt. She waited in the glass-enclosed front vestibule until the class goers spilled through the doors in their tights and exercise attire, with rolled-up yoga mats slung over their shoulders. A few smiled as they passed, others were busy chatting with the person next to them.

When the coast was clear, Willow entered. It was a large, airy space, scented with the slight twang of sweat and a healthy dose of essentials oils. Willow detected lavender for relaxation. A melodic twinkle came from a raised fountain, blending peacefully with the soft music drifting from surround-sound speakers. The room was bathed in soft, comforting colors to enhance the serene atmosphere.

She kept her voice as soft as possible when calling out a questionable, "Hello?" She felt like a library voice was required here.

A woman appeared in a doorway on the far side of the studio. She was swathed in pale, foamy green that accentuated her coloring. Being of mixed race gave her skin an exotic tone.

"You must be Willow," she said with a warm smile. "Come on back. We'll talk in my office." When she turned, the flowing robes she wore over her tights swirled around her like sea foam.

Her office was an extension of the studio and echoed the meditative vibe. There was a spatter of like colors in deeper hues, seen mostly in vases, a jade Buda statue, and a piece of abstract artwork on one wall.

"I'm Sharika. Welcome to *Restore Your Soul.* Please, have a seat."

Willow seated herself in a sumptuous chair made of vegan-friendly leather. She returned the warm smile. "Thank you. I'm Willow."

"What can I do for you today, Willow? Your call was intriguing, if not a bit vague."

"As I said, I need your help with an investigation our firm is conducting that concerns Gideon McMurray."

Sharika kept her composure, but her demeanor changed. She no longer sat so comfortably in her chair, and her smile wavered. "I'm afraid you may have wasted your time. I'm no longer in contact with Mr. McMurray."

"Yes, that was my understanding. I'm not here to question you about his whereabouts. I'm merely looking for background information. You do know him, correct?"

"I do," she answered cautiously.

"And you were once involved in a relationship, giving you unique insight into his personality. What can you tell me about him?"

Searching for the right words, Sharika sought answers in the far wall. "Gideon," she began slowly, "was a lost soul looking for a place to land. But he was too restless to stay in any one place for long."

"If I'm not being too personal, may I ask why your relationship ended?"

"I, too, was once a lost soul, but I've finally found my place in the universe." Sharika motioned to the room around her. "I'm in a good place now. My life is about inner peace and self-acceptance. I didn't need the chaos Gideon brought into it. Nothing seemed to fill the void within him, creating a restlessness inside him. That restlessness wreaked havoc on my own chakra."

"I can appreciate that. Do you happen to know how to reach him?"

"Apparently, he either blocked me or changed his number. I tried reaching him once after we parted ways but had no luck."

"And when was this?"

"I haven't seen nor talked to Gideon since shortly after the first of the year."

After another slight pause, Willow asked, "Are you familiar with a woman named Moon?"

Once again, Sharika's countenance changed. She looked like she had tasted a sour lemon. "I am," she confirmed with a tight nod.

"What can you tell me about her?"

"I'm really not—"

"Please," Willow interrupted. "This is important."

Sharika chose her words carefully. "In lieu of a party, Gideon and I spent New Year's Eve at a poetry reading in a little pub we liked to frequent. Moon was there, reading an impressive short poem she had written. She left before anyone could speak with her, but she left flyers listing her upcoming speaking schedule. I vaguely mentioned that one of the events sounded interesting. Gideon wanted to surprise me so he bought tickets, but at the last minute, I couldn't go. I encouraged him to go without me, which proved to be a mistake on my part. Gideon is... easily influenced," she admitted. "He gets carried away with whatever he currently deems a worthy cause. Those causes change often, and without rhyme or reason."

Going back to the topic of Moon, she continued, "Caught up in her message, he attended another of her sessions, then another. I could see the signs of a new obsession developing within him. I did attend one speaking event with him. On the surface, it sounded divine. An extended retreat with nature, discovering a deeper, spiritual connection with our inner selves and the world around us. I promote those very things. But there was something dark about her messaging. Something almost... sinister." She hesitated over the word.

"When I declined Gideon's next invitation, he canceled our upcoming date to attend another of her speaking events. The last time I saw him, he had just returned from a rally she held to promote her Lunar Immersion Experience. There was something in his eyes... I knew I didn't need such a strong source of negative energy in my life. It would be harmful to my chakra and inner peace."

"Can you tell me what you mean by negative energy?"

"Like I said, there was something about her overall message. I'm at peace with my life, and I want to stay that way. Her message wasn't healthy. It was like she was promoting a very radical culture, almost like a—" She stopped short of saying the word that was on both their minds.

"Cult?" Willow supplied quietly.

"Yes. Exactly like that. I know I more or less

abandoned Gideon, but he was already brainwashed. Nothing I could have said or done would have changed that."

"Of course not. It was an impossible situation. And I think that makes it imperative that we find Gideon as quickly as possible."

Sharika nodded in agreement. "The retreat culminates with the full moon. Often that includes a ceremony with sacrifices offered up to the gods. Things like incense, prized personal possessions, even blood sacrifices. It was never mentioned, of course, but I have a very disturbing sense that could include animals. Or ... worse."

"Do you have any idea—*any*—of how we could find Moon?" Willow asked urgently.

"She has a website, if that helps. And she may be conducting rallies, trying to recruit enough attendees to fill her next retreat."

"One of my partners has requested more information via the website, so maybe that will lead to something."

Sharika stood, signaling that their session was over. "I'm sorry, but I'm due to start a meditation class soon. I need time to refresh and clear my own head, so that I can help others do the same."

Willow followed her lead. "I understand. Thank you for your time. And if you should happen to hear from Gideon—"

"I won't," Sharika said confidently.

"In case you do, or in case something else comes to mind, please take my card. Don't hesitate to call me."

"Of course." Her smile was still warm, but

Willow sensed there was something amiss.

There was something Sharika wasn't telling her.

When Everleigh dropped in unannounced at *Brushy Creek Logging*, she happened to catch the foreman at the office. 'Doddy' Dodson was in charge of the Scrimshaw Mountain project.

"Sure," he told her. "I met with Gus McMurray personally. He invited me in for coffee, and we had a nice conversation. Before I could give him my spiel, he let me know real quick that he wasn't interested in having his place logged. Not even when I told him what we were paying. From the looks of his place, he could have used the money, but I could see that his mind was made up. Wasn't no use in trying to talk him into it, so I had coffee and left."

"You were just there the one time?" Everleigh clarified.

He nodded. "Just the once. Wouldn't mind going back, to be honest. He makes a fine cup of coffee."

"I'm sorry to tell you this, Mr. Dodson, but Gus McMurray was killed yesterday morning."

The foreman looked genuinely surprised. "Killed? Car accident? Tractor?" he guessed.

"No. From all indications, it was murder."

He sat back in his chair, stunned. "Well, I'll be damned," he muttered under his breath. "I knew they were ruthless, but I never thought..."

"Who was ruthless, Mr. Dodson? Who are you talking about?"

"Wh-What?" He looked startled, having

temporarily forgotten she was in the room. He waved his dismissal. "Nothing," he claimed. "Don't listen to me. I hardly knew the man, but I'm still in shock. I was just there last week."

"That didn't sound like nothing," Everleigh persisted. "Who's ruthless? Are you saying you know someone who was ruthless enough to do this?"

"Of course not!"

His denial was less than convincing. Everleigh settled into her chair more comfortably. "We can sit here while I badger you for another five minutes, or you can do the easy thing and just tell me who you're referring to." Her affable smile was disarming. "Your choice."

After a moment's hesitation, he confided in the red-haired spitball. "I try to respect landowners' wishes. If they give me a flat-out no, I don't bother trying to convince them. McMurray was dead-set against anyone logging his land, so I moved on to better prospects. My competitor doesn't give up so easily. I know for a fact that they went to him at least three times."

"You mean Mulfred Logging?"

He rubbed the back of his neck. "Yeah. Look, I'm not trying to badmouth the competition. They just use different tactics than I do."

"Murder is a bit drastic, wouldn't you say?"

"Without question!"

"But you think you know of someone who might be so ruthless?"

"I'd like to believe not," Dodson said, "but...you just never know about folks these days. They see dollar signs and go crazy."

"Can you give me a name?"

He started to shake his head, but Everleigh presented him with her most beguiling smile. "Come on, Mr. Dodson. You can't drop a bombshell like that and suddenly clam up! And I swear, I'd never betray your confidence. No one will ever know you gave me a name."

His sigh was heavy. "It's not like their buyer is any secret," he admitted. He glanced down at the card she had given him while introducing herself. "What did you say your interest in this was?"

"The day before he was killed, Mr. McMurray hired our company to investigate a personal matter for him. My two partners were meeting him at his home and, unfortunately, were the ones to discover his body. It was a gruesome sight. Naturally, we feel compelled to finish the job we set out to do, especially if his death is somehow connected. You can understand that." As always, her smile was charming.

"Yeah, I suppose." His reply was somewhat reluctant. "Look, I don't want to be caught in the middle of this. I'll give you a name, but only if you keep mine out of it."

"I promise. And, like you said, it's no secret, right?"

"That's true. Okay, so the buyer for this area goes by the name Maverick. His real name is Rick Gaines, and he goes in with guns blazing. He uses a heavy-handed approach to get people to sell their land outright. After they log it and raze it for anything else of value—rocks, limestone, sandstone, whatever it is—they chop it up into lots and market it as exclusive, high-end mountain home sites. Like I said, different approaches and different goals."

"It sounds like Maverick is very aggressive. I wonder how he reacts if someone refuses his offer."

"I suspect not well." His phone rang. "I need to get this."

"By all means." Everleigh stood to leave. "Thank you for speaking with me."

"Sure." He already had the phone to his ear. "Dodson," he barked. The foreman had been more than cordial to her, but Everleigh suspected his employees and business associates saw a different side of him.

Once in her car, she looked up the address to Mulfred Logging and determined she didn't have time to get there before they closed. She did the next best thing by requesting an appointment with Rick 'Maverick' Gaines. Without telling an outright lie, she mentioned a piece of property he might be interested in. He could make what he would of her message.

9

KARNIE

She had ground the bones nice and fine, and blended them into a salve made of magnesium, cow's milk, and ground bits of copper for Merv Ridley. Now Karnie was waiting for young Elroy to get here and take her down the mountain.

She finally saw his old pickup bounce its way up the dirt driveway, such as it was. If not for the boy coming every couple of weeks, the trail would grow up.

He climbed out, carrying a box.

"Got something for you," he said. He placed it on the scarred kitchen table for her to look through. "Payment from Rita Moss for helping with her morning sickness, and from Doc Hays for restocking that tea." He gave her a look of reproach. "You know you don't charge him enough. He turns around and sells it to his patients. He pays you pennies on the dollar."

Karnie thumbed through the envelope of cash.

"He pays me plenty. Long as I'm able to buy a few things now and then, I ain't got much need for cash."

"That reminds me. Give me your list, and I'll pick it up next time I go into town."

Karnie looked back through the box of supplies. "Won't need much. I see flour, sugar, a big box of salt, and some coffee in here."

"Oh. I forgot the other one. Be right back!" He dashed out the door, grabbed a small cooler and a paper bag from the front seat, and hurried back in. "Just look in this cooler! It's yours, too, by the way."

"Just for morning sickness?" Karnie didn't understand why Rita would send so much. This would make her fifth child. Money had to be tight.

"No, ma'am, this all is from that new customer."

Digging through the cooler filled with ice, Karnie's mouth watered at the sight of a well-marbled ribeye steak. She seldom had the luxury of eating beef. Lou was her prized milk cow, making fresh beef a real treat.

Never one to show her true emotions, the old woman's reply was low key. "That'll make me a tasty dinner. What's in the paper bag?"

She pulled out a set of linens. "What in tarnation are bamboo sheets? Like those spindly rods that take over and spread? Why would I want to sleep on sticks?"

"The package says they're real soft. All natural, too. You should at least try 'em."

Karnie worked her finger under the packaging and felt the silky-soft fiber. "I reckon my old ones are gettin' thin," she allowed, sounding gruff. "Reckon these are worth a try."

"Sure!" The young man sounded excited, even if she wasn't. "There's a towel in there, too. Big and fluffy. She gave me some just for bringing this stuff up here!"

Most people paid her in items she couldn't source for herself. Things like food staples and useful household items—spools of thread, needles, yarn for crocheting, maybe a new cook pan or eating utensils. Occasionally, they sent personal items, like warm socks for winter, those pink rubber-like shoes by the door, or reading material. No one had ever sent her something extravagant like fancy sheets and towels or ribeye steak.

"Who did you say she was, again?" Karnie asked suspiciously.

"Some lady who calls herself Moon. She's a pretty thing, with long, blond hair and good-smelling perfume."

"What's she want with all those bones, anyway? I already sent one batch. Now she wants more?"

"She didn't say why she wanted them. Maybe she's a charmer, like you. Maybe she uses them to heal people. Or maybe she makes jewelry out of them. I've seen that before, you know."

"That's a custom that goes back for generations, Elroy. Native Indians been stringing bones into necklaces and such for centuries."

Karnie made certain the cooler's lid was closed before she picked up her leather pouch and started for the door. Elroy trailed behind, still coming up with ideas for the use of bones. He was clearly taken with the woman and looking for ways to defend her odd request.

"I'll get the bones for her, Elroy, so you can quit your yapping."

The younger man—close to thirty now but still living at home beneath his mother's thumb—took no offense. He was used to her gruff ways. He didn't have many friends, but he counted the old woman as one of his best.

The Ridleys lived at the base of Knob Mountain in one of those double-wide houses that came in by truck. Coming round those sharp curves with such a monstrosity must have been a chore, but that wasn't Karnie's concern. The factory-made house was nice and roomy, full of electrical gadgets and shiny surfaces, but she preferred her hand-hewn logs and tin roof any day of the week.

"Thank you, Karnie, for coming down and seeing to Merv." Gladys Ridley greeted her at the door with a warm smile.

"How's he doing?"

"Well enough to complain, weak enough to stay in his chair most days."

Gladys led her into the front room, which was almost as big as Karnie's entire cabin. She motioned to the man sitting in an easy chair, one they called a recliner.

"Merv!" she called loudly, trying to be heard over the blaring television set. "Merv, we got company! Turn that thing off!"

He used the remote control to turn off the biggest flashing screen Karnie had ever seen. Why would someone want something like that in their house? She couldn't hear herself think when she stepped through the door, and the colors on it were too bright. Downright harsh in her opinion.

"Morning, Karnie," he said to their visitor.

"Morning, Merv. How's the arm?"

"Healing a bit, I think."

"I brought you something." She pulled a small jar from her satchel. "Soon as they cut that thing off you," she nodded to his cast, "use this salve on your arm. In the meantime, I have a charm for you, and some bone broth."

"I've seen advertisements on the internet for that stuff," Gladys said. "Even the movie stars are using it now." She nodded vigorously, as if their endorsement were all she needed.

"This is mighty strong," Karnie cautioned as she handed her a dark, thick liquid. "Weaken it with boiling water and let it cool. Use less water for soup, more to make tea. Make sure he drinks the whole jar."

"I'll do it," Gladys promised. She carried the jar to another room like it was a precious possession.

"I'll need two bowls, one of them with water," Karnie instructed. She didn't ask permission before clearing the clutter off his side table. She needed the space to do her work.

Gladys walked into the room with care, cautious of splashing water from the bowl.

Karnie accepted the bowls and placed them on the table. She emptied the contents of a small leather pouch into one and sprinkled a powdered substance into the one with water. She stirred it with a small stick to mix it well.

"Ready for your charm?"

"I reckon so."

Karnie placed one hand on his plaster case. With the other, she took a pinch of granules from the first bowl and sprinkled them on the floor as she spoke.

"From dust to bone, from bone to dust,
Make them strong, help them mend.
Go now! Pain be gone.
Bind these bones 'til they be strong."

She sprinkled more granules all around, tossing a pinch over her shoulder.

Karnie dipped her fingers into the water. She flicked a splash into Merv's face, taking him by surprise. She flicked more all along his body.

Karnie repeated the process for a total of three times.

"I reckon it's done," she said when she was finished. She handed the square of leather to Merv. "Tie this leather to your bedpost. After seven days, have Gladys bury it in the backyard. Do as I told you, and you should be stronger in no time." Karnie packed up her things and replaced them in her satchel. "Gladys, leave the granules be. Don't sweep them up," she instructed. "Elroy? I'm ready to go."

"Wait," Gladys said. "I have to pay you." She scurried off to another room.

Karnie didn't like being gone from the mountain for too long at a time. She knew she was just at the bottom of it now, but it wasn't the same. The air was too thick down here, almost stifling.

She waited impatiently for the other woman to return.

"I hope you like it," Gladys said nervously.

Everyone knew the Bone Witcher was hard to please.

"What is it?" She took the bag without looking inside.

"It's a...well, it's a..." Gladys looked around nervously, realizing how personal it would sound in the company of men, "a robe." She read the look on Karnie's face, and her own fell. "But if you don't want it..."

"It'll do," Karnie mumbled. What was it with folks today? Were they trying to make her soft?

"That's not all that's in there," Gladys was quick to say. "There's some clothespins. The wood ones for hanging your wash and the metal kind for holding things together."

"Did you put what I told you in there?" Merv asked.

"Yes, yes. There's nails, screws, and whatnot. Merv says those always come in handy."

"Thank you, Merv." It was the most useful payment she had received today, including the cash Doc Hays had sent. "You mind my orders, now."

"I will," he promised to her retreating back. Karnie was never one to linger.

On the way back up the mountain, they rode in comfortable silence until Elroy said some words that often made her leery. "I've been thinkin'."

The fact was, his thinking was sometimes downright dangerous.

"What about, Elroy?" she asked warily.

"They say there's gold in Bentwood Cave. Is gold a metal or a mineral?"

"Both, I reckon."

"Then you can witch for gold, right?"

"Never heard of that before," Karnie scoffed.

"Think about it. Bones have minerals in them. Gold is a mineral. So, why can't you find that, too?" Elroy reasoned.

"I ain't never heard of it, that's all."

"You should try it. Hey! We could go up to the cave and give it a try!"

"I ain't going to Bentwood Cave to look for no gold," Karnie said emphatically. "What's gotten into you, anyhow? Why the sudden interest in gold?"

"Gold is worth a look of money."

"I done told you. I don't need much money. What Doc Hays gives me is plenty."

"Well, maybe I do." The young man sulked.

"What do you need money for?"

"So that I can get a girlfriend. Girls like men with money."

Karnie narrowed her eyes and studied him. "This new interest in money don't have something to do with that Sky woman, does it?"

"It's Moon," he corrected. "And, no, I've always wanted money. A girlfriend, too. And it just seems that all that gold is just sitting there in that cave, goin' to waste."

"What makes you think there's gold just sitting there?"

"Nobody ever claimed to find it, and something like that is hard to keep secret. Plus, everyone knows Alfie Bolin hid a stolen payload there. If it was a thousand dollars then, it'd bound to be worth a million today. Maybe even a billion!" Elroy's voice took on the mystic quality of a true dreamer. "Think what we could do with a billion dollars, Karnie!"

The old woman tucked her hands under her arms and snorted as she stared out the side window. Everyone knew the Bolin gang preferred Murder Rocks in Missouri for their hideout. The boy was smitten, no doubt about it.

"First thing I'd do is buy a set of earplugs," she muttered.

10

Everleigh still wasn't certain how it happened, but two hours later, she found herself sitting at a table, waiting for Maverick to arrive.

Before she even returned to the office, he had returned her call and agreed to meet with her. It was close to dinner time, so he suggested they meet at *Hardwood Bar and Grill* outside of Harrison. It was a rustic old building that bordered on shabby—not the fashionable kind—but the food was good, and the prices were reasonable.

Everleigh arrived first, ordering a mixed drink while she waited. It was a luxury she rarely indulged in, especially as the mother of an impressionable eleven-year-old daughter. (Laura Beth was always quick to correct the blatant error; she would be twelve in less than a month, after all.)

Before Everleigh could fall into depression wondering where the time had gone, a hulk of a man in the proverbial red flannel shirt walked up to the table. She almost laughed at the sight of his shirt and bushy beard. He fit the stereotype of a logger to a 'T.'

"Ms. Alexander?" His voice was loud and gruff, just as she suspected.

She nodded with a welcoming smile. "And you're Mr. Gaines?"

"Maverick. Nice to meet you, ma'am."

Afraid he might crush her fingers in his strong handshake, she pulled her hand from his as discreetly as possible, but not before she experienced his anticipation of a lucrative deal. "Please, have a seat," she said, motioning to the seat opposite hers. She had requested a booth against the wall out of habit, which turned out to be a good thing; she wasn't sure the wooden chairs would hold him.

Maverick ordered a drink for himself, ordering a basket of greasy onion rings as an appetizer. He didn't bother asking Everleigh what she preferred. She wasn't certain if he planned to share, either, which was fine with her. She didn't want to fill up on an appetizer. She had been looking forward to one of *Hardwood's* famous chicken fried steaks since he mentioned meeting there.

With ordering out of the way, the big man turned his attention to Everleigh. "You said you had land for sale. I'd like to hear about it."

"In all fairness, I didn't say the land was mine to sell. I said I knew of a piece of property you might be interested in." She softened his mistaken assumption with a charming smile.

The smile didn't work. His face clouded as he thundered, "Is this some sort of trick?"

"No, no," she rushed to say. "Not at all. Just hear me out."

"I'm listening." He crossed his beefy arms in

front of him, making it clear she had limited time to make her case.

"I know of a prime piece of property that could be coming up for sale very soon, and I think I can get it for you at a bargain price. Assuming, of course, you offer me a cut of your savings."

He narrowed his eyes. "Are you a real estate agent?"

Everleigh rolled her eyes and gave a 'pfft' sound. "Oh, please! Nothing like that."

"Then what? What's your game, little lady?"

"No game. I told you. I want a cut of the amount you'll save, which I promise you will be well below market value."

He was listening but still looked skeptical. The waitress delivered the onion rings and his whiskey. He popped one of the breaded treats into his mouth. The sizzling circles were steaming, but he never flinched. "If it's not yours, how can you guarantee it's for sale? And for a bargain price?"

"I know the owners, and the son is easily influenced. Especially by whatever woman he's involved with at the moment." Again, she left her next statement up for interpretation. "I should know," she said suggestively, sitting back with a satisfied look on her face. With a fling of her hand, she tossed her red curls over her shoulder.

He smiled lasciviously, assuming he knew what she meant. "You have my attention." He tipped his drink to her before taking a generous slug.

"As soon as we come to an agreement, I think you'll find him to be a very motivated seller."

"Before I agree to even consider your offer, I

need more details. Where is this land?"

"Scrimshaw Mountain."

"I've been all over that mountain. Talked to all the landowners. Already got most of 'em eating out of my hand."

"What about Gus McMurray?" she asked. She watched his face for a reaction.

With nostrils flared and his mouth opening involuntarily, he looked spooked. "What about him?" he barked.

"Is Mr. McMurray eating out of your hand?"

He shifted in his seat. "Not exactly," he admitted.

Everleigh continued to speak of the deceased in present tense. It was part of her strategy. "I think I can change that. His son isn't nearly as attached to the land as his father is."

"There's no reasoning with his old man," Maverick grumbled.

"When was the last time you tried?"

He looked wary of her straightforward question. Without quite meeting her eyes, he shrugged. "A few days ago. He kicked me off his property."

"That must have made you mad. You don't look like the sort of man many people say no to."

His chest puffed with pride. "Not normally, no. But that old man was crazy. I could have made him rich."

Everleigh pushed her luck, eyeing him speculatively. "Do you anger easily, Mr. Gaines?"

Something in his eyes darkened. He leaned across the table, blowing his warm, onion-scented breath over her. "Believe me. You don't want to find out, missy."

"That sounds like a threat, Mr. Gaines." She held her ground, leaning in toward the stench. "And here I was, trying to make a deal."

"Over a dead man's land."

Ah, so he did know about the murder. Had he heard the news, or did he have first-hand knowledge of the fact?

She pushed her luck. "Not just a dead man. A murdered man. Did you threaten Mr. McMurray before, or after, he was murdered?"

Amused by the question, he smirked. "There'd be no reason to threaten a dead man, now would there, little lady?"

"Touché. So, definitely before." She cocked her head to one side. Her blue eyes didn't even waver. "The question is, how long before?"

The waitress delivered their meals with a smile. "Here you go, folks." She concentrated on taking the plates from her tray without tipping it, but one look of their tense stare-down, and the smile vanished. The tray wobbled precariously before she got it under control.

He ignored the intrusion and the clatter. "Best watch yourself, little lady," he growled.

"In case you've forgotten," Everleigh told him, "my name is Alexander. Not missy. Not little lady. Ms. Alexander."

"Don't worry. I won't forget," he promised darkly. When the waitress would have hurried away, he caught her arm. "Make mine to go. I'll pick it at the bar."

He rose to his feet, glaring at Everleigh the whole time. "Thanks for the dinner, *little lady*," he sneered. He finished his whiskey in one gulp and stalked away.

"I cannot believe you did that!" Willow chastised. "What were you thinking?"

Everleigh had a chance to cool down while she ate her very delicious steak in peace. After she asked for the tab and paid—Maverick had indulged in another pricey drink at her expense—she drove to her mother's to collect Laura Beth.

"I wouldn't have volunteered to keep her if I'd known you would do something so foolish! It doesn't sound like this Maverick person is a man to be trifled with," Willow continued to rant.

"I didn't *trifle* with him, Mother," Everleigh said with a roll of her eyes. "I put him in his place. Besides, you're missing the point. He already knew that Mr. McMurray was dead. We don't have a newspaper anymore, and I doubt it would be all over social media. Besides, it would be highly improper for the police to release a name before contacting the next of kin."

"Gossip tends to overlook the improper part," Willow pointed out. "That's what makes it even juicier."

"It's only been two days. It takes time for news to come down the mountain."

"Not when it comes down in an ambulance with lights and sirens."

"Yeah, why the sirens? They weren't in that big of a rush. It's not like they could help him at that point."

"I suppose it was a statement of importance. Hence, the rumor mill."

Everleigh leaned back against the cushions. "You say Laura Beth is in the shower?"

"Yes, and we've eaten dinner. Landee had her do her homework after school."

"Thanks, Mom. I really appreciate all that you two to do for me."

"You know I love having her here, and Landee is thrilled to keep her, too. I know it's not easy being a single mother, but you've done an excellent job of raising my granddaughter."

"*We've* done an excellent job of it. It takes a village, or at least a great family." Everleigh reached her arms above her head and practically purred. "Once the angry hulk of a lumberjack left, I had a delicious chicken fried steak and an equally delicious margarita. The evening turned out pretty great, you know."

"I'm glad you enjoyed yourself, sweetheart. Next time, maybe you can go out with friends. I'm always free to watch Laura Beth."

"Yeah, well, take your own advice. You should get out, too. You've lived like a hermit since the divorce."

Willow laughed in disagreement. "During that time, I've earned my PI license, totally renovated the downstairs of this building, started a detective agency, and helped dozens of clients find the answer to their questions. I hardly call that being a hermit!"

"But somewhere in there, you should have taken some time for yourself. You haven't gone on a single date in five years!"

"I beg your pardon. I've had several dates."

"Dinner with that handsome US Marshal was for surveillance. And attending events while working on a case and making public appearances with a pretend date doesn't count."

"There's nothing pretend about Sid."

"Oh, he's real, but that was hardly a date. He's our attorney!"

"Yes, but while I was in Springfield for that training seminar, I went out for drinks with a very nice man."

"Did he kiss you good night?" Everleigh prodded.

"That's hardly any of your business!"

"So, that's a no," her daughter smirked. "No kiss, no date."

"Shh. I hear Laura Beth coming out of the bathroom. No more talk of dating."

After they were gone, Willow sank into the cushions of her couch. Her daughter was right. Socially, she had lived like a hermit since Marcus left her for another woman. Not only had he gotten the house and most of their money in the divorce, but he had gotten their social circle, too. Most of their friends were actually *his* friends. They followed his lead by ditching Willow and falling in with her replacement. Mandy was fresh and bubbly, with a brain to match. But she was charming, and in Marcus's career as an investment banker, charm was everything.

She had a few friends from high school who were still in the area, but everyone was busy with their own families. On the rare occasion when they got together, she felt like the fifth wheel. The others were all married, leaving her the solo among them.

"I need to find a support group for divorcees," she muttered. "We could call ourselves The Discarded Dames." The name had a sad ring to it.

Willow looked around her living room, thinking she should be ashamed for feeling sorry for herself. It had taken a lot of hard work and determination, but she was creating a satisfying life that suited *her*. Not Marcus. Not his friends nor his stuffy business associates. Her.

Once she had finished renovating the downstairs, Willow started on the top floor. Her first project was to create an apartment for herself. It stretched the full depth of the building, offering vistas from three of the four sides. From the front windows, she had a great view of the town and the rugged hills in the distance. The back windows overlooked a handful of residential homes, but the main focus was the many lower bodies of water surrounding Table Rock Lake and the rolling hills beyond. The peaks weren't as pointed and steep as the ones to the south, but they were just as beautiful. The side windows lacked the grand views of the others, but she could see what happened on the corner street below and the businesses that faced it.

Her apartment was more than big enough for her, with plenty of room for her family and whatever entertaining she might one day do. Besides a generously sized master bedroom and an indulgent bath, she had two more bedrooms, another full bath, and a powder room. There was a large living room and a large kitchen. When she could find the time, Willow loved to cook.

She was still toying with the idea of creating additional apartments she could rent out for extra income. It seemed a shame to let the rest of the space go to waste, but she would need to save up the money—and the energy—to tackle another big project like that.

Especially when she was still in the process of renovating herself..

11

They hadn't turned the 'Open' sign on yet when someone rapped on their door.

"Deputy!" Everleigh said in surprise as she admitted their early morning visitor. She glanced across the street. Mrs. Helm hadn't even opened yet, confirming that it was closer to eight thirty than it was nine. That was the time their normal workday began.

"I'm sorry to come calling so early, ladies. I was hoping to catch you before you had clients." Deputy Damien Boggs tipped his hat in greeting. "Can I have a minute of your time?"

"Certainly. Let's go in here where there's more room." She swept her arm toward the conference room.

"Would you like some coffee?" Ireland offered. She was already in the other room, enjoying her coffee while sitting on the couch.

"No, thank you. This won't take long."

Willow took a seat beside her mother, leaving

the deputy an armchair. "What can we do for you, Deputy?" she asked curiously.

"I've been canvassing Mr. McMurray's neighbors, asking if anyone noticed any strange traffic in the area lately."

"And have they?" Everleigh asked.

"That's part of our official investigation, ma'am. I'm not at liberty to comment."

"Then I don't understand what that has to do with us."

"It's been a few days since the murder." His eyes shifted to the two older women. "It's understandable that you'd be in shock at first. But sometimes, after a few days have passed, you remember things you may not have mentioned the first time. Things you didn't realize you knew because you were so shaken at the time. Has that happened to either of you?"

"No, not that I'm aware of," Willow replied.

"Nor I," her mother agreed.

"You don't recall meeting any other vehicles coming down the road on your way in?"

Ireland shook her head. "Just the tractor we told you about. I believe it was Roy Huff driving."

Boggs consulted his notes. "Yes, that fact has been confirmed."

Ireland turned her palms upward in a helpless gesture. "I'm sorry, but that's all we have to tell you."

Those obsidian eyes shifted to Everleigh. "Can you tell me why you were seen leaving the remote office of Brushy Creek Logging Company?"

"Sure," she said agreeably. "I had just left."

"That much is obvious, Ms. Alexander. The

question is why you were there in the first place."

"I was there on behalf of a client."

"Can you be a little more specific?"

"Like you, I'm not at liberty to comment."

"We're conducting a police investigation, Ms. Alexander. It's your duty to tell us everything you know."

"Are you saying the logging company could be connected to Mr. McMurray's death?" Willow was quick to ask.

"I said no such thing. I was pointing out that police investigations supersede private cases."

"Only if they're related. Unless you assure me they are, I'm not inclined to share your opinion, or our information," she said coolly.

"That could be considered obstruction of justice."

None of the women seemed concerned. They all knew it was an empty threat, including the deputy.

He turned back to Everleigh. "You were also seen in *Hardwoods* having dinner with Rick Gaines, aka Maverick. He's running the Mulfred Logging campaign up here."

"Your information isn't right. I had a drink with Mr. Gaines. He left before I ate. It was delicious, by the way. Have you eaten there, Deputy? I highly recommend the chicken fried steak and margarita."

He wasn't amused by her attempt to throw him off track. "What was your meeting about?"

"Why do you think it was a meeting? Maybe we were just having a drink together."

Deputy Boggs looked between the three in pure frustration. "Dealing with you women is like a three-ring circus!"

Everleigh looked at her grandmother with a mischievous smile. "I believe someone's told us that before, don't you?"

"Once or twice," Ireland agreed. "Since I love circuses, I take that as a compliment."

"Look. I know you think you're funny, but this is a murder investigation. And the sheriff is riding me hard for not agreeing with his theory that this was a burglary gone bad. I'm not willing to ignore other possibilities just yet. It's my duty to follow any lead I find."

Ireland stood to put her coffee cup away. She stopped beside his chair, slyly touching the deputy's shoulder. "That must be frustrating. Why won't he listen to your concerns? I think you should try talking to him again. Maybe he'll listen this time," she suggested.

His tone was sullen. "It won't do any good. That man is stubborn. He does things the old way—make a snap decision and stick with it."

"He may not listen to you, but we will," Ireland encouraged. "Why don't you tell us your theory about what happened that day?"

"I don't have a theory. I just don't believe we have enough evidence to make that decision."

"What more do you need? The place was ransacked. It stands to reason it was a robbery. Can you explain why you think differently?"

If he noticed her light touch still on his shoulder, he didn't let it show. He was too frustrated to mind the simple comfort of a soothing touch.

"I don't," Damien Boggs admitted. "but even if

we find the person who broke in and it goes to court, the prosecution will point out that doesn't make him a murderer. It's not like we have an air-tight case. The sheriff didn't take any fingerprints at the scene. He didn't bag any evidence. Took a look at the blood on the pitchfork, the holes in the body, and declared it the murder weapon. I'm sure he's right, but he just hung it back up on the wall. Didn't take it in for any sort of testing. And he didn't call for an autopsy. Told me if I wanted one, I could pay for it myself," he sulked.

"You think he wasn't really stabbed to death?" Willow asked.

Ireland felt him tense beneath her fingers, and she subtly shook her head, meaning she should be the one to pose the questions. He was under her gentle influence, and any distraction could break the connection.

"He was stabbed, all right, but it's not a given that that's what killed him. He could have been hit over the head first, or maybe last. A final blow could have killed him."

"Are you suggesting there was a second person in the attack?" Ireland asked.

"I'm not suggesting anything. I'm saying we simply don't know, and without all the evidence, we won't." When he threw up his arms in frustration, Ireland's hand fell away. He offered one last detail while under her influence. "The sheriff didn't look for defensive wounds, or flesh under his fingernails. McMurray could have fought off his killer, but now, we'll never know. The sheriff already released the body to the funeral home."

"I understand your concerns," Ireland sympathized. "I wish you could talk to him again and convince him to reconsider."

"There's no convincing that man of anything." Suddenly uncomfortable, he stood abruptly. "I need to get back to work. But remember. If you know anything, anything at all, it's your duty to come forward."

"We will, Deputy," Willow assured him. She didn't promise when they might share that information.

"Good luck with canvassing," Everleigh said. "It's a good thing he doesn't have a lot of neighbors."

"Yeah, but the sheriff is having me canvass the entire mountain." Complaining about his assignment, he put his hat back on.

Everleigh's eyes widened. "The *entire* thing?"

He sounded dejected. "Yeah. The entire thing."

With time to spare before opening, the partners spent a few moments speculating after the deputy was gone.

"The sheriff is conducting a very sloppy investigation." Willow didn't sound surprised.

"But to just put the rake back on the wall?" Revulsion shimmied through Ireland's shoulders.

"The deputy mentioned a possible blow to the head. Did you two see anything like that?" Everleigh asked.

"No, but I can look back at my pictures."

"And I have a friend who works at the mortuary. I could discreetly ask her," Ireland offered.

"Find out if the casket will be open. That would indicate no significant damage to the head," Everleigh reasoned.

"He raised the possibility of two assailants. And that the logging companies could be involved. What do you make of that?" Willow asked.

"I don't think Rick Gaines, aka Maverick, would need any help killing an old man like Gus. I think he's capable of doing that all by himself," Everleigh said. Her phone binged, alerting her to a message. She read through it before reporting, "This is from Moon, or at least her organization. They really take this cloak and dagger routine seriously. Her next meeting will be a week from today, but she doesn't divulge the exact time or place until the day before."

Her mother raised a speculative eyebrow. "Secretive, much? That practically screams scam."

Everleigh disagreed. "I think it's meant to be seen as even more intriguing, not to mention exclusive. Remember, she's appealing to people who need a deeper purpose in life. What's better than their own private club?"

"Club, or cult?" Ireland asked. "I'm surprised she even sent that much, considering we're a PI firm."

"Are you kidding? I used a fake name and a fake email address."

"Good thinking."

Willow looked at her watch. "It's almost time to open. I have to go into Branson today, so I think I'll poke around in a pawn shop or two. Not my favorite place to shop, but we struck out with Sharika, and we can't speak with Moon until next week. We may as well start looking for the camcorder."

"Have fun with that," her daughter said in a saccharine voice. Her stance on the topic was easy to discern.

Willow wasn't dissuaded. "It's better than twiddling our thumbs for another week." She waved toward Everleigh's desk. "You do your thing on the computer. I'll do this."

'This' took her to five different pawn shops. Of the two stores that had a video camera in stock, neither were from the era she needed.

By the time Willow reached Border that evening, dusk smudged the sky with inky blues and muted grays. It was a magical time in the Ozarks, a time when the fairies—or the little people, as the mountaineers often referred to them—came out to play. She didn't believe in the mythical characters, but sometimes, it was fun to imagine they might exist. Surely in the fairy world, no one had to deal with murder and deceit.

On a whim, she decided to treat herself to dinner. There were dozens more dining options in Branson, but she hadn't realized how tired she was until the ride home. She really didn't feel like cooking.

She pulled into the parking lot of the only seafood restaurant in their little town. She slid into a slot between an oversized dually truck and a holdover Volkswagen van straight out of the 60s. It even had flowers painted on the side.

The hostess greeted her with a smile. "One this evening, or will you be joining someone?"

Dining solo had been difficult in those first years after her divorce, especially in public. Willow had avoided it as best she could, but eventually, it hadn't felt so awkward. Now, looking forward to a nice dinner that she didn't have to cook for herself, she cheerfully confirmed, "Just me."

The cheerful feeling didn't last. She felt it again. Danger mingled in the air alongside the savory scents of fish and oysters. Requesting a table against the wall, Willow felt the need to have something solid behind her back. She needed to see the danger she sensed coming her way.

She barely glanced at the menu. She knew she was having shrimp and a refreshing mojito. It was the perfect pick me up after a long day of searching, and not too heavy to dull her senses.

After ordering, she looked around at other patrons. She recognized only a handful of people. There was Vera who worked at the post office, Reverend Blue's son and his young family, one of the men who exterminated her building, a woman she vaguely knew in passing, and, to her dismay, Sheriff Mathers.

Was that where the impeding danger came from? With any luck, the sheriff wouldn't see her, and she could eat in peace.

After a day of handling dozens of second-hand objects and door handles, Willow needed to wash her hands. Weaving her way to the restrooms in the adjacent dining room meant Mathers was more likely to notice her, but it also gave her a chance to see other diners. The sense of danger could be coming from someone or something other than the sheriff.

As she picked her way to the back, she spotted a familiar face in the far corner booth. The woman was dressed in a much more colorful outfit than yesterday, but there was no mistaking Sharika. She was in a hushed conversation with a woman Willow didn't recognize, and from the looks on their faces, it was an intense discussion.

Sharika wore a bold-colored blouse with traditional African tribal symbols scattered across it. The outfit was at odds with the persona of the *Restore Your Soul* owner. Could the flowing robes, soft voice, and all that talk about inner peace and a balanced chakra be an act? Was that the secret she held back?

Willow stopped at their booth, infusing a smile into her voice. "Sharika? I thought that was you. How are you this evening?"

"I'm, uh, fine." For a moment, she looked flustered, until she gathered herself and managed a smile of her own. Willow thought it looked a bit strained. "And you?" she asked belatedly.

"Hungry!" She touched her tummy with a bit of a laugh. "I had a craving for shrimp and decided to splurge."

"It is the best in town," the younger woman agreed. Not wanting to appear rude, she motioned to her friend and stumbled through an introduction. "Ms. Alexander, this is, uhm, Maude."

From the corner of her eye, Willow saw the other woman's eyes widen. It was clearly a false name and not a very convincing one, at that. The name was no longer in vogue and usually belonged to women of a particular age. Sharika's blond-haired companion couldn't be older than Everleigh, at best.

The first time Willow met the yoga instructor, she sensed that something was off. The sensation was even stronger now. Not only was she hiding something, but whatever it was, it swirled with an omen.

Willow extended her hand to 'Maude.' "It's nice to meet you. I'm Willow Alexander."

"And you, as well." The other woman's smile looked sincere. When they exchanged handshakes, the bracelets on her wrist jangled.

"What interesting bracelets," Willow remarked. She took a closer look and changed her mind. "Are those... bones?"

"They certainly are. Hand-crafted by local artisans," Maude boasted, presenting her unusual jewelry for closer inspection.

Willow knew that Native Americans often used bones to decorate clothing, ceremonial headpieces, and sacred jewelry pieces. The ones that Maude wore were nothing like any pieces Willow had ever seen. Some were carved into mini skulls. Others had painted symbols that brought to mind devils and demons. The odd pagan-themed bracelets made Willow uncomfortable.

"Mrs. Alexander is a private investigator," Sharika informed her friend. Her voice sounded stiff as she added, "Isn't that a fascinating career choice?"

The warmth slipped from Maude's voice as she snatched her arm back. "It certainly is." Her eyes were green and wide, reminding Willow of a cat's. "What made you choose that profession, if you don't mind me asking?"

"Not at all." Like her companion, there was something off about Maude. She held herself in a poised position that could almost pass for casual, if not for the tightness around her eyes and mouth. "I suppose it's my curious nature," Willow said.

In a cool voice, 'Maude' made an observation. "I should think that could become dangerous at times."

There was a strange challenge in the other woman's eyes. Willow didn't understand it, but she knew it was a threat of sorts. She replied with cool confidence. "I often deal with the criminal element, so anything is possible," she replied.

The other woman's nostrils flared.

Sharika's eyes darted between the two women. She was clearly uncomfortable with the turn of conversation.

If Willow hoped to learn anything more from the yoga instructor, she knew antagonizing her friend wasn't the way to do it.

"Well, I just wanted to stop by and say hello. I'll let you two get back to your meal. Sharika, it was good to see you again. And Maude, it was nice meeting you."

"You, too," the other woman lied right back.

Neither of their smiles were convincing.

Willow hurried through washing her hands. If she had any intuition at all, she knew the women would leave as soon as she turned her back.

She wasn't quick enough. The women were already gone, leaving their half-eaten meal and a handful of cash on the table. If she hurried, she might get a fleeting glance of their retreat. For some reason, she thought they might climb into the hippie van she saw in the parking lot. The cheerful flowers were a far cry from skull jewelry, but somehow, it fit.

The waitress intercepted her near the door. "Oh, hon, your dinner is ready. You're not leaving, are you?"

A familiar voice spoke from behind her. "Of course she isn't," Sheriff Mathers boomed. "Mrs. Alexander would never run out on a tab. Isn't that right, Mrs. Alexander?"

"Of course not," Willow said indignantly. To appease the waitress' anxious look, she explained, "I saw a friend leaving and wanted to say goodbye."

The sheriff made the objection. "But your dinner will get cold."

It wasn't the food he warned her about.

Willow chose not to make a scene. Judging by the speed at which the women left their table, they had peeled out of the parking lot and were long gone by now.

"You're right, Sheriff," she said with a fake smile. "I certainly wouldn't want that. And thank you—" she peered at the waitress' name tag to get the name right "—Annette. I'm looking forward to my shrimp."

12

"Can I borrow your car today?" Landee asked her daughter over the phone.

"Uhm, well, sure." Willow couldn't remember ever hearing that particular request before. "Is something wrong with your car?"

"Oh, no, nothing like that. I'm headed out to speak with some of Gus' neighbors, and my car is a little flashy for what I have in mind," Ireland explained.

Willow's reply was dry. "So, naturally my car came to mind."

"It is more suited for this mission. I know it's an inconvenience, but would you mind coming over here so we can exchange vehicles?"

"You want me to drive the Mercedes?"

"I know you don't approve of my car, Willow," Ireland said irritably, "but it won't kill you to drive it once in a while."

Unable to think of a reason to refuse, she grudgingly gave in. "Fine, then. But do you think it's safe to visit the neighbors just yet? You're not afraid of running into Deputy Boggs?"

"I'm sure he started with the nearest neighbors—the ones most likely to have seen or heard something—before branching further out. I should be in the clear."

"And if you aren't?"

Ireland's reply sounded nonchalant. "You know me. I'll improvise."

"I'm in the middle of something, so give me about fifteen minutes before I head over."

"That's fine, dear. It should give me plenty of time to get the last pie out of the oven."

"You're baking?" Willow asked in surprise.

"All part of my plan. I'll explain while we're loading the car."

"But—"

"Oh, there's the timer. I need to rotate my pie. See you soon!" She hung up before Willow could ask more questions.

When Willow arrived at her mother's house, she was surprised to see Ireland's choice of clothing for the day. The trim, fashionable jeans topped by a casual sweater duo was a cross between Irie and Ireland—not suitable for the garden club, but still a far cry from actual digging in the soil. Inside of teased curls or a headband, her hair was brushed into a straight, simple style.

"I hardly recognize you!" she proclaimed.

"Good. That's what I'm going for." Wasting no time, Ireland handed her a picnic basket. "Here. Put these in the car. I'll be out with the rest."

"What are these?" She asked the question even as she inhaled the tantalizing aromas of her mother's homemade pies wafting from the basket.

"My excuse for visiting the neighbors. I'll be out in just a jiffy."

Still perplexed, Willow carried the basket as requested and deposited it into the front seat of her car. Ireland soon appeared behind her, putting her basket into the back seat. "Here's the keys to my car. Be gentle with my baby," Ireland cautioned.

"It's a car, Landee. Hardly a baby."

"Oh, stop pouting. It's a figure of speech."

"I still don't understand what the pies are for."

"I'll give you a full report when I get home. I'll try to be back before dark." She glanced down at Willow's older-model car and frowned. "I'm not sure how dependable your car is."

"Probably more dependable than yours," she retorted. "You know they seldom make things to last these days."

"True. Now, wish me luck and let me get started on my mission." With that, her mother climbed behind the steering wheel and went about her mysterious errand.

Ireland pulled into the driveway of the first house on her route, an aged farmhouse that could use a fresh coat of paint. Yet the yard was neat and well maintained, she noted.

Eying the hound in the driveway and hoping it didn't bite, she used a trick she had learned from the mailman. She spoke softly to the dog and tossed it a doggie treat. More interested in the snack than the unknown guest, the dog accepted the offering and waited for another.

Ireland stepped onto the porch as she tossed

the third and final treat to the hound. She rapped on the door and soon heard shuffling inside. A woman appeared in the doorway with a puzzled look on her face.

"Can I help you?" she asked. Her voice was neither friendly nor hostile.

Ireland took it as a good sign and proceeded with her plan. "I'm so sorry to intrude on you like this, but I just wanted to drop this pie off to my friend. I'm afraid I forgot the directions and am hoping you can steer me in the right way."

"Sure, hon," the woman said, even though she looked younger than Ireland. "What's his name?"

"Gus McMurray."

The woman's face drooped with a frown. "I'm sorry to have to tell you this, but Gus passed away a couple of days ago."

Ireland put her hand to her chest, feigning surprise. "He what?" She hoped she looked appropriately distressed.

"Oh, listen to me," the woman worried aloud. Her eyes darted to the older-model car parked in her driveway. It seemed to meet her approval. "Here I am, blurting it out so thoughtlessly! Please, come on in, hon."

The woman led her through the living room. It had a comfortable, lived-in look. When they reached the kitchen, she motioned toward the table and chairs. "Have yourself a seat, and I'll make us a cup of coffee."

"I don't want to be a bother…"

"No bother at all. None at all. Don't get too many visitors up here on the mountain. I'm Elsa.

What's your name, sweetie?"

"Landee."

"Landee," Elsa tried out the unusual name on her tongue. "Why, ain't that a pretty name!"

"I just can't believe it," Ireland murmured. "Gus is dead?" She did her best to maintain her stunned look as she took the offered chair. Secretly, she was quite pleased with herself. The casual outfit and Willow's old car had been the perfect choice for this fishing expedition.

"I'm afraid so. It's been quite the shock. Especially being as he was—" Elsa stopped short of finishing her sentence.

"He was what?"

"Well, I'm afraid the news gets worse," her hostess said. Starting the coffee pot, she joined Ireland at the table. "Gus didn't just die." She hesitated for effect. "He was murdered."

"Murdered? Gus? Why, I'm surprised he had an enemy in the world!"

"Maybe not an enemy, but definitely a few who had a grudge against him."

"You don't say!" Again, Ireland put her hand up to her chest.

"You didn't hear this from me, of course," Elsa began.

"No, no. Of course not." Ireland grasped her hand in what could be considered sacred confidentiality. The other woman had no clue about her special gift of persuasion.

Clearly a woman who didn't often get a chance to share juicy gossip, Elsa leaned forward. "I heard his throat was slit. Everyone knows what that means in these parts."

Ireland wasn't aware of any special significance to the act, but she nodded as if to agree.

Encouraged, Elsa went on, "Just like Ol' Sam Pixley. He was once a member of the Bald Knobbers, you know, and maybe the meanest of the bunch. They say he'd slit the throat of anyone who held out on them. The idea was they would bleed out that way, like a slaughtered pig. To send a message to anybody else wantin' to quit their gang and goin' out on their own, they killed Ol' Sam in the same way."

Ireland knew that Gus' throat hadn't been slashed, so some old legend of the notorious outlaw gang shed no light on the real cause of his death. However, the fact that Elsa considered him a 'holdout' did.

"Do you have any clue who may have considered Gus a holdout?" she asked.

"Ideas, no proof," Elsa said on a sigh. "I'd say the logging companies, for sure. Gus was one of the few to hold out on sellin' his land. Made 'em awfully mad, from what I heard."

"Logging companies?"

"They're doing another round of cuttin' up here. Do it every dozen years or so, moving from one place to another. One company, though, Mulfred, wants to buy the land outright. I hear they're wanting to do some sort of high-falutin housing development up the mountain. They're callin' it the Scrimshaw Project. They done built one of their fancy-dancy houses up there, right next to Gus' place. It's some prototype for what the whole neighborhood could look like."

Effecting a startled expression, Ireland softly gasped. She reached for Elsa's hand again and squeezed. Her voice was almost a whisper, as if someone might overhear. "You think that could have something to do with his death?"

"Well, now, I didn't..." Elsa's denial fell off, and Ireland sensed her hesitancy.

"You can tell me," she encouraged.

"I do reckon it's possible. That ramrod of theirs, that Gaines fella, is like a bulldog. Sinks his teeth in and don't want to let go. I could see him doing something bad to anyone who held out on him."

"Even murder?"

"He has a temper," Elsa admitted, "so, yeah, I think so." With the other woman's hand still gripping hers, she continued to share what was on her mind. "Then, there's his boy. Gideon was always a handful as a child, but he's even worse as a grown man. Always up to no good, from what I can see."

"Surely, he wouldn't kill his own father!" This time, the disbelief in Ireland's voice was real.

"I'd like to think not, but with Gideon... If his father didn't do what he wanted, he could have lost his temper. Cuttin' his throat seems a might drastic, but the boy was easily influenced. If he had a mind to idolize the legends in these parts, Ol' Sam Pixley might've come to mind."

When Ireland left, it was without the pie. It was the least she could do, she told her impromptu hostess, for her kindness and hospitality.

The next house on her route was tucked deeper among the scrubby trees, and in need of more attention. The sagging porch groaned beneath her feet when she approached the door.

"If you sellin', I ain't buyin'." The gruff voice came from somewhere behind the screen door, its owner half-hidden in the shadows. Ireland noticed how two small holes punctured the screen from the inside out, most likely compliments of a .22bullet. She just hoped the rifle hadn't been pointed toward an unwanted caller.

"In that case, you're in luck." She used her best smile in hopes of defusing his hostile greeting.

"If you ain't sellin' nothing, why are you here?" He stepped forward enough so that she could see his frown.

"I was bringing a pie to my friend. I hear he's been ailing," she explained. "The problem is, it's been a while since I paid him a visit, and I'm afraid I've forgotten how to get there." She glanced around, pretending to be disoriented. She knew this man would be a harder sell than Elsa had been. The best way to handle that was to talk circles around him and hope to throw him off balance.

"To be honest, I thought this was the right driveway, but there's no red door. Delta wanted him to paint it that color, you know, and he only did it to make her happy. I realized now that this isn't their house. The sad matter of the truth is that I haven't been up here to call since before she passed. I didn't realize how many trees could die in that time, or how I'd forget the lay of the land." Her free hand fluttered near her face. "Does that ever happen to you? You pass a place a hundred times and think it will always look that way, but take away a few trees or move a lane over just a few feet, and suddenly, it's like you don't know where you are."

The man blinked in rapid succession. Stroking his long, white beard, he seemed perplexed by the little spit of a woman babbling in such a friendly manner. He didn't know her, did he? These days, his memory didn't keep up with all the facts and faces he had known over the years. Almost ninety years of living did that to a man.

He was slow to reply, still trying to decide if he should know her. "Uh… I reckon that's happened a time or two. But the only red door I recall is about a mile up the road, at Gus McMurray's place."

"That way?" she asked, following his line of sight.

"Won't do you no good to go up there, though. He ain't home."

"Oh, dear, have I missed him?" she asked in a worried voice.

"You could say that. Ambulance come got him a few days ago."

"He's gotten worse, then? I saw him last week and he said he didn't feel well. I hope it's not too serious?" She posed it as a question.

"Reckon you could say that. He's dead."

"Dead?"

He spoke matter-of-factly, if not unsympathetically. "It happens to us all, sooner or later. My day can't be too far off."

"But I just saw him!"

"You done said that. Say, what's that under the towel? Smells awfully good."

"It's—It's a pie." She sounded just stunned

enough to be convincing. "I made it for Gus, thinking to cheer him up."

"A might late for that," he pointed out. "But, say, it might cheer me up."

Ireland worked her mouth in a gesture of being shocked speechless. After clearing her throat, she 'managed' to push out a weak, "Do you think I could bother you for a glass of water?"

He looked none too pleased about the request, but his eyes wandered back to the pie. "I reckon we could make a trade."

"Yes. Yes, of course," she murmured. "I'll carry this into the kitchen for you."

The old man led the way through a very cluttered front room. It reminded Ireland of Gus's ransacked house, but she imagined this mess could be attributed solely to its owner.

She carefully stepped across a discarded newspaper, now crumbled and torn from his heavy foot.

"Trees didn't die, you know," he said out of the blue.

It took her a moment to understand the random statement. Then she remembered her excuse of not recognizing her whereabouts because of trees dying or driveways shifting. "They didn't?" she asked obligingly.

"Nope. Those darn logging companies took 'em down. Tried to get me to sell but, by God, I ain't giving my timber to no one! That's about what it amounted to—just givin' it to them—for the paltry amount they offered me." He stomped into the kitchen where he proceeded to jerk a cabinet door open and take a

Tupperware juice glass out. No bigger than it was, he obviously didn't intend for her to stay long.

"Oh, my," she said, "where are my manners? I'm Landee. I didn't catch your name."

"Didn't give it," he said abruptly. He turned and motioned to the old Formica-top table with its three crooked chairs gathered around it. "Might as well have a seat, since you're here and all."

"Thank you." She accepted the water, noticing how some of it lapped over the edge when delivered in his unsteady hand.

"Yep, died of a slashed throat," he said without preamble.

Ireland fought the urge to correct him. Gus had been stabbed in the chest, not slit across the throat, but admitting such would defeat her purpose. Her goal today was to gather information from his neighbors, and being proved a fraud wasn't the way to go about it.

In spite of herself, she reached for her own throat as if to protect it. "A slashed throat?"

"From ear to ear, from what I heard."

"Who would have done such a thing?"

The old man went back to the cupboard, where he pulled out two small plates. "Might as well have some of that pie."

"I'll pass, but help yourself."

He shrugged and put the extra plate away. "Don," he said as he sifted through a drawer in search of a fork. "Don Becker."

The fact that he had a ready name surprised her. "That's who killed Gus?"

"Hell, no! That's who I am. Don't know who

killed Gus."

The elderly man had a strange way of answering questions in a belated fashion, but at least he was talking to her. From the expression on his face when he first came to the door, it was more than she had hoped for.

"Gideon must be distraught over his father's death," she prodded.

"Probably don't even know about it. That boy always was flighty, and he's worse the older he gets. Might not come back around for months."

"I know he was gone for a while after Delta died." She hoped she sounded like this was first-hand knowledge and not something Gus had passed along to Willow and Everleigh.

"Without that boy of his coming and going, I'm surprised they found Gus' body so fast. He don't get much company. I seen one of those hippie vans coming out of his drive one day, but not much else."

"When was that?"

He dropped heavily into his chair as he took his first bite of pie. He made a sound of appreciation as he took another bite. "Not too long ago."

"Do you know who was driving?"

"Never seen her before."

"So, it was a woman?"

"I said *her*, didn't I?" He paused to look at her closely. "How'd you say you knew Gus and Delta?"

"I didn't." She took a sip of water, searching for what little she remembered about the late couple. "My uncle's wife was a third cousin to Delta, on her mother's side." It was vague enough not to raise any flags. "I would see them from time to time and happened to run into Gus just last week. That's why I brought the pie." A huge slice of which was quickly disappearing from Don's plate.

"Mighty fine pie, it is." He nodded with enthusiasm, finding a stray crumb in his beard and stuffing it into his mouth. He clearly didn't want a bite going to waste.

"What was that about a logging company cutting timber up here?"

"Started showin' up about a year ago, wantin' to buy all our trees. Pushy lot, they are, 'specially one. Wouldn't put it past the one to kill Gus just to get his land. 'Specially with his boy gone and all."

"What was the name of the company?"

"Started with a M, or maybe a N. Guy who ran it was called Gunsmoke."

"Gunsmoke?" That was a new one to her.

"Maybe not Gunsmoke," he said on second thought. "Rawhide? It was one of those old westerns." He waved his fork in the air. "The kind of real TV they used to make, none of that fluffy nonsense they show nowadays."

"Would it have been Maverick?" Ireland guessed.

"That's it! Maverick. That's what that guy was called. He and Gus didn't get along at all."

"Really? How do you mean?"

"Gus kicked him off his place, but the guy was ornery enough to come back. Gus told me they had a few choice words to say, and the man threatened him, saying he'd get his hands on that land, one way or another. Stands to reason he was the one to use the knife."

"Were you and Gus friends, Mr. Becker?"

"Friends enough, I reckon."

"Is there anyone else you can think of who had a grudge against Gus?"

He thought about it as he finished the last of his pie. "Maybe Billy Clyde Fowler."

"Billy Clyde Fowler? Why would he want to kill Gus?"

"There was all that ruckus about Gus sellin' him a sick horse a few years back. In turn, Billy Clyde killed a few of his chickens. They have them a right good feud going." Don Becker corrected himself. "Least ways, they did. I reckon that's over now, unless he was the one to kill Gus. Iffen he did, the spirits won't let him rest. That man will be tortured for life."

Ireland knew that most of the older people in the mountains believed in spooks and spirits. She made no comment other than to ask another question.

"Killing sounds a bit drastic, don't you think?"

"Not with the Fowler temper. They can be a mean lot." He eyed her plastic glass. "You done with that water?"

Knowing she had outworn her welcome, Ireland thanked him for his hospitality. He followed her to the door, where he surprised her by saying, "If you find yourself with an extra pie sometimes, I'd be willin' to take it off your hands. Pumpkin and apple are my favorite."

"I'll keep that in mind, Mr. Becker," Ireland said with a smile. "Thank you again."

He grunted a reply she couldn't make out and abruptly shut the door.

13

The final details of Moon's secretive meeting came on Wednesday. They would gather on Friday at a small, out-of-the-way café in the tiny town of Mule Holler. The eatery closed at two, ensuring privacy for the meeting's seven pm start time.

Excited about the upcoming event, Everleigh was already planning her outfit. She would need a disguise befitting not only the occasion, but also the fake identity she used to register.

Mrs. Helm's call burst her bubble of excitement.

"Have you looked out your front windows today?" the old woman shrieked.

"No, ma'am, I haven't. We use the back entrance, and of course, Mom just uses the stairs. We haven't even opened the shades yet."

"Maybe you should."

Everleigh frowned as the elderly woman slammed down her receiver.

"Uhm, Mom? That was Mrs. Helm. She said we should open our blinds and look out."

Willow did as requested. One glimpse, and she cried out, "What in the world!"

"Is that... raw eggs?" Ireland asked, peering at the windows more closely.

"We've been egged?" Everleigh sounded slightly amused. "It's not even Halloween. April Fool's Day, either."

"Why on earth would someone do this?" Ireland cried in dismay.

Willow's voice was more subdued. "It's a warning."

"Of what? That hens are staging a revolt of some sort?" Everleigh grinned.

"This isn't meant as a joke," Willow retorted. "This is someone's way of telling us to back off."

"Actually, I think this is a good sign," Ireland interjected in her positive way. "It means we're getting close enough to make someone nervous."

With the city police force temporarily vacant, the Border County Sheriff Department had taken over their jurisdiction. Willow wasn't surprised to see Sheriff Mathers personally respond. He never missed an opportunity to harass them and warn them of some supposed violation.

He took one look at the women on the sidewalk and the egg-smeared windows behind them. "What seems to be the problem, ladies?" He wore a smirk on his face.

"See for yourself." Ireland rolled her hand toward the damage.

"Looks like you've been pranked." He chuckled. "Kids will be kids, you know."

"We both know this isn't the work of kids,"

Willow told him in an even voice.

"We do?"

"This is clearly an act of vandalism, and you know it."

"Take a look at all the other businesses," Everleigh said, motioning up and down the street. "If this was a prank, why were we the only ones singled out?"

"You must have pissed off some of the egg farmers in the area," he suggested. He turned his head to spit, the tobacco juice narrowly missing Willow's shoe.

Willow's reply was terse. "We don't know any egg farmers in the area."

"You don't know any egg farmers, eh?" he questioned.

"Surely, you aren't referring to Ms. Judy Reilly. She has backyard chickens, but I hardly think a sweet little old eighty-something-year-old woman did this."

"I'm referring," he said with a jeer, "to the commercial egg farms we have around here. You know those big ol' long, metal barns on the way out to Scrimshaw Mountain? Those are chicken houses. Hens houses, to be exact, where eggs are produced. There's more over near Knob Mountain. You been out either way recently?" His keen gaze bore into hers.

Yep, definitely a warning.

"Even if I have, I don't recall going off road and mowing down a bunch of innocent chickens. Why would one of the egg farmers be mad and retaliate like this?"

"All the same, I'd stay away from there if I was you ladies. No need to make matters worse."

"Worse?" Ireland asked. "Our front windows are one big, raw omelet."

"If you think eggs make a mess, just imagine what chicken litter would look like, ma'am. You should be glad this is all they done," the sheriff said cockily.

"Is that a threat of some kind?" Willow wanted to know.

"Now, why would I be threatening you?"

"That would be our question."

"You're barking up the wrong tree. And unless you saw who did this, I'm not sure what you expect me to do about it. Looks like a job for a window washer to me."

"I've come to expect very little from you, Sheriff Mathers." Willow's words were clipped. "But I do want our complaint documented, in case we have any other incidents."

"It's in our call log," he assured her. "Now, if you don't mind, I have some more serious matters to attend. Actual crimes, you know?"

"Vandalism is a crime, Sheriff. That's why it's called *criminal* mischief."

"I don't need you quoting the law to me, young lady."

Ireland stepped in to keep her daughter from saying something they would all regret. "Of course not, Sheriff," she cooed. "We simply want to be heard, like any other law-abiding citizen in the county. And we appreciate you coming out and personally handling this matter yourself. It's nice to know our sheriff stands behind local businesses. Being a woman-owned business, we need a man to look after us from time to time."

Ireland Garret was too charming of a woman to take offense at. Willow could have sworn she saw the sheriff blush.

Ireland touched his arm as she walked him to his car. "Before you go, I don't suppose you know anyone who could help us with these windows, do you?" she asked.

Mathers rubbed the whiskers along his chin. "I do have a couple of men working off their community service hours. I'll see if I can send them around to give you a hand."

Not interested in seeing her mother flirt with the sheriff, even if for the common good, Willow turned away and went back inside.

She, too, had more important matters to attend.

In this southern part of Branson, there were more natural areas than there were towns. The area was home to Johnny 'Mr. BassPro' Morris, and his mission to preserve wildlife, the area's rich history, and the sheer grandeur of nature. She passed Top of the Rock Ozark Heritage Preserve, the entrance to Big Cedar Lodge, and the Top of the Rock Golf Course. The closer she came to Branson, the more populated it became; subdivisions, shopping centers, and one of the many BassPro Shops. In comparison to the granddaddy of them all in Springfield, this one situated on the banks of the old White River was small.

Most people thought of Branson as the "Live Music Show Capital of the World", with its host of theaters and spectacular productions like Dolly Parton's Stampede and the Shepard of the Hills play. There were caves, lakes, and nature trails, not to mention Silver Dollar City amusement park and several interactive museums, making it a favorite destination for people of all ages and all walks of life.

But the truth was, the true town of Branson was so much more. Away from the congestion and the tourist attractions, it was simply a small town tucked into the heart of the Ozark Mountains. It still had a quaint Main Street running through the center of the town, with shops and hometown cafés that clung to the concept of days long gone. The people were friendly, welcoming, and diverse. Beyond the flash and glamour that made the area famous, lay hidden jewels that managed to escape the commercialism and pull of tourism. These were the mom-and-pop businesses, the ones that the locals preferred and frequented.

Willow knew where some of the best antique shops were, and most of the resale shops. She had frequented them often enough, looking for stolen or lost items clients hired her to retrieve. Some offered a major clue on their bigger cases, which she hoped was the case today.

By noon, she was tired, hungry, and discouraged. After three days of unproductive searching, her mission had rolled into a blur of storefronts and muddled merchandise. Someone recently told her about a small café they had discovered nestled among a strip of nostalgic buildings near Main. Deciding it was as good as any place to recharge, the GPS led her to a street she had never explored before. It looked much like the streets in Border.

"And here I thought I knew the town like the back of my hand," she mused. She found a parking space in front of an antique shop called *Years Ago Antiques and Curiosities*. "That looks interesting," she noted. "I'll check it out after lunch."

The café was noisy and crowded and filled with locals. Willow didn't recognize any of them, but she knew the look. They were regular people, grabbing a bite to eat on their lunch break or to meet up with friends.

The waitress found her a spot to eat and rattled off the specials. She chose the soup of the day and half sandwich. The soup was creamy tomato basil. One bite of delicious perfection, and she knew it was homemade.

Willow lingered over a cup of really good coffee—so few places made a good cup anymore—but time was wasting. At the moment, they had an edge on Mathers. The sheriff didn't know about the video recorder or that Gideon had cleaned out the barn and likely sold it for a few bucks. Once he learned *Intuitive Investigations* was investigating on their own, he would get suspicious. And he would definitely shut them down.

Now rejuvenated and ready to continue her mission, Willow started next door.

A cheery, old-fashioned bell announced her arrival. The store was everything an antique store should be. It was warm, cozy, and inviting. She spotted a few high-end furniture pieces, but most were set up in vignettes that would look good in anyone's home. The store didn't have rows and rows of shelves, stuffed full of someone else's past. What shelves she saw were tastefully arranged and the merchandise neatly displayed. The store had nooks and crannies to pull customers in, eager to explore every inch.

"Welcome to Years Ago!" a man's voice called from somewhere in the back. "I'll be out in a sec. Browse all you like."

"Thank you," she called to the unknown person.

She was looking for a camcorder, but dozens of other treasures snagged her attention. She hadn't gotten much from the house in Springfield. Marcus was ruthless in his demands, even though Mandy made it clear Willow's style was far from her own. Willow hadn't fought him. She wanted only sentimental favorites that brought back pleasant memories, not bitter reminders of what had once been. Now that her apartment was finished, she needed to fill empty walls and naked shelves. She found plenty of possibilities here.

"Sorry about that," the voice said as it came nearer. It was a pleasant baritone from what sounded like a middle-aged man.

In Willow's experience, most of the shops were run by two kinds of people. On one end of the pendulum were the young people—college students, most likely, waiting for a job befitting their expensive degrees or high school students needing gas money. They were just there to collect a paycheck. If they couldn't find it on the internet or remember that their grandparents had one like it, they knew practically nothing about the goods they sold. Their edgy haircuts, body piercings, and torn jeans were at odds with their surroundings.

On the other end of the pendulum were the grandparents, most of whom owned the stores. Mom and pop businesses. Their dress code required comfortable shoes and a sweater, even on the hottest of days. For some, it was a hobby, something to do after retirement. Dreams of traveling the globe or spending endless days fishing or reading by the lake grew tiresome, not to mention expensive. Some needed the small stipend to combat the havoc that inflation played on their Social Security checks. For still others, the stores were their lifetime career; it *was* their retirement plan. The lucky ones still loved the thrill of the hunt, finding and sharing just the right treasure. The unlucky ones had fallen into a rut, but it was better than sitting at home with that book.

There were, of course, a few proprietors who fell somewhere in the middle. Most of them were women, and Willow recognized them by their enthusiasm. They were full of energy, always rearranging displays and bringing in new merchandise. They took pride in their store, and it showed. If they had employees, they were well versed in the products and showed the same enthusiasm as their boss. Matching shirts with the store logo were often involved.

That's why Willow was taken aback when the nice-looking, mature man stepped around the corner. He appeared to be a well-preserved fifty-something-year-old just slightly older than her own fifty-two years. He had dark good looks, a neatly trimmed goatee, and startling blue eyes. Silver was beginning to weave through his goatee and the black hair he wore slightly longer than most men his age. His shirt sleeves were turned up to reveal strong forearms, a few tasteful tattoos, and the hands of a working man.

He was now wiping those hands on the tail of the carpenter's apron. As he reached around his trim waist to untie the ends, Willow couldn't help but appreciate the way it hung low on his hips.

"I was in the back," he explained, "working on a clock." To her relief, he was more concerned with getting the machine oil off his hands than he was her reaction.

"No problem. I was enjoying browsing."

"That's what we're here for. Help yourself."

She turned toward a display of old clocks. "Are you working on one like these?"

She assumed he nodded. "A mantel clock that should ring on the hour, but—" A melodious chime from the back room interrupted his words. "I stand corrected." His voice held a touch of humor. "It seems the pendulum is working now."

"You have a great store. The merchandise is so eclectic, yet it flows together beautifully." She turned back toward him with her sincere assessment.

"My wife taught me the art of blending styles," he replied modestly.

"Tell her I said she has excellent tastes, and a true talent when it comes to displays."

"Unfortunately, she passed away three years ago."

"Oh! I'm—I'm so sorry!" What she intended as an earnest compliment turned into an embarrassing faux pas. "My condolences."

His face was tighter than it had been before, and his eyes were sad, but he managed a half-smile. "Traci left her mark on the store and shared a lot of her secrets with me before she passed. I think I'm finally getting the hang of it."

"I think so, judging from the looks of things. How long have you been here? I'm just now discovering it."

"Forever. This was my parents' store before Traci took over. I cut my teeth on that old counter there," he motioned behind them to the register, "but I seemed to be a 'bull in a china cabinet,' as my mother would say. I wasn't allowed out front until I was strong enough to move furniture."

Willow absolutely refused to sneak a peek at his muscles. She was here on business, not to ogle the unexpected proprietor.

"Can I help you find anything?" the man asked.

"Actually, I'm hoping you can. I'm Willow Alexander with *Intuitive Investigations*." She dug into her unfashionably large bag to find a business card.

"Tobias Cameron, at your service." He bent at the waist in a half-curtsy. "What can I do for you?" He took the card, glanced at the names, and turned his sharp blue eyes to hers.

She went with the simplest explanation. "I'm looking for a miniDV camcorder from the very early 2000s. We believe it was sold by mistake at a resale or pawn shop, but we have no clue where. The seller is out of town."

His eyes narrowed in thought. "A miniDV recorder, you say?"

"We think so. Actually, it's just an assumption. But that seems to be the recorder of choice for low-budget films of the day."

"Hang on. I may have something like that in the back."

Willow followed him to the counter, too excited to browse while she waited. She heard sounds of shuffling and sorting coming from the back room before Tobias Cameron appeared in the doorway with a cardboard box.

"I'm gathering enough old cameras and photos to do a display on early photography. I thought things like camcorders and the home movie camera might add interest." He moved a few pieces before pulling out a compact camcorder. "Like this?" he asked.

Willow's heart skipped a beat. It looked just like the one she had seen on the internet. And... hadn't she and Marcus had one like that? They carried it with them when they went on vacation. Those had been few and far between, planned strategically between his clients' needs. Heaven forbid the stock market plunge and leave a client in panic, desperate to rethink their investment strategy. Family vacations were often interrupted or rescheduled at the last moment.

She pulled herself back to the present. "I think so," she breathed. She touched it gingerly, as if it were fragile and could disintegrate at any moment. "Do you happen to remember how you acquired it?"

"There should be a tag on it...Yes, right there. I use a low-tech method to keep track of all my purchases. A good old-fashioned ledger." His playful grin was disarming.

"Would it be too much trouble to look it up for me? This is very important, and could tie into a murder."

"Sure. But it may take me a minute."

"In that case, I'll browse some more."

A good ten minutes later, Tobias called her name, but not before she found the perfect wall hanging for her living room, an antique lamp, and a small trinket that reminded her of Laura Beth. She carried all three to the counter.

"I couldn't help myself," she said sheepishly. "So far, this investigation has cost me an extra two hundred dollars."

"Then hopefully my findings will make up for the loss."

When the bell announced another customer, he left Willow in suspense. She was tempted to grab the ledger and look for herself, but she wasn't familiar with his 'low-tech' system. It seemed to take forever, but he finally returned.

"Now, where were we?"

"Left in suspense." The moment she said the words, she hated how accusatory they sounded. The last thing she wanted to do was alienate someone who was willing to help.

His reply was brief and terse. "Other customers."

"Of course. And I'm sorry. This is just really important."

"Okay." He accepted her apology without fanfare. He consulted his ledger again. "It was a walk-in. I don't normally take things unsolicited, mostly because they could be stolen, but when I saw the video camera..." He paused, as if choosing his next words carefully, "I made an exception."

To Willow's dismay, the other shopper brought her selection to the register, interrupting them again. She felt like screaming when the door opened, and two more women walked in. They immediately went to an old sewing machine, the kind with a paddle wheel and a base with drawers.

"This is what I was telling you about!" the younger woman gushed. "Isn't it just perfect?"

Her companion—Willow guessed her mother—looked skeptical. "You actually like this? I thought you didn't like antiques."

The younger one wrinkled her nose. "I don't. But these are all the rage on TikTok. You gut the cabinet, paint the wood, and turn it into a makeup vanity! Genius!" She clasped her hands together, quite pleased with her find. "Lindsey will be green with envy!"

"If you're sure..."

"Oh, thank you, thank you, thank you! This will be perfect for our little apartment! I'm so sick of fighting three other girls for the bathroom counter!"

"How are we supposed to get that in the car? It looks heavy."

"I'm sure the nice man behind the counter will help us. He looks strong."

Tobias, who was looking a bit green at their plans to mutilate a piece of history, arched his eyebrow in a subtle gesture they couldn't see. Despite being frustrated beyond belief, Willow almost giggled.

Almost. They came to the register and told

Tobias they wanted the sewing cabinet. The mother paid, and the young woman effected a helpless simper. "Could you possibly help us load it? It looks so heavy, and you look so strong." Her eyes moved to his arms in genuine appreciation.

"Sure. I just need to help this lady first." He motioned toward Willow.

The woman looked at her phone. "Oh, but my class starts soon! I'll barely have time to make it as it is!" She brazenly turned to Willow. "This nice lady doesn't mind. Do you?"

Willow bit back a sharp retort. It really was best to have this conversation in private. She grudgingly agreed in a terse voice.

It took another fifteen minutes for Tobias to get out his dolly, heft the piece onto it, roll it out the door and down the sidewalk, and fit it into the small vehicle. It wasn't an easy task, but he finally succeeded. He came back smudged with dust and perspiration.

"Sorry about that," he apologized sincerely.

"I know you have a business to run." It wasn't exactly acceptance, but it was close enough.

He went back to the task at hand. "Okay, so you were wondering about the seller."

"Yes, that's right."

Using his finger as a placeholder, he looked at her without lifting his head. "I don't normally divulge names, you know."

"This is very important, Mr. Cameron. It could be related to a cold case, as well as a current murder. I really need that name."

He consulted his book again. "It says GM. I

remember him now. He said his father was selling off his junk. His word, not mine," he clarified.

"Hmm. The initials help but aren't definitive," she murmured to herself.

"I should have gotten his full name, but we were busy that day. He was getting antsy waiting on me. Some of the other things he brought in were more valuable, so I made an exception to my rule against walk-ins."

"I'm actually glad you did." She offered a rueful smile. "I'm getting tired of running around from one shop to another. I was afraid I would have to expand my parameters." Her fingers hovered over the latch to keep the film secure. "May I?"

"Sure, but you may be disappointed. I took out the film."

Disappointed was an understatement. Willow was crushed. "You what?" she cried in dismay. It bordered on hysteria.

"I always do. I try to respect the previous owner's privacy, in case they forget to take the film or memory card out. You never know when it could contain sensitive images."

Willow was distraught. "But... But..."

"I'm sorry, Miz Alexander." Like most people in the area, his accent was more Southern than Mid-Western, rounding the prefix to something soothing and less formal sounding. "It's store policy."

Willow hung her head as she composed herself. She had been so close...

"I may still have the memory card in the back," he offered.

Her head snapped up. "You do?"

"Maybe. I can't promise anything. I usually tag it, throw it all in box, and take it to a buddy of mine to review. If I think it's someone's long-lost memories—faces, not landscapes—I try to return it to the rightful owners."

Brightening, Willow asked, "Can you look? Please? I can't stress how important this is!"

His blue eyes narrowed. "If it's so important and connected to two murders, why haven't the police been around? I've had the camera for a couple of months now."

She hesitated before admitting, "The sheriff doesn't have this particular piece of evidence. The owner of the video camera hired my agency to track it down."

"Withholding evidence from law enforcement is illegal, not to mention immoral."

By now, Willow's nerves were fraught. "I don't need you to preach to me, Mr. Cameron," she snapped. "I fully intend to turn my findings over to the authorities once we've done a thorough investigation. We owe it to my client."

He crossed muscled arms over his chest. "What's the punishment time for tampering with evidence these days?"

Willow closed her eyes and counted to ten. She made it to six.

"Look, Mr. Cameron. I'm not withholding evidence. This is highly sensitive, and I'm not at liberty to divulge confidential information from my client. Please believe me when I say there are mitigating circumstances, and my findings will be revealed to the authorities as soon as I have all the pieces to the puzzle."

"And you think this card will do that?"

"If it contains what I think it does, absolutely. It will confirm my eyewitness' account and solve a twenty-five-year-old mystery."

His look turned skeptical. "Are you talking about the murder of those boys who were here to make that film?"

Willow was never good at lying. "Maybe," she said unconvincingly.

"I knew them, you know," he said in a quiet voice.

Her eyes flew to his in surprise. "You did? How?"

"I was their history professor at the university. That particular course was on colloquial culture and folk lore. We were studying legends and myths."

Willow was fascinated by his revelation. Not only could she see him as a history professor, but he knew the missing students! "This is even better than I hoped for! You actually knew the boys?"

"As well as a professor can ever know his students. But yes, I did know them."

"And you never saw them again after their trip?" she confirmed.

"No. Two lived on campus, one commuted from home. None of them returned. If they disappeared voluntarily, they did so without goodbyes and without any of their personal possessions."

"Do you—would you be willing to speak with my partners and me? We would compensate you for your time. This is hardly the place to have a private conversation."

The door opened, and a couple walked in, reaffirming her point.

He looked hesitant at best, skeptical at worst. "Maybe."

"Please, Mr. Cameron. You knew those boys. You, of all people, should want to see justice done."

"If you're trying to make me feel guilty," he said in a hard voice, "take a number. Their parents blamed me. The other students blamed me. The head of the department expressed his displeasure, as did the dean. But most of all, I blamed myself. For years, I regretted ever teaching that course. For bringing up legends I was aware of. I even used the Legend of the Flaming Woman as an example when I assigned my students a major project." His deep voice was bitter with regret. "Care to guess what the boys chose as theirs?"

"It wasn't your fault," Willow assured him. "That movie had come out. Pure sensationalism. It had an irrational premise, but it was popular on high school and college campuses. They probably imagined their own fame and fortune, not to mention a good grade. You couldn't have possibly known they wouldn't come home."

He clearly didn't believe her. "I don't know what good it would do for me to talk with you. I don't have the card."

"You might. You won't know until you look."

"I can't promise anything. Even if I find it, it may be too degraded to view."

"All I can do is ask."

The weary proprietor huffed out a sigh. She had clearly worn him down. "I will, but it won't be today. I have customers to serve and plans for the evening. I'll try to look tomorrow, but even if I find it, I can't guarantee when my buddy can get around to it."

"At least you'll try. And you'll never know how much I appreciate it." She put a hand over her chest to express her sincerity. His eyes flashed to her finger. Was he checking to see if she wore a wedding ring?

"You'll call me when you know something?"

"I promise."

He's probably thinking anything to get such a pesky woman out of his hair!

"Even without the card, if you could find an afternoon to speak with us, it could prove a huge help. You're the first person we've spoken to that actually knew the boys. Please consider it." Not too proud to beg, she implored, "Please?"

Hearing the couple come up behind her, Willow pushed her purchases toward him, along with the recorder. Pretending to be a normal customer, one without an ulterior motive, she said, "Thank you for your help. You had exactly what I was looking for."

She paid and started to turn away. "You'll call me if you find that other item I'm looking for?"

He tipped his head. "I will." Turning his attention to his next customer, he had nothing more to say.

14

The door to *Intuitive Investigations* flew open with a bang, the force slinging it back against the wall.

Everleigh yelped in surprise as she jumped up from her desk. In the process, she spilled what was left of her coffee.

"What!" Ireland's response was more of a startled cry than a question. "What's going on?"

"That's what I want to know!" a man thundered from the doorway.

Everleigh recognized the man with dismay. "Maverick," she said in a fallen voice.

"What did you do?" he demanded.

Having recovered from her initial shock, Ireland came forward to defend her granddaughter. Her voice was indignant. "Sir! I don't know who you are or what you want, but you do not speak to my granddaughter in that tone."

He looked unimpressed with the dainty woman and her haute ways. Ignoring her, he sneered at Everleigh. "Getting your granny to defend you, are you, little lady?"

"I've already told you," Everleigh said from

between clenched teeth. "My name is not *little lady*."

"Only babies and little ladies need to hide behind their granny's coattails," he goaded.

Wishing she still had coffee to fling in his face, Everleigh crossed her arms over her chest and glared at him. "You can't even get an insult down right. The tired phrase is apron strings. You know, because a woman's place is in the kitchen." Disdain dripped from her words.

"I'll insult you any way I want," he growled.

Willow walked into the room in time to hear his last comment. She immediately stiffened. "I don't know who you are or what you want," she said in no uncertain terms, "but no one comes into our office and insults us."

"That's right," Ireland said, glaring at the man still standing in the doorway. "State your business and leave." The icy look in her eyes matched that in her voice. "And close that door!" she snapped.

Stunned into submission, the giant of a man did as told. Sounding marginally less volatile than before, he wore an angry scowl as he demanded of Everleigh, "What did you tell him?"

"What did I tell who? What are you talking about?" Coffee had poured onto her favorite pair of shoes and was now seeping its way down to her toes. She was as cross about that as she was about him barging into their office.

"What did you tell Homer? Are you trying to get me fired?"

"First of all, I don't know who this Homer is. Second, I'm sure you can handle getting fired on your own without any help from me." She slipped her foot from a soggy shoe. "Could be your attitude," she suggested.

"Homer is my boss. What did you tell him?"

"I didn't but tell me his last name, and I'll be happy to file a complaint."

"Nathaniel Homer is the head of Mulfred," he informed her coldly. "He's coming down on me hard for this mess you created."

"Talk about creating a mess..." she muttered, looking down at her shoes.

Willow's mouth was set in a frown. "Let me guess. You must be the infamous Rick Gaines."

Ireland's snort was most unladylike. "No wonder," she muttered. "We've heard a lot about you. None of it good, by the way."

"I'm not talking to you two." He rudely dismissed the older two women and pointed a beefy finger at Everleigh. "I'm talking to her."

Everleigh's red curls came flying up. "*Her* has a name. Everleigh."

"Well, *Everleigh*," he spat, "you'd better hope I don't get fired over this, or there will be hell to pay!"

"Speaking of paying, you owe me for a very expensive pair of shoes. I spilled coffee on them when you came barging through the door like a madman."

"I am mad! Mad because of the trouble you've caused. What have you been saying about me?"

"After today," Willow said, crossing her arms over her chest, "we can think of plenty."

"This isn't funny. Do you know how upset Homer is?"

Everleigh refused to bow to his bullying. "No clue." This was almost fun, she thought, watching his face contort that way.

While Everleigh found his reaction entertaining, her mother found Maverick's outburst interesting. "Just why is your boss so upset?"

"He says this entire project is in jeopardy now."

Ireland took a guess. "The Scrimshaw Project?"

"Yes, the Scrimshaw Project!" He was obviously exasperated. "And now the police are all over the place, and people are asking questions. He's getting nervous. And when Nathaniel Homer gets nervous, it doesn't turn out well for the rest of us."

"Why would he fire you?" Everleigh asked, curious in spite of herself. "I thought you were the boss."

"Of this division. Nathaniel Homer is the owner and CEO of *HardWood International*. Mulfred is just one of the companies he owns."

The news surprised Ireland, but it made sense. Purdy said Homer was a bigwig of some sort, but she hadn't realized he owned the company hoping to buy up the mountain. "Homer lives in that big house we were talking about," Ireland informed Everleigh. "His land backs up to Gus McMurray's place."

Maverick turned his sharp glare to the older woman. "How do you know that?" he barked.

"It's hardly a secret." Even though her source had been less official, she replied coolly, "Anyone with access to Border County records can find that out."

"Why are you poking around in Homer's business?" the big man asked suspiciously.

"Who said I was poking?" She looked entirely innocent when she daintily held up her hands.

"I don't know what you think you're doing, but stop it now." His voice was low and rumbled with a threat. "Stop poking your nose in where it don't belong, stop stirring up trouble, and stop making my boss nervous! And you'd better pray like hell he don't fire me, or else I'll be back."

He left the same way as he had come, with a flying door and a big bang.

"Wow. What a jerk," Willow said. She marched to the door and closed it with a bang of her own.

"I see why everyone on the mountain thinks Maverick is just crazy enough to have killed Gus," her mother said.

"And just *look* at my shoes!" Holding up the soggy evidence, Everleigh still mourned the loss of her favorite footwear.

"And to think you approached that man on your own!" Willow chided. "What were you thinking? The man is clearly unhinged."

"You need to stay away from him," Ireland agreed. "If he gets fired, I have a bad feeling he'll make good on his threat."

Everleigh dressed with care for the meeting. She knew that the more desperate she appeared, the more eager they would be to recruit her. Lost souls were their target. Those people who were so eager to fit in, always trying just a little too hard to be accepted, only to fail miserably.

She layered on heavy eye makeup, the more dramatic the better, and clothes she found at one of the thrift stores she recently visited. It was the sort of outfit she would normally never buy. A woman her age with an impressionable child at home had no business wearing such a short skirt over fishnet hose and chunky heeled shoes. The look came straight from the 80s. She put a coat on over the garb as she hurried out to the car, thankful that Laura Beth was spending the night with a friend. If a neighbor happened to see her, she would say she was headed to a costume party and do her best not to die from embarrassment.

No one called her name as she slunk behind the wheel of the car and put it in reverse. Now, to drive through town without being pulled over. She needed to arrive anonymously at her meeting.

Everleigh had often heard of places referred to as a hole in the wall. They were normally seedy little joints that served cheap beer and greasy food. But this was a hole in the rock. Literally. Whether man-made or built inside what would have eventually become a cave, Hidden Rock Café had three walls made of real stone, with the front built of bricks. Mortar sealed the seams so that it all fit snugly together.

She waited outside the door like a dozen and a half others, noticing that some of the other women were dressed similar to her. Everleigh made a point to stand there awkwardly, hunching her shoulders like she hoped no one would notice her. Most of them didn't, but one woman gave her a shy smile as she self-consciously tucked a lock of hair behind her ear.

"Evie Perkins!" the bouncer's loud voice boomed.

"Here," she said, making her way to the front of

the line. "I'm here."

She had used a shortened version of her real name and Landee's maiden name as her disguise, knowing the powers that be would look her up and learn everything they could about her. They would 'discover' that Evie had trouble keeping a steady job. She had lived in shelters and questionable apartment buildings. She drifted from place to place, never landing anywhere for long.

"Fill this out at the table," the man said gruffly. He handed her a sheet of paper that covered both front and back.

Ah, the hook. Everleigh mused to herself. *Find our vulnerabilities and milk them for all they're worth.*

The café wasn't much. There was no way the tiny kitchen could produce more than a few orders at a time, she speculated, but it likely wasn't a problem. A limited number of tables fit into the cave like a jigsaw puzzle.

The ambiance was nice, she had to admit. The soft lighting and soothing music gave it an intimate feeling. To chase away the natural cold temperature of rock enclosures, low-burning flames—compliments of either electricity or gas—offered warmth and ambiance by way of fireplace or fire pits.

Everleigh found a table near one of the pits and took a seat. Across from her was a young man who looked as ill at ease as she did.

Turning her attention to the form, she read the first question.

What prompted you to come here tonight? (Circle all that apply.)

Bored. Curious. Searching for something meaningful in life.

Everleigh circled the last answer, knowing it was just the reply Moon and her 'Orbits' were hoping for.

There wasn't an empty seat in the house—nor standing room along the natural rock walls—by the time Moon came out.

She came out in simple white robes, tied at the waist with ropes. Her long white-blond hair flowed around her shoulders, with leather sandals adorning her feet. The jewelry circling her neck and slender wrists glowed eerily white in the dim lighting.

"What is she? Some female version of Jesus?" Everleigh mumbled to herself.

She must have spoken louder than intended, because the girl beside her sent her a cautionary glare. It was Tracey, the one from outside with the shy smile. She had joined Everleigh at the small table but was still painfully shy.

From the front of the room, the woman with the pale hair and soothing voice commanded the room's attention. "My name is Moon, and I will be your spiritual guide this evening. Come with me on a journey like no other, while we explore the universe around us, and that within us. Join hands with me now, and say this prayer to the gods as we offer up a sacrifice of good will and blessings."

Everleigh couldn't help but shiver.

Something about this meeting was *very*, very wrong.

15

"So? Don't keep us in suspense," Ireland said. "Did you learn anything useful last night?"

The younger woman twisted her lips. They gathered for an informal Saturday session while Laura Beth was at a friend's. "Yes, and no. Yes, I think there is something definitely up with Moon's Lunar Immersion Experience. The questionnaire asked some very specific, if not leading, questions. It was subtle, but just enough to stir the seeds of discontent within your life."

"Like what?" Willow asked with a frown.

"Oh, things like *Do you ever feel like you're drifting through life, waiting for the right direction to take*? Or *Do you feel like an outsider in your own skin*? Things like that. It would be easy for almost anyone to identify with those descriptions at some point in their lives, even if they weren't desperate. I can see where someone who's vulnerable or particularly impressionable could get caught up in the Cool Aid she's serving."

"Someone like Gideon?"

"Someone exactly like Gideon."

"Do go on," Ireland encouraged.

"After the forms were collected, Moon introduced herself and what she claimed was her calling in life. It was her wish to 'give everyone the inner peace and fulfillment she felt in everyday living.'" Everleigh gave a theatrical rendition of the quote. "She laid it on thick, talking about a deeper meaning in life and the utter tranquility that comes from knowing one's purpose on this planet."

Knowing her daughter well, Willow looked skeptical. "And you managed to keep a straight face during all this?"

"I admit, it was hard," Everleigh said, "so I kept pinching my leg. I figured a little pain might keep me from laughing."

"No one noticed?"

"Actually, the girl sitting next to me mistook it for self-inflicted pain. Her preferred method is cutting, but she said she wasn't judging me."

"It sounds like Moon's potential recruit suffers from a serious emotional problem."

"Based on what I saw and heard, Tracey's far from the only one. Everyone in attendance was, as Moon put it, 'looking for direction in their life.'"

"I wonder how many poor souls will think she's the person to provide it?" Ireland clucked her tongue.

"I'm afraid the majority. A few got up and left when she finished her spiel, but most of them asked for more information. She and her Orbits, as she calls them, met with them personally for a few minutes, promising to get back with them with a personalized suggestion on how to achieve their own inner peace."

Willow's voice was dry. "How thoughtful of her. And you?"

"Oh, I think with all the things I checked off on that list, my personalized plan will be very long!" Everleigh chuckled.

"And no doubt very expensive."

"I could almost see the dollar signs in her eyes."

"Did you find out anything at all about Gideon?"

"That's where the 'no' part of my answer came in. I did my best to crack her, but nothing worked. In case she went back to him and asked, I didn't claim to personally know Gideon. I said he and I had a family connection, and that there was some news concerning a mutual family member that I needed to discuss with him."

"Her reaction?"

"Let's put it this way. I wouldn't call it warm. She seemed personally insulted that I wasn't willing to let her be our go-between."

"But she admitted to knowing him and where he was?"

"She wouldn't admit it with words, but I felt her put her guard up. She knows, but she's not saying. I'll try again when she calls for our consultation."

Willow looked surprised. "You think she'll still call you? She's not suspicious of you?"

"I'd say she's greedier than she is suspicious. I made it clear that even though Gideon wasn't likely to remember me from our childhood, I heard he had only good things to say about her and her program. I think she fell for it."

"You're not afraid she'll look for you on social media and discover who you really are?" her mother asked worriedly.

With a cheeky grin, the younger woman replied, "Dad didn't shell out all that money on my education for nothing. More important than my degree in computer science, I made some good friends in college who happen to be first-rate hackers. Back in the day, they took me under their wing and taught me a thing or two. We still keep in touch. And when I told them I needed a new social media identity…" She shrugged as if the rest were self-explanatory.

It wasn't enough for her mother. Willow wanted details.

"They altered a few pictures, backdated a few posts, and created a convincing backstory for my alter ego, Evie Perkins."

"Perkins?" Ireland asked.

"After you, Landee. I figured it was a name people in the area might know and recognize, particularly around Dalton Holler. One with enough family branches to confuse anyone trying to climb that particular tree." Her blue eyes twinkled with merriment.

Willow was still worried. "I just don't want you getting in too deep with this Moon person. And if she runs a cult as we suspect, I'm doubly concerned for your safety."

"I'm being careful, Mom. But, yes, I think they'll buy it. However, to be specific, I would be the one buying it—and at a very steep price, I might add—so it's crucial that my cover is very convincing. One of my friends is a true genius, and he was able to hack Gideon's social media and add Evie as a friend. They tagged each other in a few comments." She snickered. "Supposedly, anyway."

"Maybe you should quit telling me about their genius ways. What they're doing is against the law, you know."

"What my friends are doing, or what Moon is doing? Besides, you haven't heard the most disturbing part yet."

"That wasn't disturbing enough?" Ireland sounded aghast.

"She offered a sacrifice to the gods last night. Something about good will and blessings."

"*Sacrifice?*" Willow cringed.

"Yes. Bones, mostly, but I found it quite disturbing."

"Bones? What kind?" Willow thought of the ones on Maude's wrists and the kind that some people witched for.

"I didn't dare ask. But I have to admit, it was spooky." Even today, a shiver worked through her body. "Something very strange is going on with Moon and her Lunar Experience."

"We need to be very careful moving forward, particularly where this Moon person is concerned," Ireland cautioned. "I don't have a good feeling about her." She paused as a shiver racked her shoulders, as well. "*Bones?* That's the devil's work!"

Willow chewed her lip before gathering the nerve to mention another set of bones. Three sets, to be exact.

"Speaking of bones… So far, what we've been doing hasn't gotten us any closer to finding the boys' killer. I think it's time we change our tactics."

"What else can we do? We're looking for Gideon. We're looking for the camcorder. What else can we do at this point?" Everleigh asked.

"We could look for the boys' remains. We would at least know our other efforts aren't in vain."

"How do you propose we do that?" Everleigh sounded incredulous. "The officials didn't find their bodies twenty-five years ago. By now, I hardly see how *we* can find what's left of them."

"*We* can't. But I know someone who can."

"Who?" her daughter demanded.

"Karnie," Willow said quietly. "We can ask for her help."

Everleigh stared at her mother. "Are you serious? Karnie, the crazy mountain witch? She hates everyone! You'll be lucky if she doesn't throw *us* off the ridge!"

"She's also known as the Bone Witcher," Willow argued. "She can actually find old graves and buried bones. If we find the boys' bones, we'll know for certain they were killed."

"But we'll still need the camcorder to prove who killed them."

"Finding those remains would reopen the case. Even without the video camera, the FBI has ways of finding the killer. There's been amazing progress in technology over the last twenty-five years."

"I just don't think risking our lives with a crazy witch is necessary!"

"It wouldn't be *our* lives," Willow corrected.

"I'll go. Just me."

"Absolutely not!" Everleigh was adamant. In protest, she jumped up from her seat. "They say she hates strangers. They say she'll cast some evil spell on you." She flung her arm out dramatically. "Or worse!"

Quiet until now, Ireland spoke out. "It's all right, Everleigh. Your mother will be safe."

"How do you know that? Mom's a stranger. She might never come back down the mountain!"

"Your mother isn't exactly a stranger," Ireland corrected. "Karnie would never hurt her."

Dumbfounded, Everleigh looked at her mother. "Is that true? You actually know her?"

"Yes." Her forehead crinkled. "At least, I did. She may not remember me."

The red-haired woman abruptly took her seat. "How do you know her? Why haven't you ever said anything before?"

"It happened a very long time ago," Willow admitted. "And it's a long story, one I'd rather not tell right now. It's already been over a week since Gus came to us. We need to make progress on this case."

"But..."

"Don't worry," Ireland assured her granddaughter. "It's fine, sweetie. Your mother will be safe."

"How can you be so certain?"

Ireland touched her arm. "I just am," she said.

Experiencing her grandmother's confidence for herself, Everleigh relaxed somewhat.

Willow stood to refill her water. When her phone rang, she asked one of them to grab it from the coffee table.

Looking at the screen, Everleigh raised an eyebrow. "Who's Tobias Cameron?"

Willow had taken one of his cards and programmed not only the number to the store into her phone, but his personal number, as well. "The owner of the antique store." She practically snatched the phone from her daughter's hands, eager to catch the call before it went to voicemail.

She answered breathlessly, "Hello?"

"Miz Alexander?" a pleasantly masculine voice asked. "This is Tobias Cameron." He paused for a nanosecond before adding, "The owner of *Years Ago Antiques and Curiosities*."

"Yes, of course. I remember you." She could feel her mother and daughter's eyes searing into her back, or else she would have slapped herself in the forehead for such an eager, inane response. They would surely interpret it as something more.

She was surprised to hear the uncertainty in his voice when he said, "You asked if I would consider speaking with you and your partners..."

"Yes!" Willow whirled back around in excitement, "Did you find the film?"

"Not conclusively, no. But I've thought about your request, and I'm willing to speak with you and answer any questions you might have."

"That's wonderful! When is a good time for you?"

"I happen to be in your area, delivering furniture to a customer. I know it's short notice, but I'm available now, if you are."

"I am! In fact, we're at the office now, working

on the case."

"Would it be okay if I stopped by?"

"Absolutely. We'd love to discuss any input you may have."

"I can be there in about fifteen minutes."

"That works out perfectly for us."

"See you soon."

Everleigh's smirky reply was immediate. "I don't suppose we have to guess who that was."

"If you guessed the shop owner where I bought the camera, you'd be correct. He happens to be in town and has agreed to speak with us. He'll be here in about fifteen minutes."

"Did he find the film?" Ireland asked.

"I don't think he said, but he's agreed to answer our questions, so, at least there's that."

"You don't *think* he said? I heard you ask him." Everleigh couldn't help but tease her mother.

"His answer was vague. At any rate, we'll know shortly."

Everleigh grinned. "That gives me time to prepare fresh coffee, and you time to freshen up in front of the mirror."

Ireland joined her granddaughter in teasing Willow. "Would I be right in assuming this isn't the stereotypical history professor with round spectacles and a cardigan sweater, puffing away on a cigar?"

"Spectacles? Really, Mother?"

Her smile was infuriating. "Like you said. We'll know shortly."

By the time the door opened to *Intuitive Investigations*, she was nervous and flustered. Teasing her about the attractive store owner made her self-conscious. She worried everything she said or did would be questioned. And what if Tobias Camerson thought she was flirting with him? She was so out of practice. She might make a fool of herself.

Willow greeted him with a forced smile.

"Hello, Mr. Cameron. I'm so glad you were able to stop by."

"Please. Call me Tobias."

Knowing she sounded stiff but unable to relax, she motioned toward the other room. "If you follow me, the others are right in here."

"If I don't follow you, will they still be in there?" His expression was unreadable.

Willow doubted he was flirting. Being a professor, it was more likely a philosophical question. With a quizzical expression, she went with a mutual, "Hmm. I guess we'll never know."

Like a true gentleman, Tobias stood aside so that she could enter first. Willow wasted no time making introductions. "I'd like for you to meet my partners. This is Ireland Garrett—" she motioned to her mother "—and Everleigh Alexander. This is Tobias Cameron, the owner of the antique store I told you about."

"It's a pleasure to meet you ladies," he replied in his pleasing voice. He offered his hand in polite greeting, earning him extra points in Ireland's eye. As he released Everleigh's hand, he glanced between her and Willow. "Alexander. Any relation?"

"She's my mom." Everleigh grinned before nodding to Ireland. "And she's my grandmother."

"So, it's a family business. I like that," Tobias said with approval.

"Would you like some coffee, Mr. Cameron?" Ireland asked. "Everleigh is quite the barista."

"Call me Tobias. All of you. And black coffee is just fine."

"Coming right up," Everleigh promised.

"Have a seat, M—Tobias." Willow caught herself from the blunder. She noticed how her mother and daughter had conveniently moved to the chairs, leaving Willow to sit on the sofa alongside their guest.

As they waited for the coffee, Ireland made small talk. "Willow tells me you have a delightful antique shop in old downtown Branson. I'll have to stop in the next time I'm there."

"Please do. My parents opened the store years ago, before my late wife and I took over."

"I'm so sorry about your wife. I, myself, am a widow," Ireland said sympathetically.

"Sadly, we have that loss in common," he murmured.

"Interestingly enough, none of us have a husband, so *Intuitive Investigations* is truly a female-owned enterprise."

Willow shot her mother a pointed glare. Ireland had deliberately slipped in that morsel of information.

"Very impressive," Tobias said obligingly.

"I was telling my mother about some of your inventory." Willow was desperate to cover up the none-too-subtle hint. "There's a few pieces I'm considering coming back for."

"Any time. If it's a large piece, I can deliver, just as I did today."

"I'll keep that in mind."

Ireland kept up the small talk until Everleigh returned with the coffee.

The talk became smaller by the minute, until Tobias addressed the elephant in the room.

16

"I know you're wondering why I changed my mind and decided to come today." He aimed the statement toward Willow.

"No matter the reason," she assured him, "we're just glad you did."

He shifted his eyes to the other two. "I'm sure Willow told you I was a professor at the university, and those three young men were enrolled in one of my classes."

"Yes," Ireland said. "That's quite a coincidence, isn't it?"

"I, for one, don't believe in coincidences," he confided quietly.

Willow wasn't sure what surprised her more: the fact that he obviously believed in fate, or how warm and natural her name sounded on his lips.

"Then you are definitely in like company," Everleigh assured him. "We believe that everything happens for a reason, even though we don't always know what at the time."

"True. And since I knew them, your mother asked if I could offer any insight into their disappearance. Because of… circumstances," he hesitated over the word, "it's not something I normally talk about. But the more I thought about her request, the more compelled I felt to come forward and talk with you."

There was no doubting the hopeful expressions on the women's faces. "So, you have insight to share?" In anticipation, Everleigh scooted to the edge of her chair.

"To be honest, I'm not sure," Tobias answered. "But I'm willing to answer your questions the best I can."

"I think the most pressing question is about the card. Did you find it?" the young woman asked.

"Like I told your mother over the phone, I can't confirm anything just yet. I took what film and cards I had to my friend, but it may take him a while to go through them all. And even then," he cautioned, "there's no guarantee the one you're looking for is in there."

"We understand," Willow assured him. "The second most pressing question is one I've already asked, but I'd like to ask again. You're certain the boys didn't come back from their assignment?"

He winced at the word *assignment*, but he didn't shrink from the question. "For the record, their names were Benny, Josh, and Terrell. And I guess you can never be absolutely certain what another person might do, but I'm 99.9 percent sure those boys never returned." His tone had a finality to it.

Ireland's voice was empathetic. "So, like us, you believe they perished on that mountain."

"I do."

"Okay, so back to Benny, Josh, and Terrell." Willow appreciated the fact that he saw them as individuals. "Tell us about them."

The former professor looked doubtful. "You really think that will help?"

"I think it will help us remember that these were human beings who met with a terrible fate," she answered softly. "Sometimes, especially on cold cases like this, it's easy to get caught up in the challenge of solving the mystery. I want to make sure we keep focused on bringing justice to these three young men and their families. It makes our mission more personal."

Tobias just nodded, but his blue eyes were vulnerable. He ran his hand over the back of his head as he stood and paced the floor.

"Uhm, yeah. Well, Josh was the jokester among them. He kept our class discussions lively with his quick comebacks and witty humor. But he was smart. He caught on fast, no matter how many jokes he came up with.

"Benny talked his buddies into taking this course with him. He was the history nerd. We got into some deep discussions, often after everyone else had left the classroom. He was the most excited of them all about this assignment. It didn't matter to him what kind of history it was. True, not true. Legend, or just conjuncture. He wanted to know it all.

"And Terrell?" he continued reminiscing. "That young man was a whiz with electronics. He could do anything with a computer or camera. His ambition in life was to put the two together and make animated learning videos for children with learning disabilities."

Tobias paced his way back to the couch and took a seat, turning toward Willow. "Like I told you at the shop, just because someone with the initials GM brought the camera in didn't mean it was the same camera that belonged to the boys. I'm not even sure you told me the connection there?" It sounded like a question, but he didn't wait for an answer. "But then I remembered. Terrell had a camera just like that. He was going to be the cameraman for the assignment, and Benny would be the announcer." A wry smile touched his lips. "I'm sure Josh would have found some way to use his theatrical skills to do a reenactment of some sort."

"They sound like wonderful young men," Ireland said. "No wonder you remember them."

"I'd like to think I remember all my students, but some of them I barely knew. These three young men were different. It was a small class, so we had a chance to really get to know one another, and they weren't afraid to open up to their old professor."

"That was twenty-five years ago," Ireland objected. "You had to have been fresh out of college."

"I admit, it was during my early years. But they made an impression on me, even before… before they disappeared."

"I know this is difficult for you to talk about," Willow said in understanding.

"Like I told you before, I feel responsible. They were there because of my class, my assignment. I'm the one who used The Legend of the Flaming Woman as an example."

"Did you tell them to make a video

documentary?"

"That was all their idea. The report was a major assignment, and they wanted to make a good grade. The documentary was a brilliant idea. Until it wasn't."

"They were being creative and thinking outside the box." Without thinking, Willow reached out to touch his knee. She felt the zing of electricity, but this wasn't the time for physical attraction. "You weren't responsible, Tobias," she stressed softly. It felt natural to use his given name.

"I'm still not so sure about that. That's why I decided to come here today. The three of them deserve justice, and if I can do my part in helping, I want to."

Everleigh felt the weight of the emotional baggage he carried. She tried to lighten his load with a distraction. "Tell me about your class. It sounds fascinating."

"It was a course on colloquial culture and folklore. We were studying legends and myths, and when I announced the assignment, Benny immediately chose the Flaming Woman. He said he had kin in the area that remembered the Hoke family, so he felt like he had a personal connection to the legend. Sadly, he didn't realize he would become a legend, of sorts, because of it."

"That's why we're determined to find the film," Everleigh stressed. "It could prove who killed those young men. Benny, Josh, and Terrell." She repeated their names as a reminder of who they were doing this for.

"How? How will that prove anything?"

"I'm afraid we aren't able to divulge that information." Willow's voice was regretful. The professor was as desperate for answers as the families were.

"You wanted my help," he reminded her. "I agreed to answer your questions. I deserve the same courtesy." There was a definite edge in his voice.

Willow looked at her partners. Providing confidential information to someone outside the case was highly unprofessional. Yet she instinctively knew this man could be trusted. What's more, he could potentially help them unravel the mystery about what happened on that mountain. Intuition told her he would make a valuable ally.

Everleigh could feel her mother's inner conflict. She mouthed the word "yes." Ireland agreed with a nod of her carefully styled hair.

"This isn't to leave this room," Willow cautioned their visitor. "What I'm about to tell you is highly confidential. I need your word that you'll never repeat a word of this to anyone."

Tobias Cameron put a hand above his heart. "I swear."

Willow took a deep breath before slowly releasing it.

"There was a witness to the murders. He says one of the boys, apparently Terrell, was recording when the first of his friends was attacked and… and thrown over the edge of the mountain." She saw Tobias flinch, but he didn't stop the sad story from unfolding. "The second friend tried to protest, but he met a similar fate. Our witness says that's when the killer heard the third boy hovering nearby. The boy was smart enough to shove the camera under a bush, so the killer never knew he was being recorded."

At that point, Tobias did interrupt with a quiet, "That's my boy. I told you he was sharp."

Willow continued, "The witness grabbed the camera and hid. He didn't come out for hours, until he was certain the killer was long gone. Only then did he leave and hide the camera in a safe place."

"Why didn't he just go to the sheriff?"

"He said he couldn't. Something about the killer being an important man in the community and worrying about retaliation on his family. He kept the secret for twenty-five years, until he finally came forward and told us what he saw."

"If he hid the camera...?" The professor had trouble understanding the problem.

Willow's shoulders sagged. "He lost it."

Everleigh was quick to defend the old man who had come to them. He had been clearly distraught and seeking absolution for his silence. "In all fairness, we don't think he actually lost it," she said. "We think his son accidentally sold it, unaware of its importance."

"GM," Tobias murmured. He frowned as comprehension dawned in his blue gaze. "Didn't I hear something on the news about an elderly man being killed when he walked in on a burglary in progress? Wasn't his name McMurray? M," he surmised.

The women didn't bother to deny his astute observation. "The goof sheriff of Border County, Arkansas," Ireland said, "was quick to dismiss it as a burglary, but we aren't so certain. However, that's not our case. Our case is to prove who killed those brilliant young men."

It took a moment for the professor to take everything in.

He stood again, too restless to sit still. "This is a lot to churn through," he murmured. "No wonder you were so persistent about that film."

Willow offered a contrite smile. "I'm sorry I was such a pest, but now you know how important it is that we find it. It proves who the killer was."

"And, unfortunately," Everleigh added, "our witness didn't give us a name. Without the film, we don't have a clue as to who it was."

"So, you believe the killer was looking for the camera and inadvertently killed this Mr. McMurray?"

Ireland answered. "Perhaps not so inadvertently, but essentially, yes."

Another frown. "But I thought they didn't know they were being recorded."

"All we can think of," Willow said, "is that he somehow found out. We don't know if Mr. McMurray let it slip, if it was his son Gideon, or someone else. But we believe somehow the killer found out, and they killed again to keep their secret safe."

"Gideon. Gideon McMurray." He tried the name out on his tongue. "I think that was the name the man used. I put down GM for short."

"That's our theory, too."

"I remember the name because I had a student with the same name in one of my classes." He paused before admitting, "I remember him for reasons quite different than my experience with the other three."

"You had him in class?" Everleigh asked incredulously. "That was him! That was the same

Gideon McMurray!"

"Really?"

"This is perfect! We need to know more about Gideon, too. No one knows where he is," Willow said.

"That sounds about right. From what I remember of him, he wasn't the most responsible of people. He could never stay on task. He dropped out before the semester was over."

"I don't think he's changed much over the years."

"Except in appearance," the professor corrected. "I didn't even recognize him."

"We think he sold the camera on another of his whims," Ireland offered. They had told him this much, they may as well confide everything. Perhaps he could help. "We think he planned to go on a spiritual retreat of sorts, and it came with a hefty price tag."

"If he had known the real value of it," Everleigh added bitterly, "he would have sold it to the devil himself. I'm sure the killer would pay a small fortune to keep his secret safe."

"I want you to know," Tobias promised, "that I'll do my very best to see if the film was still in that camera, and if my friend has it."

"Can your friend be trusted?" Willow worried.

"Absolutely. He has no ties to the community, and he's independently wealthy. He'd have no reason to betray my confidence like that. Not that I believe he ever would," he added hastily. "I trust Brad with my life."

"I just hope the card is in there."

Tobias offered Everleigh a sheepish smile. "If I'm not being too presumptuous, I could use another cup of that coffee. Your grandmother was right. You're an excellent barista."

"Why, thank you," Everleigh beamed.

"Is there anything else you'd like to know? Now that I know the whole story, I'm all in."

Hearing his words, Willow thought she felt her heart melt just a little. Her intuition seldom steered her wrong, and intuition told her that Tobias Cameron was an extraordinary man. She believed fate had sent her into that antique store because they needed him in their lives.

"For starters, let's talk about the Flaming Woman. You're a professor of history, and it was on your syllabus. Tell us what you know about it."

"Wow, you don't mince words, do you?"

Willow started to protest. "I—I didn't mean to—"

"Relax. I know you didn't. I just still have trouble with the fact that I introduced them to the legend to begin with."

"Not necessarily, dear," Ireland told him. "Rumor has it that Gideon took credit for that particular deed."

"Besides," Willow pointed out, "it was a legend, not a secret. Chances are they heard about it from multiple sources. They may have even grown up with the old tale."

"But what if I inadvertently glorified it? I still feel responsible for letting them tackle such a project."

Ireland was having none of it. She stood and made her way to him, putting her hand on his shoulder. Her voice was gentle but persuasive. "You said those young men were intelligent and talented. Your role as their teacher was to nurture such gifts. You gave them a vision, but they chose the path. You, Tobias Cameron, are not to blame for what happened."

"Thank you," he said quietly. "I needed to hear that."

"You need to believe it. Do you?"

"I—I think I'm starting to."

Satisfied she had done her job, Ireland returned to her seat. "So, young man. Tell us your version of the Flaming Woman."

He stayed for another hour.

Everleigh excused herself long enough to meet her daughter at the front door and to thank the other mother for having her. Laura Beth bound into the conference room, all smiles and excitement about her stayover.

"This lovely young lady is my granddaughter, Laura Beth," Willow proudly beamed. "Sweetie, say hello to Mr. Cameron."

"Hello."

"Hello," he replied with a friendly smile. "I must say, I am impressed." He looked around the room. "Four generations, four gorgeous women. You ladies must come from some exceptional genes."

Ireland's smile was enigmatic. "Oh, we do," she assured him.

He looked at his watch, appalled to see how late it was. "I didn't mean to monopolize so much of your time. Please forgive me for staying so long."

"Not at all! This has been a wonderful treat,"

Ireland assured him. "Right, sweetheart?" She directed the question directly toward Willow.

Put on the spot and silently vowing to kill her mother, Willow took a professional approach. "Uhm, absolutely. We appreciate your help so much. You can't know how much this means to us."

Was that a glimmer of disappointment she saw in his eyes? *Don't be ridiculous*, she chided herself. This had been a business meeting, nothing more.

Perhaps she had mistaken melancholy as disappointment. His voice was soft when he replied, "It means as much to me."

Then, collecting himself, he put on a brighter smile. "Ladies, thank you for your hospitality. If I can do anything else, don't hesitate to ask."

After rounds of goodbye, Willow offered, "I'll see you out."

There was an awkward moment at the door when she thought she may have been correct the first time. Maybe he was disappointed by her business approach to his visit.

"Well, thanks again for this afternoon. I hope I didn't keep you from anything important," he apologized again.

"*This* was important," she stressed. "Thank you so much for coming, and for agreeing to talk with us."

"I just hoped I helped in some small way."

"You helped in a very big way. I promise, we'll do our best to find justice for Josh, Terrell, and Benny."

"Thank you for referring to them by their names."

"Thank you for bringing them to life for us."

He reached for the door handle. "The minute I hear from Brad, I'll let you know."

"Thank you, that would be fantastic. I just hope he has good news."

"Me, too." He stepped outside but stopped to look back. "Don't forget about all those treasures you left at the store." His teasing smile was disarming.

"Don't worry, I won't," she said with a laugh. "I assure you I'll be back."

"I'll look forward to it, then."

Willow suspected she may have floated a step or two back into the conference room. She was certain his parting comment had double meaning. It was a real treat, having a man appreciate her again. Even Marcus hadn't in their last years together, if ever.

"Grammy, is that your boyfriend?" Laura Beth asked the minute she stepped through the door.

"Laura Beth! What a thing to say!"

"You're blushing," Everleigh teased her mother. "And I want to hear the answer to Laura Beth's question." She took a comical stance and asked in singsong, "Is that your boyfriend?"

Ireland didn't wait for Willow to huff a denial. "It should be. That man is a true catch! If I were interested in having a man of my own again—which I'm not—I would give you a run for your money."

"And if I were into older men, it would be a three-way race," Everleigh added.

"You two are ridiculous!" Willow said with exasperation. "He's an asset to the case, and nothing else."

"Daughter," Ireland drawled, "if you're half as

smart as I give you credit for, you'll soon change that."

17

There were times, like now, when Willow wished she didn't have such an astute sense of 'the knowing.'

As she rolled down the dirt path leading to the log cabin ahead, she knew she was undertaking a dangerous mission. When the killer or killers got word of this visit—and they would—the risks increased tenfold.

She also knew that, without the memory card, there was no other way to prove that Benny and his friends were dead. If this venture was successful, they would still have to prove the boys were murdered, but it was a good start.

Instinctively, Willow knew it was a risk she had to take.

Just as instinctively, she knew the Bone Witcher would help her.

As she stopped the old Corolla and killed the motor, Karnie stepped out on the porch. With her wild hair and wizened face, she looked every bit the mountain witch they called her. The shotgun in her hands didn't help the image.

"State your business," she demanded, "before I let Bear loose."

Almost on cue, an animal howled from nearby. It sounded as wild and ornery as its owner. With the telltale yip of a coyote, it was most likely a wolf-dog cross.

Willow resisted the urge to crawl back in her car and leave.

"I need your help," she called back. There was still a good distance between them.

"This ain't no visitor center. If you're lost, it's your own fault."

Willow dared move forward. "I'm not lost. Not this time."

The old woman's eyes narrowed as she studied the city woman daring to approach her. She admired her gumption.

The shotgun lowered. "Is Irie Perkins your mama?" she wanted to know.

"She is. I'm Willow. Do you remember me?"

"I reckon I do." Expression flashed across her face—could that be pleasure?—before she gruffly issued an invitation. "You made it this far. You might as well come on in and tell me what you want."

It wasn't uncommon for women of her age to use snuff. Willow noticed the bulge beneath her lower lip even before she spit. Willow side-stepped the stain as she climbed the steps and followed Karnie into her cabin.

It hadn't changed much since the first time Willow was here. She had a strong sense of déjà vu. She experienced that same off-kilter feeling when she first stepped across the threshold and found the floor tilting toward the left. That same compulsion to follow the slope to its eventual end. She saw the same wooden settle, hand-hewn and still sturdy after a century or more. The same rock fireplace with an iron pot suspended from a hook, and a stack of firewood off to one side.

She thought the gold and brown plaid chair was new to the cabin, but that was the only thing new about it. That style and that fabric hadn't been popular in at least three decades.

Karnie motioned to the plaid armchair and the cane-bottomed rocker across from it. An up-ended wood crate stood between them, serving as an end table. "Take your pick," she instructed.

Willow chose the rocker. She told herself she was being polite, saving the padded chair for the older woman's comfort. It had nothing to do with the no-doubt years of dust and grime ground into the nubby fabric.

Karnie disappeared behind her, allowing Willow time to survey the smaller details of the room. A worn wood-plank floor, freshly swept. Hand-sewn curtains on the windows, a crocheted afghan wadded upon the plaid chair, and a colorful quilt stretched across the settle to act as a cushion. A few old daguerreotypes hung on one wall alongside a modern, battery-operated clock. There was a small bookcase crammed full of books, and a basket overflowing with magazines. Willow was surprised to see the glossy cover of a fashion magazine among them, though it was admittedly a year or more out of date. She craned her neck, noting three pairs of shoes near the door. A pair of old tennis shoes, pink Crocs, and a pair of tall rubber boots.

"Here," Karnie said, thrusting a glass of rich red liquid into Willow's hands. She settled into the armchair and peered at her guest over the rim of her own glass. "You said you wanted a favor. What are you offering?"

Willow knew the old woman liked to barter her services for things she couldn't make herself. She had to wonder if that's where the pink shoes came from.

"What is it you want?" she countered. She took a generous sip of her drink and immediately sputtered in surprise, "That-That's not grape juice!"

"Of course not. That nip in the air calls for muscadine wine. Wards off the shivers."

Willow thought her shivers were attributed to nerves, but now that she thought about it, maybe they had more to do with being inside the old cabin. She thought she felt a draft swooping down through the cold firebox. Maybe Karnie saved her firewood until nightfall, when not even a hint of the sun was possible.

Taking a healthy swig of the warming drink, Karnie got down to business. "I reckon payment depends on how complicated the spell is. Whatcha wantin', girl? A love potion? Something for fertility? You look a might long in the tooth to be havin' a baby."

"No spell, and most certainly not for fertility!"

"Then what is it you want?"

Willow didn't shrink beneath the piercing gaze of the old mountain witch. She lifted her chin and announced, "I want you to find a grave for me."

She could tell the request took her by surprise. Her eyes narrowed as she reassessed her visitor. "What for?"

"Bones. Proof of death."

"Given enough time and the elements, even bones dissolve."

"But in twenty-five years?"

"Quarter of a century, huh?"

"That's right."

Karnie rubbed her chin as she calculated her rate of compensation. Willow noticed the fine, long white hairs that sprouted there, idly wondering if they had sprung up since her arrival. She discreetly touched her own chin for a similar growth spurt.

"Well, it ain't as simple as all that. First off, depends on where we need to search."

"The bottom of Kinney Knob."

"Kinney Knob, you say? That ain't far a'tall from here," she mused. Even though no glasses rested on her nose, she lowered her head as if peering over the lens. "These would be human bones, I reckon?"

"Yes, ma'am."

"We'd need someone to do the diggin'. That's rocky soil, you know. Hard to break through."

Willow hadn't thought of that. "I'll have to find someone." She was already wondering who that might be. It would need to be someone she trusted, someone who would keep their secrets safe.

Why did Tobias Cameron come to mind? The man looked fit enough, but Karnie was right. It would be hard work.

"I reckon I know someone who could help,"

Karnie said. "But it'll take at least two able-bodied men to do the job, mind you."

"Okay. I'll bring someone if you will." Willow sounded more confident than she felt.

"How quick you thinking'?"

"As soon as possible."

"Done been twenty-five years," the old woman pointed out. "Why you in such an all-fire hurry now?"

"I just found out about it."

"I figured everyone knew about them boys by now."

It was Willow's turn to be surprised. "Why do you think I'm talking about those three boys?"

"Never mentioned a number, but I'm right, ain't I?" She all but crowed in victory.

Willow sighed. "You're right."

"What's their bones got to do with you, girl?"

"I'm a private investigator." It always gave her a thrill to say the words aloud. In a strange, broken-hearted way, she had Marcus to thank for her new career. Failure hadn't been an option. "It's for a case I'm working on."

"A private investigator, huh?" She couldn't read the look in Karnie's eyes, but she hoped it was approval. Stranger still, she had this woman to thank for not just her career, but for her life.

When she smiled, it made Karnie look almost young again—at least eighty. "Then it's a good thing I saved you."

Willow's demeanor softened, too. "I'm sorry. I didn't say thank you for that, did I?"

"Your family thanked me plenty." Not accustomed to praise, Karnie went back to her calculations. "Now, about that payment. I reckon I could use a new hoe and some seeds to put in the ground."

"Done. What else?"

"It goes without saying I'll need one of those big propane bottles. My consultation fee, I think they call it, for hearin' you out."

While reasonable, that should have been the first thing she mentioned. Knowing better than to argue, Willow simply agreed. "Okay. What else?"

Karnie looked around the simple home. Over the years, there had been a few additions. A bedroom had been tacked on at the back, but she chose to keep her bed here in the main room, closer to the fire. A lean-to kitchen with its wood-burning stove was added on the right of the main room, its doorway cut from the previous window opening. Willow couldn't see into the sparsely accommodated room from there, a bit surprised when she heard Karnie's reply.

"I reckon I got most everything I need right here, but I ain't opposed to something extra."

Biting back a smile, Willow agreed. "Then we have a deal?"

"Give me a few days to round up supplies and help."

Willow wondered what supplies were required to witch for a grave, but she held her tongue. "This weekend?"

"Sunday sounds 'bout right," Karnie agreed. "No better way to worship Him than to be out and about on the Lord's day."

Willow stood to go. Now that they'd come to an agreement of terms, she suspected she had worn out her welcome. "I'll be here at eight o'clock Sunday morning."

"Go on 'round back and grab you one of those empty bottles. Refills are cheaper than buying a whole new setup," the old woman offered.

"Thank you, I may do that."

"Don't mind 'Ol Bear. He'll make a big ruckus, but he don't attack unless I give the word." Karnie didn't bother seeing her out. She was already reaching for her spittoon.

Willow found a stack of empty propane bottles at the back of the house. She assumed the ones closest to the small water heater were full, with one currently in use. She paused for a moment, admiring the woman's ingenuity. A cistern was mounted under the eaves. One pipe disappeared into the side of the house, and another connected to the water heater. Karnie may not have electricity, but she had running water, crude though the system might be.

Knowing she owed the old woman more than she could ever repay, Willow grabbed three of the empty bottles.

Willow was six when she first met Karnie.

It was a well-known fact that Knob Mountain produced the best wild strawberries in the Ozarks, and Aunt Purdy and Mama had a tradition of making strawberry pies and jam while the berries were at their peak.

Aunt Purdy's children were older than Willow and were always picking on her, teasing her about being too little to keep up with them. So on that day,

Willow decided to take her basket and hunt for her own berries. She'd prove who was the better picker, once and for all!

Determined to fill her basket first, she wandered away from the others. The sound of a trickling spring caught her attention, and she knew berries grew best near the water. The trees were dense here, making it impossible for even a little girl like her to squeeze among them. She followed the sound of the stream until she found an opening in the trees.

By then, Willow was tired and thirsty. Hungry, too. She took a dip of the fresh spring water, using her small hands as a cup. It tasted so good, she had more.

She sampled a few of the berries in her basket. She still had plenty of time to find more and show those stupid cousins of hers that she was as big and as clever as they were!

But the afternoon was warm, and the sound of the stream was mesmerizing. Willow stretched out on a patch of grass where the sun shone through, warming the ground like a cozy blanket. Soon, she was fast asleep.

When she woke, the shadows were longer than before. The air was decidedly cooler, and the sun was no longer warm. She looked around, wondering where the others were. Her mother must be worried about her by now.

"Mama?" she called into the trees. "Aunt Purdy? Where are you?"

She heard no reply, just the chirp of wood frogs and the twinkling sound of the stream.

"M—Mama?" There was a tremble in her voice when she realized she was alone.

Willow had no idea where she was. She had no idea where her family was. Maybe she should stay there by the creek until they came for her. She pulled her knees up to her chest and waited.

But as the light slowly seeped from the day, she began to cry. She was here in the woods, all alone, and her cousins swore there was a witch who lived on the mountain and baked small children into pies. Trying her best to be brave, Willow told herself she was only crying because she was cold and lonely. She didn't believe in the witch.

Until she saw her.

She appeared out of nowhere, looking every bit the wicked witch they claimed. Backlit by the dying rays of the sun, her long, wild hair appeared like a glowing fire atop her head. She wore men's pants and work boots, and she used a tall, crooked stick to manage the rocky terrain. But the thing young Willow noticed most was the huge hunting knife strapped to her side.

"Are you lost?" the witch asked.

"N-N-No," Willow said through her sniffles. "I-I just don't know where I am."

The child's answer drew a sound from the old woman. It sounded as much like a cackle as it did laughter.

"What's your name, child?"

"W-Willow."

"Come with me, Weeping Willow."

Afraid the witch would bake her into a pie, Willow sprang to her feet and dashed off into the gathering darkness. The witch called for her to stop, but she kept going, desperate to get away. She didn't want to be a pie!

Willow pushed deeper into the woods, finding that the forest wasn't impossible to squeeze into, after all. By the time she stopped to rest, she was truly lost. And what was worse, it began to rain. Now, she was alone in the dark with a real, live witch, she was cold and wet, and she wanted her mama. She even longed to see her cousins. Anyone but the witch.

Huddled in the darkness, Willow didn't know what to do. She cried herself to sleep and vowed to never pick another strawberry in her life.

It was an angel who saved her from the witch. Willow was certain of it. Through sleepy eyes, she saw the halo on the angel's head and the golden staff she held. Lifting her into her arms, the angel told her not to be afraid as she covered her with a coat. It was warm and dry inside, and it felt Heavenly. That didn't surprise Willow. Everything about an angel was supposed to be Heavenly.

Thanks to the angel, the rain had stopped. Now safe and warm, Willow drifted back to sleep as they moved through the dark forest.

She woke in a warm bed piled high with blankets. The walls didn't look familiar, and the sun came through the window from the wrong side of the bed. She sat up in bed, and the first thing she saw was a huge stone fireplace. A low fire glowed in the firebox, filling her head with the vision of the mountain witch and her flaming hair. Had it been a dream? Last night was still fuzzy in her mind. She had been picking strawberries and wandered too far away from the others. Then she had seen the witch and ran deeper into the forest, but an angel had saved her.

That was it! The angel must have brought her here to this strange cabin to protect her from the witch.

Young Willow turned her head, visually studying her surroundings before getting out of bed. The cabin was a little dark, and the furniture looked strange. Where was the television set? And why was the bed in the living room? Where *was* she?

Then she saw her. The angel was asleep in the rocking chair not far from the bed. Had she sat there all night, keeping watch over the little girl as she slept? She must be exhausted. Willow couldn't see the angel's halo now. Her long hair looked more like the witch's, all tangled and wild. But the witch's hair had been glowing red, and the angel's hair was gray.

As the child's eyes adjusted to the dim light, she noticed other similarities. She thought angels were supposed to wear white robes that floated around them, but this one wore boots. Just like the witch had. She never thought about what kind of shoes angels wore, but this one wore boots. Just like the witch. Pants, too.

Willow frowned, trying to wrap her head around it all. Were the witch and the angel the same person? She tried remembering the night before. The witch had been in the woods, but she hadn't hurt her. She hadn't cast a spell on her or turned her into a pie. The angel had been in the woods, too, and she had helped her. She wrapped Willow in something dry and warm, and carried her out of the thick trees.

Maybe she had been wrong about the witch with the flaming hair.

"I see you're awake." The witch/angel's voice was rough, like it was rusty from not being used much.

The child stared at her, trying to sort it out in her mind. "Are you a witch?" she asked bluntly.

Her responded cackle reminded Willow of the witch. Hadn't she sounded the same way? Was that her laugh? It sounded funny.

"I've been called that a time or two," the witch/angel answered.

"Do you really bake children into pies?"

Surprised by such a question, it took the woman a moment to answer. "Nah. Ain't got a pie pan big enough. 'Sides, children give me the heartburn. Some are too sweet; some are done spoiled. Leave a bad taste in the mouth." She smacked her lips, wincing like she had tasted a green persimmon.

"You're not a witch, then?"

"There are many kinds of witches, child. There's garden witches, who use plants and herbs for all sorts of uses. Kitchen witches who know how to brew up those same herbs to cure ailments. There's fairy tale witches, the kind that are mean and vengeful, and hurt little children. I reckon I am a witch, in a way. I'm a douser."

"The kind that finds water?"

"Yes. I witch for water. Other things, too, like bones."

"Bones? Why would someone want *bones*?" She wrinkled her nose with distaste.

"There's lots of uses for bones. I can grind 'em

up fine-like and use them for scrubbing. I can whittle them down to make small things. I even use them in medicine."

"You heal people?"

"I do."

"Does that mean you're a bone witcher?"

"I reckon so."

Just to clarify things, Willow asked, "But you don't eat children."

The old woman tapped her chest. "Heartburn, remember?"

"Okay." Satisfied, the little girl pushed back the covers. "I'm hungry."

After breakfast, the witch/angel said she had chores to attend. Willow followed her outside and offered to help.

"What's that?" she asked.

"This here's a flare. It's what we use up here on the mountain when we need help. I'll set this off, and the search party will know to come for you."

"Why don't you use the telephone?"

"Ain't got one. Now, stand back. And cover your ears."

Willow did as told, fascinated by the bright flame that streamed straight up in the sky.

"While we wait, might as well feed the chickens and gather eggs. Grab that basket and come with me, Weeping Willow."

"What's your name?" she thought to ask. It was rude to keep thinking of her as the witch when she wasn't at all like the witches Willow had read about.

"Karnie."

Karnie didn't talk much, but a comfortable

silence settled between them. They worked well together, and when the old woman did speak, it was to impart some morsel of knowledge on her young companion.

In the two hours that Willow waited for the search party, she learned a lot from the older woman. By that time, she thought of her as more angel than witch.

Then her parents and Aunt Purdy came for her, plus a lot of people Willow didn't know. She started crying when her mother swept her into her arms, and for the first time in her entire six years, she saw her daddy cry.

Her parents repeatedly thanked Karnie for rescuing their child. When Ireland asked how they could ever repay her, the answer was a curt, "Watch your child more closely."

It was strange how the angel acted around grownups. She almost sounded like a witch, all gruff and sharp. Nothing like the way she had been when it was just her and Willow.

Willow's father herded her to the car, eager to be on their way home, but the little girl broke free. She ran back to her new friend and gave her a big hug.

She had no way of knowing, but hers was one of the few hugs Karnie had ever received.

18

Hairpin curves and steep cliffs made Knob Mountain a formidable opponent for drivers. To Willow, driving up the inclines wasn't so bad; it was coming down that had her clutching the steering wheel with fraught nerves.

By the time she turned onto the adjacent 'main' road—still winding and narrow, little more than a ribbon of pavement that ran through the hills and hollers of Border County—her muscles were tense. What she needed was a massage.

Still thinking about the old bone witcher and her primitive lifestyle, she concentrated on the road in front of her more than she did the road behind her. Somewhere along the way, a dark-colored pickup had fallen in behind her and seemed in no hurry to pass.

Willow thought nothing of it. She felt the same way when traveling these roads. There were only a handful of places to pass, and those were in short spurts. Willow wasn't a fan of accelerating to pass someone in front of her, only to slow down again for another curve.

It wasn't until the truck gained on her that she

felt the first flash of irritation. The driver had just missed the perfect chance to pass! There was no need to crowd her bumper now.

By the time she reached town, her irritation had shifted into concern. The truck was still behind her.

Willow put on her blinker and casually turned right. The truck followed.

She made another right. Again, the truck followed.

The tension in her shoulders ramped up again. She didn't recognize the vehicle. Was it dark navy, or black? She couldn't decipher the color.

Pretending she didn't know she was being followed, Willow turned into the bank parking lot. The drive-through deposit box had cameras. With her doors locked, she felt relatively safe as she rolled to a stop. She went through the motions of grabbing one of the provided envelopes, pretending to stuff it, and dropping her blank offering into the box.

She was hesitant to lead the truck to her doorstep. Realistically, if someone was tailing her, they probably knew who she was, and where she lived and worked. Still, on the off chance it was just a case of road rage, she didn't want to make things easy for them.

Willow flexed her shoulders again. They felt so tight. What she needed was a massage!

An idea hit her. She could go to the fitness and lifestyle center. Not only would it throw the truck off, but it would give her another excuse to speak with Sharika. She could ask if the center offered massages. And if not, a relaxation session might be a good substitute. She seldom meditated but today could be the exception.

The truck followed her to the center, but when she pulled into a parking space and killed her motor, she watched in her mirror as they drove on by. At least she had solved one of her problems.

As she passed the pool area, the pungent smell of chlorine assaulted her nose. It seemed stronger today than the first time she visited. Could it be that all her senses were hyper-sensitive today?

Restore Your Soul's studio was empty when she arrived. According to the posted schedule, a meditation session would be starting soon. Willow looked down at her pants, pulled on the material a couple of times to assure its elasticity, and judged them suitable for sitting cross-legged on the floor.

She heard a voice coming from the back. Hesitant to use anything louder than a library voice, she quietly called Sharika's name.

No answer. Willow moved closer and tried again.

Still no answer. She walked forward a few more feet to try a third time.

Closer now, Willow heard a second voice. The muted voices between two women sounded contentious. Not wanting to intrude on their heated argument, she turned to retrace her steps.

Until she heard them say the name *Gideon*.

Her conscience told her this was none of her business.

Her curiosity told her that this might be her best chance to find his whereabouts.

Her curious nature won the battle. She moved

closer still, not exactly stealthy, not exactly announced. If seen, she could always feign innocence. She had called out twice, after all.

She couldn't see the women, but she recognized Sharika's voice. The other, she thought, belonged to the woman introduced to her as Maude.

"You just couldn't leave well enough alone, could you?" Sharika demanded.

"Don't pull the high and mighty act with me," the other woman shot back. "You didn't want him for yourself. This has always been about the money. Once this deal goes through, Gideon McMurray will be a rich man."

"*If* this deal goes through. I almost had him convinced, when you butted in and stole him from me!"

"You were taking too long!" the other woman snapped. "The investors are getting nervous. They need assurance that things are progressing as planned. Sweet-talking Gideon wasn't working, so I took matters into my own hands."

"By brainwashing him!"

Willow could almost hear the second woman's shrug. "If that's what it takes, so be it."

The tone of Sharika's voice lowered. "I've always known you had a bad aura about you. If you believed half of what you fed to all those unsuspecting souls, you wouldn't have so much evil inside you."

"You're one to be talking, sister dear!"

Willow's forehead furrowed. Sharika and 'Maude' were sisters? Try as she might, she couldn't find a resemblance. Judging by her exotic skin tones and hair, Sharika was partially black. In stark contrast, Maude had white-blond hair and green cat eyes. Even with a wig and tinted contact lenses, there was no denying her naturally pale skin.

Maybe she was wrong about the voice. Maude definitely had a bad aura about her, but what was that dig about brainwashing and unsuspecting souls? That sounded more like something Moon would do.

Willow barely held in her gasp. Could it be? Could Sharika and *Moon* be sisters? They had similar platforms. Both promoted inner peace and harmony, though in vastly different ways. And whether motived by love or by money, they were fighting over a man. Classic fodder for a sisterly competition.

Willow wanted to peek around the corner, but she didn't dare. What if she were right about the voice? 'Maude' had clearly been an alias, meaning the woman introduced to her at *The Captain's Table* could very well have been Moon.

Willow left as quietly as she had come.

That relaxing session with Sharika no longer sounded so relaxing.

"Aunt Purdy! What a surprise!" Everleigh squealed in pleasure. "I didn't know you were coming."

"It was a spur of the moment decision," the older woman answered. Technically, she was Everleigh's great-great-aunt, but the title sounded much too ancient for the vibrant woman hugging her.

Willow waited for her own hug. "This is always

a treat." After yesterday's visit to Karnie, the dark truck that followed her, and her unconfirmed suspicion that Sharika and Moon were sisters, she could use a pick me up.

"I had to make a delivery, and I decided if I was this close to Border, I might as well drop in for a visit."

"We're so glad you did!" With her arm around Aunt Purdy's waist, Ireland encouraged her to have a seat. "That delivery wasn't to Carolyn Homer's, was it?"

Everleigh picked up on the name. "Homer? As in Nathaniel Homer?"

"His wife," Aunt Purdy confirmed. "She's a customer of mine. Since she was a neighbor to poor old Gus, I decided to make a special home delivery." Her eyes twinkled with mischief.

"Did you find out anything useful?" Ireland asked hopefully.

"Unfortunately, no. It just confirmed what I already knew—her husband is a royal pain in the patootie."

As a vague memory surfaced, Willow looked thoughtful. "You know," she recalled, "I think I may have met them before. Marcus and I were attending a black-tie fund raiser of some sort, and I remember a couple with that name. It struck me that they were such an odd, mismatched pair. She was quiet and very likable, while he was loud and boastful."

"That description certainly fits. They're opposite in looks, too. She has fair skin and blond hair. He has a swarthy complexion and what was probably dark hair when he was younger."

"That sounds like the couple I remember," Willow agreed.

"Carolyn took me on a tour of their house—it's gorgeous, by the way, and completely over the top—and as we passed her husband's office, I saw him on the phone. It was a very intense conversation that left me feeling sorry for the person on the other end. He glared at me as if I were eavesdropping!" She was clearly offended by his assumption. "I'm telling you, that Nathaniel Homer is not a man to be crossed. It wasn't five minutes later that he tracked us down and all but herded me out the door."

Everleigh frowned. "That sounds rather rude. I think he's more than just a pain in the patootie. He *is* the patootie!"

"What else do we know about the Homers?" Willow asked.

"Not much. I know they moved here from Little Rock. The Scrimshaw Project is his brainchild," Aunt Purdy told them. "He plans to clear cut the mountain, turn the logs into milled lumber, and use the land for a fancy housing development. His house is a prototype for his vision of a luxurious mountain neighborhood."

"No wonder Maverick stormed in here like that," Everleigh reasoned. "He's probably getting a big bonus if he secures enough land for the development."

"You've met Maverick?" Aunt Purdy asked.

"Unfortunately. You know him?"

"Like you, unfortunately. He's paid a few visits to our neck of the hills, too."

Ireland looked horrified. "Surely, he doesn't

plan to log our hills!"

"He may try, but he won't have any luck," she answered confidently.

"I certainly hope you're right."

Aunt Purdy wore a knowing smile. "Is that protectiveness I hear in your voice? A bit of nostalgia?"

"Of course I'm nostalgic about my birthplace." Landee defended herself.

"For heaven's sake, Ireland!" A rare note of impatience slipped into her aunt's voice. "If you're so nostalgic for it, go back and see it! And your mother," she added shortly.

"Let's not start that up again." Ireland looked cross.

"One visit, and I won't say another word."

Everleigh looked between the two of them warily. She had never seen them argue before. "What's going on? It's not like the two of you to fight."

"We're not fighting," her grandmother denied, but her voice sounded tight. "We're having a difference of opinion."

"When Mom and I go at it like that, you call it fighting."

The bell above the door jingled as a delivery man came through the door, buried beneath an armful of boxes.

"Here, let me help you with that," Everleigh said, jumping to her feet.

"Thanks. They're not heavy, just bulky."

"You're right." She tested the weight of one she held. "These three don't weigh a thing."

"Fine by me," the man grinned. "I'll put these

heavier ones here on your desk." He politely touched his cap. "You ladies have a nice day."

"I know what those two are," Everleigh said when he was gone, nodding toward her desk. "One is an order of envelopes, and the other is a gift for Laura Beth. But what are these three?" The packaging offered no hint. "And look. They're numbered." She handed one box to her mother and the other to her grandmother.

"I have number one," Ireland said. "Shall I?"

"By all means."

She used the letter opener on Willow's desk to slice through the brown tape. Beneath the flap were packing peanuts, the pesky kind that stuck to her fingers like taffy. She dug through them with a mumbled complaint, until she found a bright pink piece of paper folded in half.

"What's it say?" Everleigh asked.

Her grandmother frowned. "That's strange. All it says is '*You.*' Who has number two?"

"That would be me." The redhead reached for the letter opener.

Inside the second box rested more peanuts and a green note. Unfolding it, she read it aloud with an even bigger frown. "*Were.*"

"Okay, I have number three. Let's see what this one says." Willow opened the box and raked through the Styrofoam peanuts until she touched the third note.

"Red paper," she murmured as she retrieved it.

"The color of danger," Aunt Purdy pointed out.

Willow's fingers were unsteady as she unfolded the paper. Instinct told her it wouldn't say *pranked.* Though doubtful, the window egging could have been a childish prank. But this... This felt far more sinister. Apprehension zinged down her spine.

"Well?" her mother demanded. "What's it say?"

"*Warned,*" she read quietly. She strung the words together and repeated, "*You were warned.*"

The women looked at each other, the worry and concern plainly etched upon their faces.

After a moment, Willow noted, "There's no return address. Nothing legit, anyway. A name that spells nothing, a cryptic PO Box 123, and a zip code just as fake."

"I'll call the delivery company, for all the good it will do," Everleigh said. "It's unlikely, but they may be able to trace the sender."

"I think we should call the sheriff, too," Ireland said. "If for no other reason than to document it, right along with the egging incident."

Sheriff Mathers took his time showing up. He could have apologized for the delay and cited being detained by another matter. Instead, he ambled in with a coffee in his hand and a toothpick dangling from his mouth.

He practically blamed the women for the incident, saying they should have a better class of clientèle. He took one picture of each box, jotted down minimal details, and left with no promises to keep them informed.

"That was a waste of time," Everleigh grunted. "He doesn't plan to do one thing for us."

"I loved your comeback about needing a better class of law enforcement," Aunt Purdy said with a chuckle. "That look on his face was priceless!"

"Have you ever wondered," Ireland contemplated, "why he is so hostile over this case? He's clearly not taking the harassment seriously, although, granted, that could be because it's us. But he doesn't seem to be overly concerned about any of it. He was quick to rule Gus' death as a random theft gone bad. He was more concerned about finding you on Knob Mountain than he was about finding the boys' remains. It just strikes me as strange."

"I assumed it was because it involved us, but you do have a point," Willow agreed.

Aunt Purdy made an interesting observation. "Did you know his father was the sheriff when those boys went missing? It was big news at the time, so of course Hank Mathers went through the motions of doing a thorough investigation. But when the news outlets and the state police gave up, he did, too."

"There's mention of the case on all the big anniversaries," Ireland noted. "Five, ten, twenty. With the twenty-fifth anniversary coming up, there could be revived interest in the cold case."

Everleigh looked incredulous. "Mather's *father* was the sheriff then?"

Willow twisted her lips. "Do you think his father knew more about the case than he let on? Mathers may be trying to protect his good name by keeping his reputation intact."

"His father died several years ago," Aunt Purdy said.

She shrugged. "You know how people talk. If the father was a dirty cop, a lot of people would say the son is, too."

Ireland agreed. "That would certainly explain

why Mathers hasn't been too concerned about solving the old murders."

Willow nodded. "Gus kept saying it would be a mistake to tell the law what he witnessed. Maybe the sheriff was friends with the person who killed them, and he was protecting him."

"I suppose anything is possible," Aunt Purdy admitted. "I knew the man, but that's not to say we were close friends."

"No matter how close you are to someone, you never really know what people are capable of doing."

"How very true," Willow murmured. Her ex-husband came to mind.

"So," Everleigh made the logical conclusion, "if Mathers wanted to protect his father's reputation and somehow got wind that Gus planned to tell what he knew, does that make *him* a suspect in Gus' murder?"

The thought was sobering.

"It makes more sense, in a way, than blaming Maverick," Willow agreed. "That's been one thing that keeps bothering me. I agree that if Gus was standing in the way of closing the Scrimshaw Project, Maverick had the best motive to kill him. But how does he tie into a murder from twenty-five years ago? My understanding is that he's only been with Mulfred for five or six years. He's originally from Kentucky, so I don't understand his connection to Kinney Knob or why he would want to murder Benny and his friends."

"Excellent point," Ireland agreed. "It doesn't make a lot of sense when you think of it like that."

Aunt Purdy verbalized what they were all thinking.

In a sober voice, she said, "I think the sheriff just moved to the top of the suspect list."

19

She stood outside *Years Ago Antiques and Curiosities*, trying to drum up the nerve to go inside. Willow hadn't spoken to Tobias since Saturday, and now she had to ask him for an impossible favor.

She couldn't think of anyone else she trusted to accompany her to Kinney Knob. He said he would do anything to find justice for his students, but had he really meant it? Especially with something like this?

Karnie was an obstacle within herself. Most people were afraid of her. Those who weren't frightened were still leery. She had a gruff, unfriendly demeanor and an unsettling appearance.

The other obstacle was the physical aspects of her request. Willow wanted him to hike the ridge with her and then dig up an unmarked grave. Chances were that it would take multiple false attempts before—and if—they were successful in finding the boys' remains.

Not the boys, she reminded herself. *Benny, Terrell, and Josh.*

Sadly, Willow didn't know many men she could

ask for help. She nor Everleigh had a boyfriend or a steady male figure in their lives, so her current possibilities for recruits were sitting at zilch.

"Not zilch," she said aloud. "At least, not until Tobias kicks me out of his store. If he thought I was crazy the first time I came in, just wait until today."

She had to quit stalling. If he turned her down, she would have to find someone else. She sensed that with Karnie, there were no second chances.

Willow straightened her shirt as she got out of her car. On the way to the front door, she gave herself a pep talk. She could do this. He said he would do anything to help. He was a good man. She could make this happen.

Her confidence wavered as she opened the door.

It vanished when she saw him with his arm around a petite brunette.

"Thanks again, Tobey," the woman said. "I'll call you when dinner's almost done.'"

"Can't wait."

"Love you." She pressed a kiss to his cheek.

"Love you more," he said, laughing as she pranced down the aisle. Both had silly smiles on their faces.

Tobias watched until the woman left, slightly shaking his head in amusement. Only then did he notice Willow. "Oh," he said. "Hi, Willow. I didn't see you come in."

"I didn't want to disturb you."

Willow, what a fool you are, she berated herself. *You honestly thought he was flirting with you the other night? He's in a relationship!*

"You wouldn't have disturbed me. I'm glad you stopped in."

Because he wants to make a sale, she reminded herself. Was she wrong to have come here?

"Willow?" he asked in concern. "Is everything all right?" While she was busy arguing with herself, he had made his way toward her.

"Uhm, yes. Why do you ask?"

"I said something to you, and you didn't seem to even hear me."

"I'm sorry. I guess I'm just…"

"Just what?"

"Nervous."

He almost looked pleased.

At least one of us finds humor in this! Just ask what you came to ask, and salvage what's left of your pride!

It was odd, she realized, how a person could hiss to themselves silently.

"I'm here to ask a favor," she blurted out.

"I told you that I'm happy to deliver anything you'd like to buy."

"It's not that. I, uhm, need your help."

"Is this about Benny and his friends? I'm happy to help."

"Wait until you hear what I'm asking."

"Just a sec." He jogged to the counter, pulled out a cardboard sign, and jogged back to the door, where he put the sign in the window and locked the handle. "I put out the 'Be right back' sign. We can go to the back and talk."

"Oh, but I don't want to interrupt your day."

"You aren't." His smile was enigmatic as he

took her elbow and steered her toward the back. There was an opening behind the counter, obviously leading to his workroom. When she stepped through, she saw it was also a small office/kitchen/seating area. He moved a box and motioned to the settee.

"Ignore the frilly pink cushions. My sister was cleaning out her daughter's room and thought I might want to sell it in the store. Hard pass, but I said I could use it in here."

Willow couldn't help but laugh at his comical expression.

"Do you want some coffee? Water?"

"I'm fine, thanks." She would make this as quick and painless as possible.

"So. What's the favor?" He sat on the small couch beside her, and much too close for her comfort.

Willow opened her mouth to speak but realized this would be harder than she imagined. How did she explain Karnie without sounding crazy?

"Wow, this must be a big ask," Tobias guessed.

"It is. Tell me. Are you familiar with the term *bone witcher*?"

"Sure. They're dowsers. Instead of water, they witch for graves, or bones. There's supposedly one over in Arkansas on Knob Mountain."

"Yes. Yes," she said enthusiastically, bobbing her head like one of those dolls. Other than looking like an idiot, she surmised, things were going good so far. "That's the one I'm talking about. Her name is Karnie."

"You know her?" he looked surprised.

Best to just blurt it out. "Yes. And I asked her if she'd be willing to help us search for the remains of your students."

Tobias sat back against the frilly cushions, appearing a bit stunned. "And?"

"I'm meeting her Sunday morning."

"Where do I come in?"

"Well, that's the thing." Willow's confidence wavered. She looked down at her hands, picking at her nails. "Naturally, even if we find the bodies, we can't exhume them. We'd have to call the authorities, and there would be paperwork and—"

"Willow." He used his professor voice. He knew she was stalling, just as his students often had. Josh had been one of the worst.

"Fine. We need someone to help dig, and we both agreed to bring someone. The problem is, I don't know anyone, and I was thinking... That is to say, I hoped..."

"I'll do it, Willow," he said quietly.

"It's just that—wait. Did you say you'll do it?"

"I told you I'd do whatever it takes to find out who killed them. I meant it."

"Thank you. Thank you, thank you." She was so relieved, her shoulders slumped as she fell against the pink cushions.

"You really doubted I'd help?"

"You caught the part about digging, right? I knew you'd be supportive, but physical labor is a different thing altogether."

"You don't think I'm up to it?" There was a teasing tone in his voice.

It took great discipline, but Willow didn't allow herself to look at him. Her eyes might take their own assessment.

"It's not that. It's just a lot to assume on my part."

"I'm ready, willing, and able. I'll pick you up, and we can go in my truck. Sound good?"

"Are you sure you don't mind?"

"Positive."

"And your… friend? She won't mind?" Willow realized it sounded as though she thought the cute brunette would be threatened by her, which was ridiculous. "I mean, it's a weekend, and she might have other plans for you."

"What friend?" Tobias looked genuinely confused.

"The one you're having dinner with tonight. The one you were talking to when I came in."

"You mean Angela? She's not my girlfriend. She's my sister," he corrected. "You're sitting on her couch, as a matter of fact."

"Your sister?"

"I have two."

Flustered and highly relieved, she covered it well. "Yet you ended up with the store."

He lifted his shoulders in a shrug. "Traci loved it. My sisters, not so much."

She had been wrong about him having a new girlfriend, but there was no denying he had a wife he still mourned. She sat forward. "I really should go."

"Are you sure? You just got here," he protested.

"I've already kept you long enough."

Tobias looked toward the front door. "I guess I should unlock the door." He sounded regretful.

Together, they walked to the front. "How can I ever thank you for agreeing to Sunday?"

His answer was simple.

"By catching the killer."

20

"You'll need to give me directions to this Karnie woman's house," Tobias told Willow on Sunday morning.

"It's just better if I show you, rather than tell you. I'm not good with north of so-and-so, or go west from there. I'm more of a left/right/turn past the coffee shop woman."

Tobias chuckled at the description. It was a sound that warmed her through and through.

"I know how to get to Knob Mountain." His expression sobered. "After the boys disappeared, I went up there to see it for myself. There's no way they could have survived a fall from Kinney Knob."

"It's a steep ridge," she agreed, "with a long overhang. There's probably a thirty-foot drop, if not more. Even then, it's onto treetops or more rock."

"Authorities and volunteers combed the area when it happened. How will we even begin to search after all these years?" There was already a note of defeat in his voice.

"They were looking for fresh signs of blood and

broken tree limbs. Karnie takes a different approach. She'll be looking for remains."

"It still sounds overwhelming."

"I know, but at the moment, it's the best we have." After a long moment, schooling the disappointment from her voice, she added, "If you want to turn back, we can."

"Not at all. I'm willing to give it my best shot. At least we have good weather for it."

The morning sky was already filled with sunshine and big, fluffy clouds.

"The sun is shining, all right."

He heard the lackluster note in her voice. "I hear a 'but' in there."

"No but," she denied, forcing a smile. "It is shining. It looks like a beautiful day."

"Then what was that I heard in your voice? And don't say 'nothing,'" Tobias warned.

She struggled with how much to tell him. He was still a relative stranger, even if she had asked such a monumental favor of him.

"Caution, I suppose you could call it."

He accepted her answer for what it was: a half-truth. She appreciated that he didn't force the issue, and soon, they were talking of more pleasant things.

When they reached the point of their final assent, he peered uncertainly at the steep incline. "We're going up there?"

"You can't see it from here, but we're almost there. Her cabin is in the woods past that clearing. Turn at that boulder, and the road leads up to it."

"You call this a road?" he soon mumbled.

"Yes, it's a road," she said with a laugh.

He took his eyes off the path long enough to look at her. "You have a nice laugh."

"Watch the road!" Willow warned. A wrong move could be dangerous this high up.

As they came into view of the cabin, they saw an older-model pickup already there.

"That must be her help. Karnie doesn't drive."

Tobias looked surprised. "How does she get down from up here?"

"Resentfully."

He chuckled at her witty reply as he parked behind the other truck. "Wow. What an awesome old cabin."

"No one knows when it was actually built. Some claim it just sprang up from the ground."

"It looks like it," he murmured.

When he gazed at the old structure in something akin to reverence, Willow realized how much he loved history. She had no doubt that he was an amazing teacher.

She gently broke the spell. "Thank you for coming with me and for helping me load all that stuff in the back."

"May I ask why you brought all that?" He hitched a thumb over his shoulder as he opened his door. "Propane tanks, a hoe, vinegar, groceries. It looks like you did her shopping for her."

"Karnie prefers goods over cash. This is payment for agreeing to help us."

"You'll owe more when she finds the bodies?" He opened the tailgate and pulled out plastic tubs filled with sundries.

"*If*," Willow stressed. There was no guarantee

their efforts would be successful.

"I choose to remain optimistic. We're going to find their bones and prove they died up here in these mountains."

"As for more payment" —she tugged on another tub— "we didn't discuss it, but I'll definitely reward her if we're successful."

"I'll do my part, too. I'm as determined as you are to solve this mystery. I owe that much to Terrell and Josh, and particularly to Benny."

As they trudged up the path to the cabin, Willow whispered under her breath, "I should warn you about Karnie's appearance. She looks a little… well, like a witch."

As if on cue, the 'witch' stepped out the door. She wore her typical garb, but her wild gray hair was contained, best as could be, into a long braid down her back. Frayed and frizzy ends sprung up around her head like a crown.

"Bring it all in, 'cept for the fuel." She barked the instructions before disappearing back into the cabin.

"Is she always this gruff?" Tobias wanted to know.

"For Karnie, that was polite."

Once their eyes adjusted to the dim light in the cabin, Willow and Tobias carried the tubs to the table.

"Karnie, this is my helper for the day, Tobias Cameron."

"Nice to meet you, ma'am," he said politely.

She grunted in reply and pointed toward the man behind her. "This here is Elroy Busey."

The thirty-something man offered a friendly

hand. "Pleasure, ma'am. Nice to meet you, Mr. Cameron."

"Call me Tobias."

"And I'm Willow."

"I'm Elroy," he repeated needlessly. He wore a big smile on his face. In his estimation, he had just made two new friends.

"Anything cold in them boxes?" Karnie wanted to know.

"No, ma'am. But there's three butane bottles in the truck, some kerosene, the hoe you wanted, and a surprise."

The old woman harrumphed, muttering something about not liking surprises. Willow was sure she would like this one, no matter what her reaction might be.

"I'll help bring 'em in," Elroy offered.

When the men left, Willow motioned to the two tubs on the table. "You can keep the tubs, if you like."

"Might take one."

Willow nodded. "They make good storage. I keep seasonal things in them, like quilts and blankets." She tried to make small talk to bridge the awkwardness between them. Karnie had a knack for making people uncomfortable.

"Might as well help me unload 'em while we're waiting," was her gruff reply.

Willow pulled out a variety of canned goods and stacked them on the slab of oiled wood serving as a countertop. Karnie pulled out pantry staples like flour, sugar, cocoa powder, black pepper, and salt.

"Who's that man?" Karnie asked.

"He's a former history professor at the university. He knew the boys who went missing."

"That why he's here?"

"Yes. They were in his class on colloquial culture and folklore. They were studying myths and legends, and the boys decided to do a video project for their big grade."

Karnie heaved a sigh. "I reckon it was about the Flaming Woman."

"It was."

"Why can't folks just leave it be? Can't the poor woman rest in peace?"

"I guess not."

She grumbled a complaint as the men came back in. Tobias carried a set of three LED lanterns.

"What's that?" Karnie barked.

"Battery-operated lights," he told her. "They're extremely bright."

"What do I need them for?" The old woman sounded gruff, but Willow saw a glimmer of interest in her eyes.

Smiling, Willow offered possible uses for the surprise gift. "Reading... extra light when you're sewing... for anything, really. These bulbs don't drain batteries like normal flashlights do and will last for ages. You can adjust the brightness, too."

"Leave 'em here on the table. Might find some use for them," she grumbled.

Tobias examined the cabin with an appreciative eye. History and the test of time seeped into every dimly lit corner, every wooden plank, every rafter, and every log. The scent of smoked meats and kerosene hung in the air, sweetened by the lingering aroma of baked apples and homemade bread.

"Oh, wow. Is that an old settle?" he murmured when his eyes fell upon it.

"What about it?" Karnie asked suspiciously.

"It's gorgeous!" The history buff ran admiring hands over the ancient piece. "This is excellent craftsmanship. Crude, but it stands the test of time. It's hickory, I believe, which is known for its sturdiness."

"One of my grandpappies made that," she announced proudly. "Not sure how many generations ago. Most likely built with the cabin."

"When was that?"

"Nobody knows for sure."

"It's amazing." He referred to the cabin as a whole. He found everything about it fascinating. Even the single upholstered chair, propped up by a brick where one leg had broken off, had a certain sort of charm to it. Like everything else, it looked well lived in.

"That's a great fireplace." His eyes moved to the kitchen. "Do you still cook on that stove?" He sounded awe-struck.

"What else would I cook on?" She sounded irritable.

"Those cook the best meals, don't they?" His disarming smile took her by surprise.

She seemed to soften before their eyes. "I reckon so," she agreed.

"This entire cabin is amazing. I could spend hours in here, admiring every single thing about it."

"We'd never make it to Kinney Knob. We've

already wasted time." She was grumbling again. "If anyone needs to relieve their bladder, do it now."

Feeling self-conscious, Willow needed to ask, "Uhm, where's your outhouse?"

"Out back or use the indoor facilities." She motioned to the back of the cabin.

Willow was pleasantly surprised. She assumed the cistern and water pipes were only for the kitchen.

Some of the pleasantry leaked away when she opened the back door. A lean-to had been added to the cabin, but the seams and corners didn't align properly. Chinking attempted to meld the two together; slices of daylight spilling between them debated its success. She shivered when she thought about the cold air that must accompany it in the dead of winter.

The 'indoor facilities' were crude. The commode was ancient. It was the kind with the water tank up high and flushed by pull-chain. The claw-foot tub had water handles and a spigot, but the sink required use of a hand pump. She dared wonder where the pipes emptied, but she assumed the small hot water tank outside filled the tub.

"We'll take Old Cuss with us to carry the diggin' tools," Karnie announced when they were ready to leave. "Elroy has her loaded up already."

"Old Cuss?" Willow questioned.

The younger man nodded. "Karnie's prized donkey. I loaded him up with some extra water, too, and flashlights."

"I'll take ya to the ridge first, so you can see where the boys fell from. Ready for a hike? It's a might high from here," she warned.

Willow foolishly thought if the old woman could make the climb, she could handle it with ease. Halfway up, she lagged behind the others. Her breathing was labored, and her leg muscles screamed with exhaustion.

Tobias noticed she had fallen out of line and was behind them now, struggling to keep up. "Hold up," he told the others. "Can we take a breather?"

Karnie snorted, saying something about city slickers under her breath.

They found boulders and fallen logs to sit on, and everyone but Karnie pulled bottled water from their backpacks. She took two sips of water from a canteen hanging from the mule's pack and remained standing. Willow wondered if it was because she found it difficult to get up, or if she simply wasn't tired. Either way, she admired her stamina.

They continued after a brief rest, hiking the rest of the way up to Kinney Knob.

"This here is where the Hoke steel once stood. That's what started all this notion about the Flaming Woman." She repeated the story as her uncle had told it. "That there's Bentwood Cave. Some say outlaws buried treasure there, but nobody's ever claimed to find it." She glared at Elroy with a warning. "And ain't none of us going to try to retrieve it, neither. Right, Elroy?"

The young man kicked a pebble with the toe of his scuffed boots. "No, ma'am, I reckon not."

A crooked juniper tree grew beside the mouth of the cave, no doubt giving the cavern its name. Passing in front of it, Willow noted the black hole receding into the rocks. Not a fan of confined spaces, she thought it looked dark and ominous.

"Best I can tell, the boys were up here when they were pushed." Karnie led the way onto the rocky overlook referred to as a knob.

"Will it hold all four of us?" Willow asked cautiously. She wasn't a fan of falling from life-threatening heights, either.

"Quit your lollygagging around, girl, and come on out."

Elroy, Willow noticed, was still behind her. Was he less confident than their guide?

Tobias took her elbow and encouraged her to take a step forward. Soon, they stood near the edge, and overlooking the amazing vista.

"Wow," she breathed in wonder. "The view is fantastic from here. I can see for miles."

They took a few moments to soak in the beauty of the Ozarks, admiring the hills and hollows that stretched below.

"Before we go, I need to cast a charm for luck. Stand in a circle and when I speak, lift your faces to the sun."

They fanned out to form a circle of four, with Karnie facing the ledge of the knob. Willow stood directly across from her. Karnie pulled a handful of fine grains and granules from her pocket and tested the wind's direction.

The first wind test failed. The few grains she released blew to the far left of where the boys' bodies would have presumably landed. She shifted the circle so that when she released the next few grains, they flew in the correct direction.

Satisfied, she lifted her face to the sun, closed

her eyes, and spoke in rhyme.

"From here to there, the path will show
The things you seek, the way you go.
Your search go swiftly, your search go sure,
The search go wisely, with causes so pure.
Follow the trail left behind,
What you seek, you shall find."

She blew the remaining handful of granules into the wind. Willow wasn't expecting a face full of grit and couldn't help but sputter.

Ignoring her, Karnie instructed, "Each of you wear this amulet 'round your neck." She handed out small pouches attached to slender strips of leather.

Tobias looked skeptical. "May I ask what's in here?" he asked.

"Sage, sweetgrass, lavender, and cayenne pepper to ward off evil spirits and keep you safe." She clapped her hands together with a smack. "We're wasting daylight. We need to get goin'."

Willow found that descending Kinney Knob was just as strenuous, if not more so, than climbing it. Defying the slope of the land and the gravity pulling her forward required different leg muscles than climbing. More than once, Willow felt her foot slip, and she would struggle for control.

Saving their breath for maneuvering the tedious course, there was little talk between them. Karnie grunted a few times as she led Ol' Cuss down, particularly the times when Willow slipped. Elroy finally volunteered to walk in front of her to keep her from tumbling down the dangerous rocks.

Their search had officially begun.

21

"We look here first," Karnie announced. The ground tapered to a more even surface, making it easier to stand.

She wasted no time going to work. She pulled two copper rods from her backpack before slipping it off her shoulders. She took a deep breath of concentration, chanted a few words no one else could hear, and set out on her mission.

A few feet from the tree, Karnie began witching.

The rods were slender and bent into somewhat of an "L" shape. She held the shorter end as a handle, her grip loose but secure. The longer ends pointed in no particular direction as she kept them parallel to the ground and slowly moved forward.

The rods moved this way and that, at times in polar opposite ways, at times pointed in the same direction. At no time did they cross.

After repeating the tedious process all around and among the trees, she seemed satisfied no bones were hidden below.

"I ain't gettin' nothin'," she said. Just as she would have relaxed her arms, the rods moved again. As they closely crossed one above the other, she changed her mind. "Never mind. There's something here."

"Really?" Willow asked with excitement.

Elroy beamed. "I told you she was the best at witching!"

"Should I bring the shovel?" offered Tobias.

"Don't bother," the old woman said. "Whatever it is, it's small. Most likely a bird or a squirrel."

"How can you tell?"

"Can't tell you the animal, just the size. Watch the rods." She pulled back, and the rods went back to random positions. When she crossed over the spot again, they gravitated inward until they were crossed. She moved forward a few inches, and they uncrossed once again. To be thorough, she crossed the would-be grave from the side and got the same results.

"Can't be too big," she insisted.

"Out of curiosity, can we find what it is?" Tobias asked.

"Curiosity, or doubt?" she asked. There was no accusation in her voice.

"A little of both, I suppose," he admitted with honesty.

Karnie raked her foot over the piles of dead, soggy leaves from last fall. She used the heel of her foot to dig slightly into the earth.

"See for yourself," she said, pointing to the ground.

They all peered down at the petite bones that had probably belonged to a bird.

"That's amazing!" Willow said.

"I'm impressed," Tobias agreed.

Karnie didn't respond to their praise. She peered up at the overhang of Kinney Knob, calculating trajectory. "I'll witch yonder a little ways," she motioned further along the slope. "Elroy, get them bones. They might come in handy."

"For that lady who collects bones?"

"If she don't want 'em, I can use 'em for poultices and powders."

Willow thought of Maude and the bones she wore as jewelry. She thought, too, of Moon and the bones she offered in sacrifice to her gods.

She kept the thoughts to herself and followed the others.

The further down they went, the steeper the slope became. Karnie instructed Elroy to find Willow a walking stick like hers. He wandered off on his own and soon came back with a slim, sturdy branch almost as tall as the younger woman. He had already trimmed the twigs and knots off with his knife.

"This will make walking easier," he assured her.

"Thank you."

She was amazed at how well the simple stick helped. Her foot still slipped at times, but she felt more confident with the stick as an aid.

Saying not a word, Karnie stopped abruptly. She pulled out her witching tools and started her search.

Without the hindrance of trees, the search in this area was much wider and more thorough. It came with similar results. They found the carcass of what could have been a large bird, plus the remains of two smaller creatures. The shovels came out when the divining rods revealed an area at least three feet long.

"What is that?" Willow asked, gazing down at the small ditch the men had dug.

"Looks like some sort of cat," Elroy answered. "Probably a mountain lion or panther."

"Yeah, there's the skull," Tobias agreed.

While Willow looked on in interest, Karnie was unimpressed. "We'll try a might longer before we move on."

She walked another several yards, her rods still parallel with the ground.

Elroy noticed when she traced a path several feet long and at least a yard wide. He yelped with excitement.

"She done it again!" he whooped. "Karnie found something, and it's big. Real big!"

Willow and Tobias exchanged looks. This could be the moment they were waiting for.

The men carefully began to dig. They hadn't gone too deep when they found the first bone.

"Hmm. That's a big bone, but it doesn't look human. Not sure what that is," Tobias said.

Elroy became more excited. "Maybe it's a dinosaur!"

"Best you just dig, Elroy," Karnie said. Her voice sounded weary. It wasn't the first time she had heard such an outlandish statement from him.

The men tediously worked to uncover more of the shallow grave. As the deteriorated bones became more visible, they realized the body had never been buried. The mud and dirt coming off the mountain had simply piled upon it, hiding it from view.

"Ain't nothing but a horse!" Elroy said in disgust.

"Could be a mule," Karnie speculated.

They were all disappointed. Willow broke the gloom with a suggestion. "How about a short break?" she asked with forced brightness. "These men look like they could use it."

"Reckon so. But we can't tarry too long," the old woman warned. "There's still a lot of ground to cover."

This time, she perched upon a tree stump that stood well off the ground. Willow and Tobias shared a fallen log, while Elroy retrieved a saddlebag from Ol' Cuss. He handed the bag to Karnie, then proceeded to offer the donkey a handful of grains and water that he poured into a pan.

"Might as well have a bite while we're waitin'," Karnie said.

She took apples from her bag and tossed one to each person, followed by a generous slice of red-rind cheese.

Tobias guzzled down one bottle of water and started on another.

On their way again, Willow appreciated the way the rugged mountainside tapered off to a gentle talus slope. By the time they stopped again, they were on a plateau.

As Karnie dug in her backpack for her trusted wands, she had another warning for the group. "We could be wrong about this. It might not be the place. If it ain't, our search will start all over."

Willow closed her eyes and listened to the wind ruffling nearby tree branches. Standing perfectly still, she took slow, steady breaths and cleared her mind. *'Be still and know'* was her favorite Bible verse. It was also her personal mantra.

"We're close," she whispered softly. "It's somewhere nearby."

Tobias studied her with a curious expression, but he didn't question her quiet sense of certainty.

Karnie's lined and weathered face crinkled into one of her rare smiles, and she nodded in appreciation.

Elroy grinned like a child given a piece of candy. "You got the knowing, don't ya?" It was more of a realization than a question.

Willow avoided Tobias' gaze. "I suppose some would call it that," she said.

Karnie walked all around the log, witching the ground for hidden or buried bones. The pieces of copper rotated at random but never crossed for any length of time. She expanded the perimeter of her search, discovering only small, unidentified bones.

"Try over there," Tobias suggested. He pointed to a rotted log overgrown with vines and briers and covered in mold spores. It rested against a large boulder.

They understood his train of thought; a body could roll down a steep incline as easily as a log could. When met with resistance—a boulder, for instance—any momentum would come to a halt. There was a chance this was the final resting place of one of his former students.

Karnie's divining rods remained indifferent.

She made another sweep nearer the log, and the wands began to move toward one another.

"They're crossing!" Elroy whooped. "Hot dog, this could be it!" He seemed not to realize that this sort of celebration wasn't befitting the solemn occasion. If the rods had detected a human body, it would be confirmation of a tragic death.

"There's something here," Karnie agreed. "Too soon to say what."

"I'll get to diggin' and see exactly what it is."

"I'll help." Tobias was already breaking ground with careful scoops of his shovel.

After removing several layers of dirt, Tobias told the watchful women, "There's bone here, but I'm not sure what kind. Most of these are small and seem to be scattered. We'll need to widen the hole."

As he and Elroy broke a sweat with their efforts, Willow searched the area for shadows. She expected to feel something dark when they found the bodies. Some shiver of danger down her spine. Some oppressive air that stifled her lungs. The tingle of impending doom.

There were none of those things.

Even before Elroy spoke, she knew this wasn't the place.

"Ain't nothing but a deer," he said in disappointment. "It probably bedded down here to die." He rested against his hoe handle and complained, "This ain't working."

Willow knew they were close. This wasn't the place, but it was nearby. She could feel it.

"Over there." She pointed to their left. The ground there was rippled, sinking lower in some spots, while others were mounded with soil and sod.

Karnie approached one of the sunken areas. If this were a gravesite, twenty-five years in the elements would have caused the soil to break down and settle. It would create a cavity in the earth, just like this one.

When the divining rods crossed, the onlookers held a collective breath. The crude tools remained crossed as Karnie carefully walked forward. Whatever lay beneath the ground, it was far larger than a fox or a deer.

It could always be another equine, but something in the air told Willow the discovery was far more sinister than that. A shiver crawled its way down her spine.

She wasn't the only one to feel the tension. No one spoke as the men dipped their shovels into the dirt, extracting the soil in small, mindful scoops. It was a tedious chore, but neither complained. As the hole grew deeper, and the men were knee-deep within, Willow got on her knees and sifted the discarded soil through her fingers. Small bones could be delicate and hard to see at first glance.

The men kept digging, until only their torsos were above ground.

She heard the distinct chink of Tobias' shovel hit against something solid. As he sucked in his breath, his eyes sought hers. Somehow, they both knew. These were the remains of Josh, Benny, and Terrell.

"Stop," he told Elroy, catching his arm to still him. "I found something."

Elroy saw the gravity in his face and

immediately stood back. Tobias needed the space to fall on his knees and carefully brush away the dirt.

Willow leaned over to see what was happening. Even Karnie moved closer.

Someone—perhaps all of them—let out a small whimper as the bone came into view. The length suggested it could be from a human leg. To be certain, Tobias brushed away more dirt, careful not to dislodge the bone itself.

He abruptly sat back on his heels. He was visibly shaken by what he had found. "You may want to look away," he cautioned Willow.

"What-What is it?"

"There's more bones beneath it." His voice lowered. "One of them is a skull."

Covering a gasp behind her hand, Willow sank back against her heels. It was true. The boys had been murdered and carelessly tossed into a single grave. The enormity of the find hit her hard.

She saw the shadows now. Dark and menacing, and tainted with danger.

The men helped each other out of the hole, mindful not to disturb the remains. Elroy stood upright, but Tobias' energy suddenly drained away. He pushed back to sit beside Willow, who still knelt by the hole.

Oddly enough, it was Elroy who kept a calm head and took charge of the situation. "I'll call the sheriff."

"What county are we in?" Willow asked. She hoped he would say anything other than Border.

He didn't.

"The very edge of Border County. I reckon

Mathers will be the one comin' out."

"Figures," Willow muttered.

Elroy consulted his cell phone for service. No bars.

"I may have to walk a piece to get a signal," he told the others. "Maybe back up to the knob."

"We'll be here," Tobias assured him quietly.

Stillness settled with his departure. It was a solemn task, watching over the exposed remains.

Willow rearranged her legs and settled more comfortably on the ground. They could be in for a long wait. "Oh, Tobias," Willow whispered quietly, placing a comforting hand upon his arm. "I'm so sorry. This has to be difficult for you."

Staring toward the grave, he answered with a raw, "At least we know for certain now."

They sat in silence for a long moment. After a while, he reached out to seek her hand. There was nothing romantic about the gesture. He was looking for comfort in a friend. Willow returned the grip, and they sat for another long moment, hands joined and hearts heavy.

"Need some water?"

Karnie's rough voice startled them both. They had forgotten she was there.

She handed them each a bottle of water. She didn't bother saying she found them in Willow's pack; Karnie avoided plastic whenever she could.

"I reckon that clears up a few things," the old woman said. She lowered herself to the ground with little difficulty. Willow watched in admiration, knowing she would be far less agile at that age, whatever it might be.

The self-proclaimed witcher settled into the freshly dug dirt, unconcerned about stains and grit. "Should put your mind to ease," she said, spitting her snuff in the opposite direction. "Some folks wondered if they just walked off the mountain and went on with their lives somewhere else. This settles that."

"I never doubted they were dead," Tobias said, "but I always hoped they had died of natural causes. One slipped off the edge of the cliff," he imagined, "the others tried to help their friend, and they all fell to their deaths. I never considered the notion of murder. Not until Willow brought up the possibility."

Tact was never Karnie's strong suit. "No other reason to pile those boys in one grave," she said bluntly. "Only saw two, but odds are all three are in there."

Their cocoon of comfort lost some of its warmth. Tobias pulled his hand free from Willow's and said on a sigh, "I imagine so."

What little conversation they had was fragmented. It came in spurts, as Tobias and Willow's minds struggled to make sense of what they had found. Even though they had been searching, hoping for these very results, it still left them in shock.

At one point, Tobias spoke to Karnie. "It was amazing what you did today, finding this grave like you did. I'd heard of grave witching—or bone witching, whatever you want to call it—but I'd never seen it done. How did you learn the art?"

"Just somethin' passed down to me through the years," she said, spitting once again.

"It was fascinating to watch. Thank you for finding my students. It's long past time for their families to have closure." He didn't say he needed that same closure for himself.

Karnie readjusted the snuff packed against her lower lip and spit again. She used the back of her hand to wipe her chin clean. She nodded toward Willow. "It was her that pointed me in the right direction."

"That it was."

Without looking at him, Willow knew when his blue eyes turned upon her.

"Thank you, Willow, for knowing where to look," he said in all sincerity.

She knew, too, that the next question was coming.

"How *did* you know where to look?"

Willow seldom spoke of her gift. Only a few people knew of it, but many would doubt it, should her secret come out. It seemed foolish, however, to deny it now. Tobias had seen it for himself.

"Like Karnie," she answered in slow, measured words, "I suppose it was something passed down to me through the years."

"I guess that explains the caution from earlier," he murmured softly. From the look in his eyes, she knew that wasn't the last she would hear on the subject.

For now, however, he let it go and stared at the grave once again.

"They had such bright futures ahead of them," he mused after a long silence.

"You're one of those teachers at the big school, you say?" Not one for small talk, Willow was surprised to hear Karnie reply.

"Yes, ma'am, I am. Benny and his friends were my students."

"I reckon Benny's one of them in there?" She tilted her head toward the exposed grave.

"Benny, Josh, and Terrell," he confirmed.

"There's evil in some folks. Ain't no rhyme nor reason for it, or for the folks who suffer because of it. I reckon your boys came across something they shouldn't've, and that evil came a'calling for them."

"That's my theory, too," Willow agreed. "I asked for your help because I needed proof they were murdered."

Tobias blew out a heavy breath. "Burying them in an unmarked mountainside grave is proof enough that this was no accident. Someone did this deliberately."

"Best be careful, girl, or that evil may come for you," Karnie warned. "I'll make a special charm that will keep you safe. It's best to do on a Friday, but I reckon you may need it before then." She sighed noisily. "When word of this gets out," she looked toward the hole again, "you could be dancin' with danger."

Willow felt the subtle change in the wind. A gust of chilly air swept down from atop Kinney Knob, causing her to shiver. It wasn't so much from cold as it was from apprehension.

Karnie must have felt it, too. She nodded to the amulet hanging from Willow's neck. "You best keep that with you, I reckon." Her gaze moved to Tobias. "You, too, teacher man, being as you were part of today."

An army of emergency vehicles descended upon Knob Mountain. Dust swirled as the string of cars and trucks swarmed the narrow state highway. The cry of a dozen sirens shattered the coveted mountainside peace. On a normal day, blue sky filtered through the treetops, spilling light between clusters of trees and the irregular skyline. Today, flashes of red and blue dominated the normally tranquil scene.

If Willow thought the response to Gus' death had been chaotic, it was nothing compared to this.

Elroy volunteered to meet the first responders and lead them in. The remote area was accessible by horse or rugged off-road RVs, but not vehicles. Even time-worn footpaths were barely distinguishable among the shifting debris of talus rock and random boulders.

Having lived on the mountain his entire life, Elroy was an expert on how to reach the crude grave site. Spotted vegetation grew between crevices of the bedrock, but he used the bushes and grassy patches as landmarks. He effortlessly led essential personnel up the twisting trail, ignorant to the fact that most struggled to keep up.

Topping the plateau, Sheriff Mathers burst onto the scene with an air of self-importance.

His eyes fell on Willow, and he immediately bristled. "What are *you* doing here?" he demanded.

Tobias helped Willow to her feet. As she brushed off the backside of her clothes, the polite professor offered Karnie the same courtesy.

"*We* did what should have been done in the first place. We found the gravesite and remains of the three college students who went missing over two decades ago."

"Benny Golden, Terrell Washington, and Josh Banik," Tobias supplied their names.

"You don't know for certain that's those boys buried in there!" Mathers pointed to the hole he had yet to examine.

"If not, you have a serious problem on your hands, Sheriff." Tobias' tone was almost a threat. "There are at least two bodies in that unmarked grave, and probably a third. I can't be sure because I didn't want to disturb the site. What I am sure of is that there's no coffin, no marker, and no explanation for that grave being here other than to hide a murder. Multiple murders, to be exact. If that's not those boys in there," he reiterated soberly, "you could have a serial killer on your hands."

"Now, hold on one minute," Mathers blustered. "You can't be throwing claims around like that. Not without proof. You'll cause a panic."

"Then you'd better hope those remains belong to the missing college students."

This was a side of Tobias she had never seen before. Not, Willow reminded herself, that she knew him well. Today, they had bound them together in a way, but they were still virtually strangers.

Neither one of them offered to stand aside for the red-faced sheriff. Mathers was forced to stalk around them for a closer look into the hole.

"Looks like human bones, all right," he agreed. "Can't say for sure there's two bodies in there from up here."

"Unfortunately, I had a closer vantage point," the former professor said.

Mathers pinned his gaze on Willow. "This is the second murder scene you've supposedly 'discovered' in less than two weeks. What's your stake in all this?"

Well aware of the fact that he had possibly killed Gus, she still couldn't resist goading him. "Besides doing your job for you?"

"I've had about enough of you, Mrs. Alexander. I've told you before. Stay. Out. Of. My. Investigations."

"Neither were an investigation until I called them to your attention."

"Fine. Have it your way. From this minute on, this is *my* investigation." He pointed his finger at her face. "Stay out!"

From a legal perspective, he had a point. She couldn't interfere with an official investigation.

"Stand back," he barked, "so the *real* investigators can do their work." He motioned for his deputies, two EMTs, and someone in bunker gear to come forward. Additional people filed up the trail.

Elroy and Karnie had stepped back as the newcomers crowded into their space, and now Tobias and Willow joined them. "Not sure were all those folks was parking," Elroy whistled. "You should'a seen that line of cars and trucks down there!"

"I'm sure when it went out on the radio, everyone who heard it came to see what the commotion was all about," nodded Willow.

A deputy strode over to the foursome, his expression severe. "I'm Deputy Mario Galvez. Sheriff

Mathers has remanded you to stay here until he has time to interview you." He had the same self-important air about him that plagued the sheriff.

"Not a problem," Tobias answered in a flat voice. "I don't intend to leave until those bones do."

"That may not be possible. This will become a closed scene with no exceptions."

"Did you personally know the students who went missing twenty-five years ago?" Tobias challenged.

"No, but that's beside the point."

"I disagree. I'm probably the only one up here who knew those young men, and the only one who has a personal stake in retrieving their bodies."

Galvez drew himself up straighter. He was still several inches shorter than the other two men. "As law officers, I assure you that Sheriff Mathers and I share that same stake."

"What were their names?" Willow's question took him by surprise.

While Galvez stuttered out a non-reply, Tobias provided the information. After identifying them by their names, he refused to back down. "I can assure *you,* Deputy Galvez, that we have entirely different goals here. I'm seeking closure for their families and for all of us who still mourn for them. I'm not interested in a personal commendation or accolades for my office. As their only advocate here on this mountain, I won't be leaving unless it's in cuffs."

Without an adequate comeback, the deputy stood down. "I'll let the sheriff deal with you," was all he said as he stalked off.

Elroy rocked back on his heels. "Shoo wee! I

don't know what some of them words meant, but you sure told him off good!"

Even Willow's eyes twinkled. "I'm sure you made quite the impression on any student who didn't toe the line."

"Lines are there for a reason," he answered. His anger was still too raw to see the humor in the situation. He didn't fully appreciate the way the deputy had all but withered beneath his glare.

"Looks like we'll be here a while," Karnie grumbled.

"I'll go tend to Ol' Cuss."

22

Willow knew their gruesome discovery wasn't an everyday occurrence. Even in large cities, finding three bodies in a makeshift grave deviated from the norm. But here in rural Border County, it was unimaginable. A discovery like this created nothing short of havoc.

If it hadn't been such a solemn occasion, Willow thought their clumsy attempt at competency would have been laughable. Even from where they waited on the sidelines, it was clear that Mathers had only a marginal grip on the confusion.

He ambled their way at last. His dark scowl reached them before he did.

"Let's hear it, Miz Alexander." He didn't bother with pleasantries, nor with introducing himself. "Why were you out here in the first place?"

"Like I said before, I was doing the job that's taken twenty-five years to be done. I found the grave."

"I want to know how." He grounded out. As an afterthought, he glanced around irritably. "Who are all these people, anyway?"

"This is Professor Tobias Cameron. He personally knew the young men in that grave. This is Elroy Busey. And this," she indicated the old woman, "is Karnie."

He recognized the name. Few had seen her with their own eyes, but everyone knew who she was. Tales of the mountain witch were practically legendary.

Willow saw him recoil at the name. He tried to disguise it as if readjusting his belt, but he took a small step backward to put more distance between them.

Mathers hid his obvious discomfort behind a growl. "Are you going to answer the question, or not? How did you find the bodies?"

"A very old mountain science called witching. You may have heard of it before."

"I've heard of it, but there's nothing scientific about it! It's just a bunch of foolishness."

The others remained silent, but Karnie replied in her own way. She spit tobacco juice at his feet. It seemed poetic justice after he had done the same thing to Willow's egg-smeared windows.

"'Who dug the hole?" he demanded.

"That would be me and Mr. Busey," Tobias replied smoothly. He wasn't intimidated by the sheriff's gruff demeanor. He extended his hand, forcing the other man to take it. "Tobias Cameron," he formally introduced himself. "There were remains of three bodies in that hole, correct?"

He dropped the professor's hand abruptly.

"This is an official investigation. I have no comment."

"I have a personal stake in the situation. Those young men were students of mine at the university."

"Tell me, then. You're an educated man. Do you believe in all this hocus pocus of grave witching?"

"I have to admit, before today, I had my doubts." He looked at Karnie with respect. "But I saw it with my own eyes. We dug more than one hole today, all with bones of animals inside. Bones discovered by witching."

"Malarkey!" Mathers claimed.

A hiss came from the old woman. Her white hair had escaped its braid altogether. With the wild mass free and unruly, her face and hands smudged with dirt, and her teeth stained with tobacco, she looked more of a witch than ever. She pointed a crooked finger at him and gave him an evil eye.

"You stop that!" he demanded, jumping back another step. "You can't put a curse on me!"

"I didn't hear her speak a word. Did you, Mrs. Alexander?" Tobias asked. His eyes looked amused.

"Not a word. What about you, Mr. Busey?" She passed the question—and the amusement—on to their companion.

"Nary a thing," Elroy said.

Willow knew she couldn't disobey the sheriff's orders concerning the case, but that didn't mean she couldn't push his buttons. "You should be thanking us for all our help, you know."

"Thank you? Thank you?" His voice rose to a thunder.

"Exactly. If it hadn't been for me, it could have been days, even weeks, before you discovered Gus McMurray's body."

Come to think of it, she realized, that had probably been his plan all along. By the time he officially 'investigated' the murder, the body would have been badly decomposed. That could explain part of his animosity toward their team for getting involved.

Not to be sidetracked, Willow continued with her rant, "And can you truly say you're still working a cold case after all these years? We did you a favor by finding the remains of all three bodies for you."

"There may be three bodies in there, but it's too soon to say who they belong to! There's no telling how long they've been there. They could be revenuers, killed by moonshiners. Or rival outlaws, murdered by the Bald Knobbers."

Tobias smiled at Willow. The sheriff had unwittingly confirmed there were three bodies in the grave.

"True but highly doubtful. Even bones deteriorate over time. And speaking of Mr. McMurray... How's that investigation coming, by the way?"

"We weren't speaking of him. Not that's it's any of your concern, but we have the situation handled."

"So, that would be a no."

"That would be a 'stay out of police business!'" He looked the rag-tag group over with a sharp eye. "Is there anything else any of you would like to contribute? Like, why you were out here looking for the grave in the first place?"

Elroy didn't understand the question. "We were looking for the bones. And there they are behind you, plain as day."

The sheriff ignored everyone but Willow. "Stay out of my way, or you'll regret it!"

There weren't many people Karnie trusted, and this man certainly wasn't one of them. But she trusted Willow, and she wouldn't let someone threaten her in such a way. She pulled the last few grains of sand from her pocket, cradled them in her palm, and with narrowed eyes, blew them at the sheriff.

"You take that back!" This time, the sheriff stumbled backward. "Take it off me!" He batted at his face like a cobweb had attacked him.

When Karnie laughed, it sounded like the thing of storybook witches.

With frightened eyes, Lew Mathers all but ran back to the others.

"Did you hex him, Karnie? Did you?" Elroy asked excitedly.

"Should'a," she said, "but I didn't."

"Then what did you just do?"

"Blew dirt in his face," she answered simply. Brushing her hands off, she announced, "Me and Ol' Cuss are going back. Elroy, you stay here and see 'em to the cabin when all's done here. Go fetch the backpacks so you have food and water."

"I've lost my appetite," Tobias said.

"All the same, you need water."

She didn't say goodbye. Karnie put the rope back on the donkey and urged him to follow behind. The sheriff hadn't officially released them, but she figured she wasn't under his rule.

No one told Karnie what she could or could not do.

Streaks of red and orange drained from the day as evening crowded in.

Here among the trees, the sun bled out even faster.

The last few yards up to the old cabin were the hardest, but the welcoming glow of candlelight quickened the weary travelers' steps.

"Something sure smells good," Elroy said, sniffing the air.

All Willow detected was woodsmoke, but a fire would feel good about now. The warmth of day died with the sun, leaving a definite chill in the air.

A huge dog came around the cabin with the beginnings of a growl. Recognizing a friendly face, he fell in step with Elroy.

"This here is Bear." Elroy made the formal introduction with sincerity. "Bear, these are our friends, Willow and Tobias. You be good and give 'em a proper hello."

Willow wasn't too keen on putting her hand so near the wolf-dog's mouth. He took a sniff, deemed it worthy, and flicked his rough tongue over her skin. The canine dutifully repeated the process with the man behind her.

"I didn't see a dog when we came this morning," Tobias said, scratching Bear behind the ears.

"Karnie sent him on a mission."

"Mission?" Willow asked. "How do you send a dog on a mission?"

"Part of a binding spell to carry away evil. Tie a

loose red string round its neck, whisper the charm in his ear, and send him away. When the string falls off, the spell is done."

Willow and Tobias exchanged a silent look. After today, they were both hesitant to dismiss Karnie's talents.

When Elroy pushed the door open, unannounced, Karnie straightened from her bent position at the stove.

"I reckoned that was you. I could hear ya coming up the hill," she said. "Wash up. Dinner's ready."

"You cooked?" Willow asked in surprise.

"We all had to eat. Might as well do it at once." It wasn't the most gracious of invitations, but she doubted the recluse had had much practice.

Willow was amazed at how much better she felt once her face and hands were clean.

"I reckon they got the bones down?" Karnie asked as the men cleaned up.

"It took a while, but they finally managed." That, too, had been a chaotic scene. Nothing like the way they did things on TV, painstakingly labeling and documenting each bone individually. In real life—at least in Border County—they had used a single body bag to collect all remains.

"Your young man refused to leave until it was over, I take it."

"He's not my young man." Willow frowned at the assumed relationship. "We're simply working together to bring those boys justice. And yes, he was determined to see this through. We both are."

"Why's this so important to you?" the old

witch-woman asked, watching Willow's face when she answered.

She debated on whether or not to tell the whole truth. "I have a client who claimed to know who killed them," she confessed. "Until I knew for certain that's what happened, I didn't have a lot to go on."

She helped Karnie set the table with mismatched plates. She doubted the old woman seldom—if ever—had three extra people joining her for a meal, either.

Once they were all seated at the table, Karnie nodded to the professor. "Tobias, say grace." It was more of an order than request, but the dark-haired man didn't object. They bowed their heads as he blessed the food in his pleasing baritone.

Willow was embarrassed when her stomach growled. Other than an energy bar, she hadn't had anything to eat since the apple and cheese. Apparently, finding a grave in the middle of nowhere had dampened her appetite, but now it seemed to have come back with a vengeance.

"Everything looks delicious." Willow hoped the compliment would take the spotlight off her stomach. Laid out before them was a platter of pan-fried ham, fried eggs, apple butter, and what turned out to be the most delicious pancakes Willow had ever eaten.

"These pancakes are amazing! What's your secret?"

"Just a normal cast iron skillet on a wood-burning stove." She made a sound that was something akin to a snort. *How else would she make the pancakes*, the snort seemed to say.

"She's right," Tobias agreed. "It's a fine meal, Miss Karnie. The best I've had in a long time. There's just something about cooking on a wood stove that can't be beat."

"Karnie," she corrected. "And where'd you learn about wood stoves? I thought you young folks only used those fancy ones these days."

"My grandparents lived in the mountains. In the wintertime, Grandma liked to cook on her wood stove."

"Smart woman."

Karnie didn't encourage her guests to take a final serving. When just two slices of ham and a single egg were left, she took the platters away and set them aside—her meal for tomorrow, no doubt. She returned to the table with a jar of peaches she had preserved herself, and small servings of her muscadine wine.

Willow leaned toward Tobias with a whispered warning, "Go easy on the wine. It's potent."

"I need to charm both of ya," Karnie reminded her visitors. "Someone set their eye on you. Evil's comin' your way, but I can help ward it off. When you're done here, you menfolk can bring in some wood and Willow will help with the dishes. We need to get on with it."

With the chores done, Karnie set out a bowl of water and twenty-four pinches of bread. They were lined up in rows of four, six to a row.

"Stand here," she instructed, "beside each other. I'll be touching you, so don't flinch. Elroy, you might as well get in here, too. Never hurts to be too careful." When they were all in place, she began the charm to remove the Evil Eye that had been cast upon them.

"Eyes that look, and looker too!
I throw you back into the water!
From head, from throat,
From hands, from belly,
From legs, from feet!
Back into the water,
May it carry you away!
Carry away the looker too!"

Each time she named a body part—head, each leg and foot, and all the rest—she touched a piece of bread to its place. She used the same piece for each of them, tossing the used bread into the water when done. It took eight pinches of bread for each recitation. After performing the ritual three times, the bread was gone.

"Elroy, take this bowl to the back and toss it out so that it trickles downhill. The water and soggy bread will carry your curse away, and you'll be safe."

The ride back to Border was a quiet one. Both Willow and Tobias were lost in thought. It had been an exhausting day. The hearty meal and the strong wine had relaxed them, but the need for a charm set them on edge. Whether they believed in the ancient tradition or not, there was a reason Karnie thought it necessary, and a reason they had gone along with it.

Willow hadn't told him about the warning delivered to the office. After today, he would be on the sheriff's radar, too, which meant they were both in danger.

"Thank you, Tobias, for going with me today,"

Willow said as they neared home.

"Thank you for finding their bodies." He paused before asking, "What's next? We both heard Sheriff Mathers. This is an official case. We can't interfere."

Willow was slow to answer. Should she tell him her suspicions? It would embroil him further into the case, but didn't he deserve to know?

"I think the sheriff could have an ulterior motive for warning me to back off," she admitted. "It's possible that—" Something he had just said sank in. "Wait. Did you say 'we' can't interfere?"

Illumination from the dashboard and passing lights highlighted his jawline. She saw the way it tightened. "I want to know who killed them as much as you do. Possibly more."

Willow could understand that. She answered his question with honesty. "Frankly? It all hinges on finding that recording. Without it, even if we're lucky enough to find a viable suspect, it would still be circumstantial. We need proof."

"I'll call Brad again. I'll tell him how important this is."

They reached her building.

"I can see you in," Tobias offered.

She was glad, now, that she hadn't told him her suspicions about the sheriff.

"Absolutely not. You still have to drive back to Branson. I know you're exhausted after all that digging."

"It doesn't feel right, not seeing you safely to your door."

"I go in by myself all the time," she assured

him. "Besides, Karnie's charm is protecting me, not to mention this stylish amulet around my neck." She grinned, modeling the pouch like it was a precious jewel.

"You're sure?"

"Positive." She opened the door before he could put the truck in park and do it for her. "Be careful driving home."

"I think from now on, we should both be very careful."

23

Exhausted on every level—mentally, physically, and emotionally—Willow waited until morning to give her partners a full briefing. She had texted them last night with news of success but begged off on the full reveal.

Now, relaying Karnie's amazing methods and the heartbreaking result, the others listened in awe.

"Wow. I can't believe you found their grave after all this time!" Everleigh's voice revealed her amazement.

"It was pretty incredible," Willow agreed. "Karnie has a true gift as a bone witcher. It sounds creepy, but in truth, it's a talent."

"How did the professor take it?" Ireland asked.

Remembering the sadness in his eyes, she answered, "He was understandably upset, of course, but at the same time, I think he was relieved. At least he knows for certain now."

"As will their families."

"Mathers warned him not to tell them until it was confirmed, but I doubt he listened. He talked like he planned to tell them today."

"I don't blame him one bit. Those poor parents deserve closure!"

"I can't imagine going that long without knowing for sure. It had to have been torture for them," Everleigh agreed.

"The same way it tortured Gus," Ireland murmured, "living with his secret for so long."

"Which is why we owe it to him to find their killer," said Willow. "I'm more committed to that cause than ever. We know for certain that the boys are dead, we know they were murdered, and we know that for twenty-five years, their killer has gone free."

"Mathers will try to stand in our way, but he doesn't know how stubborn the three of us can be once our minds are made up," Ireland echoed.

Everleigh couldn't help but chuckle. "He really thought Karnie put a hex on him? That must have been hilarious!"

"You should have seen his eyes. And he kept flapping his arms, like he was caught in a cobweb and couldn't get free!" She could see the full humor in the situation now, and a giggle rose up from her chest. "He nearly broke out running, trying to get away from her."

The more she described the scene, the funnier it became. Tears of laughter rolled down her cheeks. Before long, she had them all laughing.

Hearing the door open, Willow tried to stem the flow of laughter. Anyone coming in would think she had lost her mind. They wouldn't know that when she got tired, or overly stressed, or when her nerves were on edge, she often found relief in laughter.

"Excuse us, ladies. We don't mean to interrupt."

Willow dabbed her eyes and face and tried composing herself. Little bubbles of laughter still drifted to the surface as the two men closed the door behind them. Both wore dark suits.

Ireland was the first to squelch her laughter. "Not at all. May we help you?"

"I'm United States Marshal Jennings and this is my partner, Marshal Deats. Can we have a moment with the three of you, please?"

"Officer Jennings!" Ireland's smile broadened when she recognized the man speaking. "I didn't know we would see you again so soon!" It had been less than three months since he had been here, when another case required working with the feds.

"Always a pleasure, Mrs. Garrett." His eyes sought out the other two women in the room. A polite nod acknowledged Everleigh first, before his eyes settled on Willow.

Willow dabbed her face a second time, this time with her fingers. She was blushing again. The man had a way of looking at her that always made her feel self-conscious. She found herself wondering if her hair was mussed or her face splotchy from laughing so hard.

"Why don't we step into the conference room?" Willow suggested. "There's more room in there."

Formal introductions were made as they settled around the conference table. This, obviously, was not a social call.

"How can we help you gentleman?" Willow asked. "Would anyone like something to drink before we get started? Water, coffee, a soft drink?"

The men declined and went straight to the point.

"I'm sure it comes as no surprise, but we're here to discuss the grave you discovered on Knob Mountain," Marshal Jennings said. "Mrs. Alexander, I understand you were the one to originally find it?"

"Yes. Myself and three others."

"We'll need their names and phone numbers before we go."

"I only know the phone number for one. The second person doesn't have a phone, and I'm not sure about the third."

"How did you get in touch with the person without a phone?" he asked curiously.

"I went to see her in person."

"In that case, I'll need her address."

"I'm not sure she has that either. I can give you directions, but I don't suggest you go there without taking someone she knows. She can be rather... cantankerous." Willow looked for the best word to describe Karnie.

"How can someone not have an address or phone?" Marshal Deats wanted to know.

"She lives off the grid. No electricity, no traditional plumbing, very little contact with the outside world. The only way I know to reach her is to take a remote mountain road to her even more remote cabin."

"We can circle back around to that," Marshal Lane Jennings said. "I'd like to know more about why and how you found that grave."

Willow answered the questions to the best of her ability, without revealing Gus' name or his claim of witnessing the murder. When pressed for that information, the partners stood behind their policy of confidentiality and loyalty to their client. They would only provide that information with a court-issued warrant.

Jennings had a calm, steady manner about him. He tried to establish a rapport with subjects so that they trusted him and answered his questions. Deats took a different approach. He was stern and disciplined, and he wasn't shy about touting his credentials. If they were playing good cop/bad cop, Deats was clearly the bad cop.

"Tell us about the process of finding the grave," Jennings said. "You didn't just pick a random location and start to dig, did you?"

"Not exactly."

Deats spoke up. "What's that mean? Did you stop every few feet and just start digging?"

A smile played around her lips. "I'm sure it felt that way to Elroy and Tobias. They were the ones behind the shovels." Willow looked at Marshal Jennings as she spoke.

"I really am curious about your methods. You realize you did what some of the most sophisticated equipment in the country couldn't do. You found those bodies, even after all this time."

"Who those remains belong to are yet to be determined," Marshal Deats interrupted, "pending DNA testing."

Willow didn't argue. "We're going on the unofficial assumption that the three bodies dumped into an unmarked grave on a remote mountainside near the place they disappeared belong to the murdered college boys."

Deats was persistent. "At this point, a ruling of murder has not been substantiated."

"Sorry." She didn't sound at all sorry. "We're also going on the unofficial assumption that the boys didn't bury themselves, and therefore someone else was involved. The secrecy and unmarked grave suggests murder. But your point is noted. Nothing has been confirmed as of yet."

"Short of digging up the entire mountain side," Jennings said, "how did you know where to dig?"

The explanation would sound ludicrous to non-believers. Should she tell them Karnie cast a charm, and the answer came to her by way of grains of sand? Should she reveal her own special talents? Would they believe the truth?

She settled on a more scientific explanation. It, too, was true.

"We have reason to believe the boys were pushed from Kinney Knob. Again, our source is confidential. But using that premise, we were able to project a reasonable location where they could have fallen. We checked those places first and kept moving forward."

"But you only dug in specific places, correct?" Jennings nudged her to answer, rather than pressing her.

"Yes."

"And why is that?"

"Partially intuition," she answered honestly. "And partially the art of bone witching."

Deats snorted with disbelief. "The art of *bone witching*? How did you come up with that—"

Jennings cut his partner off mid-sentence. "Please let Mrs. Alexander finish. I'd like to hear more about this bone witching."

"I don't have the gift," she was quick to point out. "Karnie claims that honor."

"Honor!" Deats hooted.

A sharp look from Jennings silenced him. "Can you tell me what all that entails?"

"I can only give you a very crude explanation," Willow said. "She holds two copper rods in her hands and walks slowly across an area. If the rods cross, they've reacted to something that contains metal, or minerals, or whatever it is that copper interacts with. It's the same premise as witching for water. A twig is drawn to water, the same way copper is drawn to another element."

"I've heard of it, but I've never seen it for myself."

"It's amazing to watch," Willow told him. "She had a perfect record, even when it was nothing but the remains of tiny birds. She found a mountain cat, an equine of some kind, a deer, and, of course, the human remains."

"That does sound impressive," Lane Jennings agreed.

"It sounds like you still haven't answered the question!" Deats complained.

"I agreed to answer to the best of my ability," Willow said coolly, "which I did. That was the process we used. There's really nothing more I can tell you."

Marshal Jennings knew when an interrogation was going nowhere. "I think that's all we need for now but understand that we may need to talk with you again. Do you foresee that being a problem?"

She met his gaze without blinking. "Of course not."

"If you learn or remember anything new, you'll let me know?"

"I promise."

"Well, then, Deats, I think it's time for us to let these ladies get back to work." He stood to leave, signaling they were officially done.

"Work?" the other marshal huffed. "They were laughing like hyenas when we came in. Hardly the sort of thing you would expect one day after making a gruesome discovery."

"What *was* so funny, if you don't mind me asking?" Jennings asked.

Willow tried holding it back, but her lips curled into a grin. "Karnie pretended to put a hex on the sheriff. He tried batting it away, which looked more like swatting at flies. He backtracked so fast, he almost fell."

They walked toward the door with Jennings and Willow in the lead. Leaning in, Lane Jennings shared her grin. "That," he said confidentially, "would have been something to see."

Her eyes glittered with humor. "Oh, it was."

A sound woke her from a deep sleep. *Was that thunder she heard?* Willow wondered as she sat up in bed.

There was a rumble in the night, more like a train than thunder. *A tornado?* Even the windows rattled.

Willow jumped up, sliding into her shoes and grabbing a nearby sweater. There was a strange orange glow outside, illuminating the room and making a lamp unnecessary.

Something hit the back of the building. Limbs from nearby trees slung off by the swirling winds? Fear rose in her throat. She needed to get downstairs to safety.

As an afterthought, she grabbed her cell phone and purse. She was almost to the bedroom door when she went back for her gun. Tornadoes didn't normally call for a gun, but she instinctively knew she might need it.

She clamored down the stairs, listening for howling winds and tossed debris. All she heard was a constant roar. The lights hadn't even flickered.

Willow knew the center of the building was always the safest place to be during a tornado. The first floor had no bathtub for her to hunker down in, but it had the conference table. It was made of solid oak and would offer at least some protection from falling objects.

During a storm, going near windows was taboo. Broken glass and flying debris could drive through a person like razor wire. Bolts of lightning had been known to come through the openings, striking a person down in their steps.

She knew the old wisdom. She knew the danger.

She knew she had to look out, anyway.

Nothing stirred outside, not even the wind. The streetlights still glowed. The bench where Bobby Ray Neyland and Tully Brown visited every Monday morning was still upright. The winter roses planted by the Main Street Project still had their blooms. Not even the donut shop had a light within; the owners hadn't yet arrived to prepare fresh dough for the day.

Outside, nothing looked amiss. Main Street was still asleep.

So, what was that noise?

A new fear seized her heart. Fire? Was her building on fire?

Willow ran frantically through the first floor. She saw no flames. Felt no heat. Smelled no smoke.

Except *there*, near the back door. Was there a fire behind the building? With unsteady hands, she dialed 9-1-1.

"9-1-1," the dispatcher answered. "What's your emergency?"

"I think my building is on fire!"

"Apartment building? How many residents are inside?"

"Just one. It's a business. And my residence. I'm the only one here." Willow wasn't sure she was making sense. Fear built inside her, blurring her good senses.

"Tell me your location," the dispatcher said. "I'll send someone immediately."

Willow could hear her typing in the information. "You need to get out of the structure, ma'am. It may not be stable. Can you tell me where the fire is located?"

"I—I don't know. In the back, I think. Possibly outside."

"What's your name, hon?"

"Willow."

"Willow, you need to exit from the front of the building. Now."

Willow resisted the urge to run to her desk and rake all her files into her purse. Not that they would fit. Did she have a pillowcase down here?

No. The dispatcher advised her to get out. Now.

"I'm leaving now," she said, struggling with the front door. With her hands trembling, it was difficult to hold her phone, her gun, and to unlatch the locks, all at the same time.

The door opened, and she stumbled out into the cold night air. There was the acrid smell of burning rubber outside, and that infernal roar. It had to be coming from the back.

"I'm out," she told the dispatcher. "I'm going to the back to see what's going on."

"Be careful, ma'am. Approach from a distance. Don't take any chances."

"I won't." She started at a speed walk, changed to a lope, and ended up jogging to the rear of the building. "I just want to see…" She took one look at the burning ball of fire and cried, "My car! My car is on fire!"

"Stand back, ma'am. Do you understand? The car could explode. Get as far away as you can. Take cover if possible and cover your ears in case of a blast. The trucks will be there soon."

Willow knew there was nothing she could do. Nothing she could salvage. Her faithful little Corolla was a blazing mass of orange and red flames.

On a normal night, it would be parked within steps of the building. She couldn't remember why— her mind was still jumbled and now numb with shock—but she had stopped further out when she came back from the post office. That, at least, was a positive in an otherwise bleak night. If she had been parked where she normally was, the flames would have licked the side of the building. She could have lost everything and not just her car.

Border depended on a volunteer fire department, so it took long, agonizing minutes for the trucks to arrive. Willow crossed the side street and waited on the sidewalk, watching her car burn from a safe distance. So far, there hadn't been an explosion, but she braced herself for the potential blast.

There. At the back of the parking lot. Willow thought she saw a shadow move. She clutched her gun closer to her side. The dispatcher stayed on the line with her, coaching her in safety precautions, but her mind was on the shadows. Was someone out there?

"I hear the sirens now," Willow told the kind woman on the phone. "I need to hang up. I need to call my daughter."

"Are you sure you'll be all right?"

"Yes. Thank you for staying on the phone with me. But the trucks are pulling up now, and I need to go."

"You take care, Willow. Everything will be fine now."

Willow disconnected the call and immediately dialed Everleigh.

In a voice thick with sleep, she answered on the fourth ring. "Mom? Why are you calling in the middle of the night?" Her voice sharpened remarkably. "Are those sirens I hear? What's happening? Mom, are you all right?"

"I—I think so. My car is on fire. Completely engulfed. It's a total loss, sweetheart." Her voice broke then, as the cruel truth sank in. "This wasn't an accident. This was another warning."

"We'll be right there. Stay away from the building and go to a safe place. Laura Beth and I are on our way."

"There's no need to wake her. I'll be fine."

"We're on our way," Everleigh repeated firmly. "I love you, Mom. Hang in there. Everything is going to be fine."

"I love you too, sweetheart. Don't drive like a mad woman getting here. I'm fine, really I am."

Now to convince herself of that...

By the time Everleigh and Laura Beth got there, the fire was little more than a smolder. The danger had passed, but Willow's nerves were a wreck. She sat on the sidewalk, shivering, wondering how she would manage without a car, and knowing the loss could have been so much worse.

"Mom! Mom, where are you?" Parked safely along the side of the building, Everleigh started around the building to find her mother.

"Over here! I'm over here!" Willow called from across the street as she waved her arms. The spot had offered a front-row seat to watch the drama play out.

Everleigh hugged her mother tightly. "I'm so sorry about your car. Are you sure you're okay?"

"Upset. Angry. But not hurt. Not physically, anyway." Willow wrapped her arms around her daughter and granddaughter.

"Are you sure?" Laura Beth's lips quivered with

the question.

"I'm positive, sweet pea."

"You're shivering, Mom," Everleigh observed. "Let's at least sit in the car where it's warm. The firemen will find you when they're done."

Landee pulled in behind them. Seeing the shiny little sports car made the loss of her beloved Corolla even more poignant. She would never tell her mother that, however, so she returned the warm hug and thanked her for coming.

"Of course I came! This was no accident, was it?"

"No. The firemen haven't confirmed it, but no. This was intentional."

Ireland made a show of looking around. "Where's the sheriff?" she demanded. "I don't see anyone from his office here!"

"Because no one has responded."

"How irresponsible can he be! This is outrageous!" her mother huffed. When she noticed how violently Willow shivered, her voice softened. "Let's get you inside. Everleigh, can you tell one of firemen where we'll be?" She urged Laura Beth to join them. "Sweet Pea, you come along with us. I think we could all use some hot cocoa right about now."

Ireland herded them around the building and through the front door. As the townspeople heard the sirens and came out to see what had happened, a few stopped them to ask if everyone was safe. Willow could only nod numbly, allowing her mother to answer for her.

The fire chief eventually found her in the conference room, wrapped in a warm blanket, hugging a cup of hot chocolate with Laura Beth curled up beside her. The child had fallen back to sleep, oblivious to the danger surrounding them.

Willow answered routine questions. No, she hadn't seen or heard anything amiss before the blaze started. Yes, she had insurance. No, she hadn't done anything stupid, like try to retrieve something from the burning vehicle. She wasn't hurt.

He asked if she knew of anyone who had a grudge against her or had threatened her in any way. She glossed over her answer, giving some vague statement about her line of work. There was always the chance of making someone angry.

The firemen were mopping up the scene by the time Deputy Boggs arrived. He spoke with the chief before seeking out Willow.

The moment he stepped through the door, he apologized. "I'm so sorry for the delay," he said. "It's been an unusually busy night, with calls scattered all over the county. Everyone was tied up. Are you sure you're not hurt, Mrs. Alexander?"

"I'm sure."

"I'm sorry this has happened to you. I know you must be exhausted, but I have a few questions for you."

"That's fine. I doubt I could go back to sleep, anyway." She motioned for him to have a seat.

"Can you walk me through what happened tonight?" the deputy asked.

"Like I told Chief Billings, I was asleep. The roar of the fire woke me up."

"It must have been loud to have heard it from inside."

"It was. And… I think something may have exploded." She hadn't thought of it when the chief asked, but now it came back to her. "The windows rattled, and I heard something hit the rear of the building."

He confirmed her recollection with a nod. "The chief told me they found a small explosive device. Someone must have thrown it under your car to start the fire."

Willow sucked in her breath as he continued.

"Dispatch said you exited the building and saw your car engulfed. Did you see anyone outside? Anyone near your car?"

Willow couldn't be certain. It appeared the shadows had shifted, but it could have been a trick of the flickering flames. In the back of her mind, she wondered if his boss could have been among the shadows.

"I'm not sure," she answered truthfully. "It was dark. I was in shock."

"I'm sure you were. Do you have anyone who's made any threats against you recently? Have you had any troubles before tonight?"

"You mean other than the first two warnings?"

The deputy looked confused. "What warnings?"

Ireland answered for her daughter. "Someone egged our front windows. Didn't you see the report?"

"I log all the reports into our system, and I'm afraid I'm not aware of any such report."

Frowning, Everleigh looked at him sharply. "Are you aware that we received a threatening message?"

The deputy looked alarmed. "A threat? When?

What was it?"

"A few days ago. Maybe three?" she guessed.

Willow nodded. "Something like that. Someone sent three boxes, each containing paper with one word written on it. Together, the message said, 'You've been warned.'"

"And you didn't think to report it?" His voice sounded incredulous.

"Of course we reported it!" Ireland snapped. "The sheriff responded both times, but he brushed it off as nothing to be concerned over."

Straightening his shoulders, Deputy Boggs' expression was grave. "Not to contradict my boss, but I disagree. I think you ladies have a great deal to be concerned about."

24

It was disheartening, knowing how concerned the deputy was for their welfare. Even more disheartening was the fact that the sheriff hadn't filed their reports.

There had been no going back to sleep for any of them, even though they went through the motions. Only Laura Beth managed a decent night's rest. The others tossed and turned upstairs in Willow's apartment, until they could give up the ruse and get ready for work.

By the light of day, the black, twisted metal looked worse than it had while burning. Eager to have it out of her sight, Willow made the necessary calls to her insurance agent. Someone would be out soon to make a report, then a wrecker could haul the sad heap away.

"With all the attention pulled to Knob Mountain, I think this would be a good time to go back to Gus' place," Everleigh said. "We were waiting until the heat was off Scrimshaw. If finding those remains doesn't cool it down, nothing will."

"I know we said that," Ireland agreed, "but what purpose will it serve? We've found the camera."

"Yes, but we still don't know if the film was in it. There's a chance it's still at Gus'. We all know Mathers didn't conduct a thorough search. Who knows what secrets we might reveal?"

"I'm game if you are," Willow said. "I think I'm too antsy to stay in the office today, anyway."

"I'll stay here with Laura Beth," Ireland volunteered, "and if the insurance adjuster shows up, I can answer most of his or her questions. You two go on."

"You're sure?" Everleigh asked.

"Absolutely. Although…" She seemed to rethink her position on the subject. "Are you sure it's safe for just the two of you to go? Maybe you should call Tobias and ask him to go, too."

Willow gave her mother an irritated look. "Stop trying to play matchmaker! The very last thing on my mind right now is romance. Everleigh and I are both big girls, so yes, we're fine to go by ourselves. Besides, Tobias has a store to run."

"He's also calling you." With a pleased smile, Ireland glanced at the Caller ID showing on Willow's phone.

She almost didn't answer. Her nerves were fraught enough today, and she didn't need her mother gloating on top of everything else.

Ireland noticed her hesitation. "It could be about the film," she reminded her.

With a bit of a growl, Willow answered her phone. Her voice came out sharper than she intended.

"Willow?" he asked uncertainly. "Is everything

okay? Did I catch you at a bad time?"

She tried to soften her voice. "You caught me on a bad day."

"Oh." He sounded disappointed. "Oh, well, I guess I could call back. I just wanted to give you an update on the film."

There was an immediate lift in her voice. "You found it?"

"Brad eliminated all but three memory cards. He's working on those today."

It wasn't quite the news she was hoping for, but it was closer than what they had. "That's something, at least."

Everleigh and Ireland had heard the excitement in her voice and crowded around. She dashed their hopes with a shake of her head. Putting her hand over the phone, she told them, "He's down to three cards, though. One of those could be the one."

"I'm sorry it's not what you wanted to hear, but I promised to keep you updated," Tobias told her.

"Don't apologize. Thank you for keeping us in the loop."

"Willow? Are you sure you're all right? You sound strange."

"Just tired. I didn't get a lot of sleep last night." That much was true.

"For a minute there, I thought something else might be wrong." She heard the lingering question in his voice.

Willow sidestepped his concern. "I'm one of those who needs her rest, or else I get grouchy."

"Then try to grab a nap, and the next time I call, maybe I'll have better news."

"I'll try, but it's doubtful. Thanks, though. And thanks for the update."

The moment she disconnected, the others pounced.

"There's a reason you didn't sleep, and you know it!" her mother protested. "Why didn't you tell him the truth?"

"Yeah, why didn't you tell him about your car?" Everleigh wanted to know.

"Tobias Cameron has been a tremendous help in this case, but that's all he is. A business associate. Having my car bombed isn't something I would divulge to other associates, so it's the same with him."

"It's *not* the same with him," her daughter insisted. "Even Laura Beth could see there was something brewing between the two of you."

"There is. Their names are Benny, Terrell, and Josh." Her voice was clipped.

"Is it because Marshal Jennings is back in town? Because I see the way he looks at you. There could easily be something between the two of you, as well."

"Yes, and it's the same thing that brought Tobias and I together," Willow snapped. "The bones of those three boys. Now. Are we going, or what?"

The drive up Scrimshaw Mountain wasn't as smooth in Everleigh's mid-sized SUV as it had been in Landee's little sports car. Willow sadly admitted it was still better than what her faithful Corolla could have managed.

"Faithful to the end," she murmured morosely.

"What's that?" her daughter asked.

"Nothing. Just lamenting how I'll manage without a car for the next little while."

"Your insurance allows for a rental, doesn't it? That should tide you over until you can buy something new. And if not, I'll be happy to take you where you need to go."

"Thanks. I just hate renting a car. And I hate buying one even more."

"It's been a few decades since you last bought one. Maybe things have changed by now."

"Laugh all you want, but having an old model car means replacing it with a new one that will cost a small fortune."

"I'm sure I could get Dad to give me the money. I'll just say it's for something else, like a new air conditioner for the house. He and the wicked witch will never know they'll be footing the bill for your new ride." Everleigh grinned at her genius duplicity.

"You shouldn't call your stepmother a wicked witch," Willow said. Her objection was weak, at best. "And I can't depend on your father to pay my bills for me."

"Dad cheated you out of what was rightfully yours. It's the least he can do."

"That may be true, but I've never wanted to put you in an uncomfortable situation. He's still your father."

"Who's uncomfortable? I still love him, but he cheated on you, then he treated you like dirt. He can cough up the dough for you to have a decent vehicle."

"It's not nice to speak ill of the dead," Willow reminded her. "My Corolla's ashes are still lukewarm."

"I'm just saying it was past time to get a new car. This just speeds things along."

"Turn here," Willow directed, happy to have the subject put to rest.

The truth was, she had been fretting about how she would pay for a new car. Business was good, but a car payment would make things tight for her third of the profits. Tricking Marcus into a healthy down payment had its appeal.

As they neared their destination, Willow alerted Everleigh. "Up here on the right is the Homer's log house. It's huge. Gus' driveway is the next one."

"I'm anxious to see this house everyone is talking about."

"Think money. As in, lots of money."

"This must be a very exclusive subdivision he's planning," Everleigh speculated. "If what Maverick said is true, it's no one wonder he's so upset about losing out on Gus' land."

"Yeah, about that..." Something about the overheard conversation still bothered her. "I had the distinct feeling Sharika and her sister, whoever she may be, were both trying to manipulate Gideon. I originally thought it was for the money he would get from the sale, but there's holes in that theory."

"Such as?"

"For one, the land wasn't his to sell. I think that's what they were doing—trying to get Gideon to persuade his father into selling."

"Unless Gideon already had power of attorney," Everleigh pointed out.

"I hadn't thought of that." Willow pursed her lips.

"Or, maybe Gus signed the contract that morning before he was killed. If Maverick did it, he may have gotten what he wanted and killed him just for spite."

"I thought we favored the sheriff for this."

"Who says they aren't working together? Maverick did the deed, Mathers covered it up." She slowed down as they approached the log house. "Oh, wow, I can only see it through the trees, but it's already gorgeous!"

"It is. After what Aunt Purdy said, I'd love to see the inside, too!"

Everleigh giggled. "You don't suppose we can pretend to be interested in buying into the subdivision, do you? We could ask for a tour of the house to see what ours might look like."

"Nathaniel Homer doesn't sound like the kind of guy you just drop in on. He would prob—watch out!"

Willow screamed the warning as they narrowly escaped a van fishtailing out of the Homers' driveway. It kicked up a swirl of dust as its tires skidded on the gravel road. Before it tangled amid the trees on the other side of the road, the driver managed to get the vintage Volkswagen under control.

"That was close!" Willow's hand was on her pounding chest.

"You're telling me!"

As the van barreled past them, Everleigh got a glimpse of the driver.

"That—That looked like Moon!" she gasped. "Why would Moon be up here at the Homers?"

"Does she drive an old van like that?"

"No clue. But that looked like her blond hair."

"Blond hair?" Willow asked. Apprehension bloomed in her stomach. "What does this Moon woman look like?"

"Pale skin, impossibly straight hair that hangs to her waist, strange-looking eyes."

"Like a cat's?"

"Yeah, that's it! I didn't know how to describe them, but that's it. They're like a cat's. How did you know?"

"Because I think Moon is the person I met as Maude."

"You're kidding!"

"Gus' drive is right up here," Willow pointed out. "And no, I'm serious. I think Moon and Maude are one in the same, and I think she's Sharika's sister."

Looking into her rearview mirror, Everleigh looked alarmed. "I also think she's behind me."

"What!" Startled, Willow twisted around in her seat. Sure enough, she saw a yellow hood with a bright pink flower trailing behind them. When Everleigh slowed to turn into Gus', Willow motioned her away. "Don't. Don't turn in. Keep going."

"Why?"

"It's a dead-end into Gus' place. Keep straight on this road. It eventually winds down and back to the highway."

"Eventually?" her daughter squeaked.

"I don't know how far. Landee said she visited one of Gus neighbors a little way down." Willow alternated between looking into her side mirror and turning around to look out the back window. "She's still behind us but holding her distance. I don't think she wants us to know she's there."

Everleigh pointed out the obvious. "She must have turned around and come back."

"Do you think she recognized you?"

"I doubt it. I had on a convincing disguise that night."

"Maybe she recognized your car."

Everleigh shook her head. "I stopped along the way and borrowed my friend's old clunker. It looked more the part than the Mom Mobile. And Joey didn't even recognize me at first, so I don't see how she could have."

"Then she must have recognized me."

"Is that why we kept going?"

"Partially. There was something about the way Moon/Maude looked at me that night. There was almost a challenge in her eyes. But her words were definitely a warning. I think she could be a dangerous person to make an enemy."

Everleigh wasn't convinced. "You said you talked to her for like three minutes. Is that really enough time to make an enemy?"

"With her it is. The minute Sharika told her I was a private eye, I felt a sense of foreboding. Both of them are definitely hiding something."

"I wonder how she knows the Homers, and why she was driving like a bat out of Hades?"

"I don't know. Someone told Landee they saw a hippie van coming out of Gus's driveway one day. That's definitely what I would call a hippie van. I even saw it in the parking lot the night I met 'Maude.'"

"That's weird. Why would she be up here visiting Gus, and now the Homers? They don't seem to be her type."

"Maybe she's not visiting," Willow suggested.

Everleigh looked at her mother with wide eyes. "*Nnooo*!" she said, but it was a hushed question of sorts. "You think she's robbing them? Casing the place to see if anyone's home?"

"It crossed my mind."

"Wait. Does that mean the sheriff could have been right? Gus' death was a burglary gone bad? And *Moon* was the one to kill him?"

"I wouldn't go that far. Burglary, yes. Gideon may have told her about something valuable his father owned."

Everleigh's eyes lit up. "Like a camcorder?"

"Hmm. It's possible, I suppose. Maybe she planned to blackmail the boys' killer."

"Let's make it easy and call him Papa Mathers," she suggested with a note of humor. "It's more personal than 'Killer One' or 'Subject A.'"

Willow rolled her eyes. "You watch too many cop shows."

"I like to refer to them as training videos. That way, I can claim the streaming service on my income tax."

"Tricky but smart."

"Dad taught me."

"That figures. But, fine, we'll say Hank, aka Papa Mathers, killed the boys. Moon found out through Gideon, killed him, and now she's blackmailing Lew Mathers into not doing a proper investigation. But why would she want Gus dead? We're still missing something."

"How do we work Maverick into that scenario…"

"Everleigh!" Willow chastised. "You can't implicate someone in a crime just because you don't like them. There's no 'working him in' if he's innocent."

Ignoring the reprimand, her daughter kept speculating. "Maybe Moon and Maverick have a thing going. Maybe they forced the sale, killed Gus, and plan to take his commission and run away to Brazil."

"You're reaching." Willow twisted in her seat again. "I don't see her now. Maybe she gave up when she realized we weren't turning into Gus'."

Everleigh checked the rearview mirror. "Uh-oh. You spoke too soon. There she is coming around the curve."

"I guess she's going to follow us back to town?"

"I hope not. This doesn't feel right."

Willow tried to be positive. "It's possible she didn't recognize me. She may be worried we can ID her if the Homer house comes up burglarized."

"That's even worse!"

"No, *that* is worse." Willow pointed at the road ahead. "I see a logging truck coming out of that clearing. We'll be stuck behind it, giving Moon time to catch up with us."

"We'll be a Mom Mobile sandwich." Leave it to Everleigh to find humor in any situation.

"Maybe the truck will turn off soon, and we can speed up. So far, she's still hanging back. She seems to think we don't see her."

Everleigh snorted. "She really should pick another vehicle for that. A yellow hippie van with flowers doesn't exactly cut it."

25

Karnie

She had a bad feeling. The danger was imminent. It was coming for the girl, and her family, too. Even the professor could be in danger. She had to do something to protect them.

She would do a separation charm, separating them from awaiting evil. It would form a strong boundary around them, so that no danger could penetrate.

The waning moon was right for such a spell. Many of the age-old charms passed down through the generations followed the signs of the zodiac. Their strength and efficiency were tied to the phases of the moon. Days of the week were important, too, but not always possible.

Willow needed this charm now.

Karnie took three day-old biscuits outside to an open field. She closed her eyes, imagining Willow with her arms around two other women and a young girl. The professor stood behind them. Their faces were blurry, but that wasn't important. She had an image in her mind. Then she imagined a devil spirit, cloaked with a hooded cloth to hide his identity.

She blew three times over the buns, imagining that with each breath, she blew the evil away from her subjects. With the third breath, she could no longer see the devil's image.

Karnie turned to face the east.

"Int-ery, mint-ery, corn,
Apple seed, and apple thorn;
Wine, brier, limber lock,
Three geese in a flock,
One flew east—"

She stopped to throw one biscuit as far as she could, then she turned to the west.

"—one flew west,"

She continued the chant, throwing a second roll into the westward winds. She rotated to face south and recited the final line.

"And one few over the goose's nest."

With the last biscuit thrown, the charm was cast.

Karnie walked back to the house, satisfied she had done the best she could to keep the girl safe.

<h1 style="text-align:center">26</h1>

"Willow!"

She could hear the excitement in his voice the minute Tobias said her name. Willow tightened her grip on the phone. "Did you find the card?" She held her breath until he answered.

"Yes! I think this is the proof you were looking for!" Tobias confirmed.

"That's wonderful! When can I come get it?"

"Right now is fine."

"I can be there in…. Oh, shoot. Never mind. I keep forgetting I don't have a car anymore."

"You don't have a car?" His frown came through in his voice. "What happened?"

"Uhm, well, you see…" Deciding not to stall, she blurted out, "Someone blew it up two nights ago."

"They *what?*"

"Someone threw a small explosive under it. It was a complete loss."

"Were you hurt? Are you okay?"

His concern touched her. Willow babbled when she was nervous. "I'm fine. My building is fine. The only thing to suffer was my car. I should have had Karnie make a charm for it, too. It was a total loss, so now I have to depend on everyone else for a ride. The insurance company is still sorting out the rental provision."

"Why didn't you tell me this when I called last time?"

"It was the day after. I was still in a daze." While true, it wasn't the reason she hadn't told him. She had been afraid telling him would sound as if she thought they were more than business acquaintances. It wasn't an assumption she wanted to make. And Landee had been listening, with that knowing smirk on her face...

Tobias was quiet for a moment. Had she offended him?

"Okay, then how about this?" he said. It was a good thing she hadn't made that assumption. He had been thinking, not sulking. "I'll bring the card to you. It's not a common size, but my buddy has all the gadgets to make it work. Is it okay if I bring him with me?"

"Of course."

"Do you have a TV we can hook up to? The screen would be bigger, and I thought the rest of your team might want to be there, too."

"You're right, they will. We don't have a TV downstairs, but we can use the one in my apartment."

"How long do you need? Brad is here with me now, and we can come anytime. The shop's already closed."

"Mom and Everleigh just left. If now's not good for them, I'll call you right back. But I have a feeling they'll drop everything to finally have some answers!"

"These Branson men break all the stereotypes, don't they?" Ireland whispered.

Filling their glasses with ice, Willow paused. The men were hooking things up in the living room. "What do you mean?"

"When you hear of a professor turned antique proprietor, you think sweaters that smell like mothballs and little round glasses. And computer nerd brings to mind dorky men with pimples on their face and bulky glasses with coke-bottle lenses. Lucky for you two, Brad and Tobias broke the mold."

Willow frowned at the ridiculous images that sprang to mind. "That's rather prejudiced of you, don't you think?" She kept her voice low so the men couldn't hear.

"I'm just saying it's a good thing those two far exceed expectations."

"Landee," Everleigh warned in a whisper, "no matchmaking, no matter how good looking they are!"

"So, you *do* think Brad is good looking," her grandmother smiled.

"I have eyes, don't I? Now, behave yourself. This is a solemn occasion, not a hook-up session."

"I think we've got it now," Brad called from the living room. "It's a little grainy, so you may have trouble seeing it."

"We can turn out the light if that helps."

"It probably would," he agreed.

"Here," Tobias offered. "Let me take those

glasses," he told Willow.

She turned off the overhead fixtures so that only ambient light filtered in via other rooms. If this was a home theater, they were settling in to watch a horror film.

Brad pushed a button on the remote control. "I'll fast-forward through this front part. Benny, as he introduced himself, is retelling the legend of The Flaming Woman." The film flew through several scenes in hilarious timing. "Here, he mentions the gold that's supposedly still inside the cave. He's moving in for a closer shot when this man steps out of the cave." He stopped the film and pointed to the man in the frame.

"Does anyone recognize him?" Tobias asked.

Ireland squinted her eyes. She even stood and walked to the TV for a close-up view. "I don't think I've ever seen him before," she finally concluded.

"I don't think I have, either," Willow said.

Everleigh cocked her head to the left. She angled it to the right. "There's something about him... He looks vaguely familiar, but I can't place him. No name springs to mind, either."

"We'll go on," Brad said, restarting the video at normal speed. "See how angry he gets when he sees the boys? He's yelling at Benny, demanding him to get off the mountain. The audio is muffled, but I can turn it up. You'll have to listen closely."

The scene played out the exact way Gus had described it. The static of the microphone and the sound of the wind caught on tape intensified the feeling of suspense. They all knew something horrible was about to happen.

It still took them by surprise.

The man and Benny started to scuffle. Benny was faster on his feet, sidestepping the man's advances, but the man was stronger. He grabbed Benny around the throat, spun him around so that his back was to him, and clamped his arms around him.

The second boy, obviously Josh, tried to defend his friend. He plummeted the man's back with his fist. When that had no effect, he jumped on the man's back, trying to break the hold he had on Benny. The man simply flung him off like a pesky ant. Josh hit his head on a rock when he fell to the ground.

Meanwhile, Benny dug in his heels, skidding across the rocky surface until reaching the spot where sky touched rock. With one final push, the man sent the college student sailing over the jagged edge of Kinney Knob.

The boy cried out, his arms flailing mid-air. When he dropped out of sight, the silence was deafening.

Even knowing it was coming, Everleigh gasped. Ireland jumped in revulsion. Willow stared at the screen in stunned silence.

Josh staggered to his feet, screaming obscenities at the man. He held the side of his head as blood seeped around his fingers. The man whirled around to face him and whipped out a knife. The lens caught the glint of steel as he brandished the weapon in Josh's face.

Josh jumped back, evading the sharp blade. He danced around the older man in circles, trying to throw him off balance. But as more blood dripped from his head wound, Josh staggered. With a single movement, the man plunged the knife into the boy's chest.

Blood covered the front of Josh's shirt. His faint gurgle was barely audible on tape. The man wretched his knife free and tossed it aside.

As he threw the bloody body over the edge of the cliff, a feral cry could be heard. Like Gus remembered, it was a terrible sound, like one a wounded animal might make. The sound sent chills through them all.

The killer whirled around, searching for the source of the cry. He demanded to know who was there.

Terrell's sobs led the man straight to him. As the boy thought to shove the recorder into the bushes, the sky tumbled, and the rocky earth tilted to one side. There were flashes of a flannel shirt, branches, a splash of blue sky, and more rock. Coming to rest on its side, the camera caught enough of the scene to tell the story. The man threw Terrell to the ground, where he pummeled his fist into the Black man's face. Over and over again, until his cries stopped, and his blood seeped into the ground.

The video rolled on, offering snippets of what happened next. The man's shoes moved in and out of the frame as he struggled to drag the limp body across rocky, prickly soil.

There was another jumble of sky and rock and leaves while the man tugged. They assumed that was the point when Gus grabbed the camera and faded back into the bushes. Brad turned off the camera as his audience sat in horrified silence.

At some point, Ireland had covered her face

with a throw pillow. She couldn't bear to see the last boy beaten to a pulp. Tears streamed down Everleigh's face, splashing onto her blouse and leaving wet swatches behind. Willow had her hand to her mouth, trying to hold in her sorrow. Hearing about the murders and seeing them happen were two different things. Tobias was visibly shaken as well, with tears shimmering in his eyes.

"That was the most horrific thing I've ever seen in my life," Ireland whispered.

Everleigh sniffed away a tear. "Poor Gus, to have seen that in person!"

"You're certain none of you recognize the killer?" Emotions roughened Tobias' voice when he spoke.

"I didn't," Willow said.

"Nor I," her mother agreed.

"There's still something about him..." Everleigh looked at Brad. "Can you send me a still shot of his face? I could run it through one of my facial recognition sites. It might offer some clue to his identity."

"Obviously, Gus must have known him," Willow pointed out. "He said something about how he was no match for money and power. I assume that meant the killer had both. And he insisted that going to the police would be a mistake."

"I made a couple of copies of the card," Brad volunteered. "And I can send them electronically, too, if you prefer."

"Thank you, Brad. That sounds great," Willow said. She heaved out a sigh. "I suppose I should hand over the original to Lane."

"Lane?" Tobias questioned.

"US Marshal Lane Jennings," she corrected quickly. "We've worked with him on previous cases, and he's already questioned me on the discovery of the bones. In fact, he asked for your phone number. Has he contacted you yet?"

"We have a meeting scheduled for tomorrow."

"For what it's worth, I was honest as I could be, without directly telling him our source was an eyewitness to the murders." She motioned to the empty screen. "Now, I guess that's a moot point. This is better than a witness. This is video proof of who killed those boys."

"And to think we doubted Gus' memory!" Everleigh frowned. "He quoted the scenes almost verbatim."

"I doubt you could ever forget something like this," Ireland mumbled. "I know I won't."

"I probably won't sleep for a week," the younger woman predicted.

When Willow dropped her head into her hands, Everleigh asked in concern, "Mom? Are you okay?"

"I'm a lot of things right now. Sad. Weary. Broken-hearted. Relieved. Confused. But one thing I'm not is 'okay.'"

Everleigh slipped her hand into her mother's. "I know. I feel the same way."

27

"I'm sorry to be blunt, sweetie, but you look terrible." Ireland's voice was softer than her blunt assessment. "Did you get any sleep at all last night?"

"Not much," Willow admitted. "I keep seeing those scenes in my mind. Those poor boys sailing over the edge of the cliff. Knowing how far they fell. Knowing what they fell onto." She slowly shook her head. "Rock. Hard, jagged rock. Every time I close my eyes, I see them."

Commiserating, Everleigh perched her hip on the side of her desk. "I know. I think seeing them, putting a face to a name, made it even worse. They all looked so young."

"And terrified," Ireland added. She rubbed her daughter's shoulder with a gentle caress. "Can you imagine what Gus went through all those years ago? It was bad enough on film. Seeing it in person must been a thousand times worse. Living with that, knowing he did nothing to stop it, must have been torture."

"I've been thinking about that." Willow sat up

straighter. Crossing her arms, she propped them on the desk and leaned forward. It was her speculation posture.

Ireland recognized the look. She took a seat in front of Willow's desk and waited.

"Gus knew the killer, and he was afraid of him. He knew the man had enough clout to come after his family. He couldn't even trust the sheriff."

"Hank Mathers," Everleigh supplied.

"Yes, the current sheriff's father." It was all old news, but Willow had to run it through her head again. "We've been asking ourselves why someone would want to kill Benny and his friends. What if we've been asking the wrong question?

"Such as?" Ireland asked.

"Why was the killer on the knob to begin with? Getting up there isn't an easy thing to do. Karnie made it look so easy, and she's a thousand years old."

Her mother cocked her brow. "A thousand?"

"Okay, not a thousand, but she has to be close to a hundred. The point is, I'm almost half her age, and I struggled to keep up. Even Tobias was out of breath at times. Elroy, too. So, the killer was either accustomed to hiking, or he had some motivation to climb that ridge."

"He could have followed the boys," Everleigh suggested. "He knew it was a remote location where no one would see him. If not for the camera, it was the perfect murder."

"That's true," Ireland agreed. "He's gotten away with it for almost twenty-five years."

Willow was slow to respond. "My instincts tell me that's not it. As hard as it was to watch, I replayed the video last night. Twice."

With a sheepish grin, Everleigh admitted, "So did I."

"Not me! Once was quite enough, thank you very much." Ireland shivered just thinking about the horrible scenes.

Willow went on with her thoughts. "There was something I noticed last night, but I didn't think much about it. But now... Did you notice how the man just appeared out of nowhere? The boys had been filming for quite a while before he showed up. While Benny told the story in vivid detail, Josh acted out the scene of the revenuers finding the still. He switched characters, pretending to be the moonshiners fighting for his livelihood."

"Don't forget how many times he was shot, pretending to be both the revenuers and the moonshiners," Everleigh pitched in. She nodded in appreciation. "Tobias was right. Josh was a born actor."

"Right. He even had time to act out the still catching fire, and the horror of the boy who took the brunt of the explosion. He was almost to the point in the story where the mother rushes to his aid and catches fire herself. And then, suddenly, the killer appeared out of nowhere."

Ireland's eyes narrowed as the theory took hold. "You think he had been on the mountain all along."

"I do. But I don't think he knew the boys were there, which is odd, considering they were making a film. Benny was talking, Josh was running around acting out scenes, and Terrell was keeping up with it all as he filmed. How could the man not have seen or heard them?”

“He was on the other side of the mountain?” Everleigh guessed.

“Or…”

Everleigh’s eyes lit up. “Or he was inside the cave!” she realized.

“Exactly. I noticed how he stepped forward, just appearing out of the shadows. But he looked surprised to see them.”

“Meaning he hadn’t been watching them, waiting for the perfect time to pounce.”

“And meaning,” Willow said, “he was somewhere deeper in the cave. The question is why? Why was he inside that cave?”

Ireland had the answer. “The gold. He was looking for the hidden gold.”

“What gold?” Everleigh asked. “You mean those old tales about Jesse James hiding his loot in caves all over the countryside?”

“The tales vary. Jesse James was from Missouri, so it’s said he mostly hid it there. Meramec Caverns was his best-known hideout. But there are plenty of rumors about other outlaws using the caves on this side of the state line for hideouts and stashing their loot. Outlaws like the Baldknobbers, and Ol’ Sam Pixley, and Dave Rudabaugh. It all depends on who’s telling the story.”

“Let me get this straight. A rich, powerful man falls for some old legend about a hidden fortune? And he personally goes into a cave to look for it?” The youngest member of their team was skeptical.

“Why do you think explorers still search the

seas, looking for pirate ships that are rumored to hold gold? What about the Titanic? The tombs of ancient kings, supposedly buried with their gold and precious jewels? They're dreamers, searching for fabled fortunes that may or may not exist," her grandmother insisted. "Dreamers who have the funds to pull off such massive endeavors. Our killer wouldn't be the first rich man to pass up the chance to get even richer."

"When you put it that way…"

"It makes sense, don't you think?" Excitement infused Willow's voice as she rolled with the theory. "Our killer was searching for the hidden gold. I remember Karnie talking about the old tales, and how no one ever claimed to find the fortune of Bentwood Cave. A lot of people believe it's still in there, hidden in one of the unexplored chambers. What if the killer was one of those people? He was deep inside the cave, didn't hear the boys moving around making their movie, and was taken by surprise when he came out. Their murder wasn't premeditated. It was just the desperate act of a greedy man who wanted the fortune for himself."

"There's more to that theory than you realize," Ireland said. "Now and then, people claim to see lights on Kinney Knob at night. They believe it's the ghost of the Flaming Woman, walking the hills while mourning her family. But those lights could be something else entirely."

Willow knew what her mother was thinking. "Like someone in the caves, searching for the gold?"

"Exactly. And if I remember correctly, the ghost legend was really strong around that time."

"I remember that! I imagine that's why the boys went up there in the first place. That ridiculous movie about the other witch had come out and rekindled interest in the Flaming Woman."

"It's definitely plausible," Everleigh agreed. "But it doesn't get us any closer to identifying the killer. That's the biggest mystery of all."

"You're right. We can rule out some people—a much younger Maverick, Hank Mathers, even a young Lew Mathers—but we can't name that face."

"Have you called the marshals yet?"

"Yes. Lane—Marshal Jennings—wasn't in, but I left a message. I told him it was urgent."

"Lane, is it?" Ireland teased.

Willow bristled. "Yes. We've worked with him enough times to be on a first name basis. It's not like some pet name I have for him."

"I think thou dost protest too much."

"I think thou likes to play matchmaker too much," Willow shot back. "I don't need the complication of having a man in my life. So, let's just drop it, shall we, and get back to work."

"I'll scour the internet," Everleigh volunteered. She had already hopped off the desk and gone back to her computer. "The facial rec programs I have aren't the best, but you never know. They might pop out the name we're looking for."

"Should I go back to Gus' neighbors and show them the man's picture?" Ireland asked. "It he was a powerful man back in the days, chances are someone up there may recognize him."

"That's not a bad idea," Willow agreed thoughtfully. She thought about their last visit to the mountain and how Moon had followed them down. "But I don't think you should go alone," she cautioned. "I'll go with you."

They didn't have much luck. Some of the neighbors weren't home, or perhaps just not opening their doors. The ones who answered thought the man looked vaguely familiar but had no name. Most suggested they speak to Elsa Bishop. Elsa knew everyone.

Unfortunately, Elsa wasn't home.

"So far, we're batting 0." Ireland frowned.

"Could be the flashy sports car. Too bad we couldn't come in the Corolla."

"I truly am sorry about your car. Any luck with the insurance company?"

"The say they're working on it." Willow stared out the window with a sigh.

"Speaking of neighbors... There is one house we haven't stopped at yet, you know," Ireland noted.

"The Homers' grand mansion?"

Ireland saw the interest in her daughter's eyes. It was just the encouragement she needed to reveal her own excitement. "Yes! Ever since Purdy told us about it, I've been dying to see the inside! Do you think they'll answer the door for us?"

Willow rethought her stance on the car. "Actually, bringing your car may have been the right thing, after all. Seeing a Mercedes-Benz in the driveway, they won't confuse us with someone peddling encyclopedias."

"Does anyone even do that anymore?" Ireland

wondered. "The internet has changed the way of the world. And not always in a good way."

"We used to say that some things never change, like history. But even that's no longer true. Popular opinion has erased a lot of hard truths."

Willow looked out her window again, appreciating the way sunlight filtered through the trees. They zipped along the mountain road, but one grove looked like another. All around them, the rocky soil rose and fell with the slope of the hills. Dormant leaves stirred in the breeze, as the first buds of the season flirted with barren treetops and ground cover plants. Spring green. It was one of her favorite colors.

"That's what I like about the mountains," Willow said. "As much as times change, some things always stay the same. I'll never get tired of looking at these hills."

"They get in your blood, that's for sure," Ireland said in a dreamy voice. "The colors bloom in your heart, and the scent of fresh mountain air flows through your veins. Once they take their hold on you, these hills never let you go."

Willow knew it was a sensitive subject, but she had to ask. Her voice was soft. "Why, Landee? Why do you never go home to see your family?"

For a long moment, her mother didn't answer. When she did, it was with a sad, resigned sigh. "That's another story, for another time."

"When, though? I'm fifty-two, and I still don't know what happened. Are you ever going to tell me? Don't you owe me that much?" She kept her voice gentle. She wasn't accusing her mother. She was hurt.

"One day soon, my love. I promise."

"I'll hold you to that."

"Please do. It's time you know the full story."

Willow let the silence sit for a moment, until she acknowledged, "But we have another story to finish now, and something tells me it won't have a good ending." She closed her eyes and took a deep breath. "It's in the air again. I feel it every time I come here. There's something up here. Something dark. Something evil. I just don't know what it is."

"Yet." Ireland added the word with confidence. "You'll work it out, sweetheart. You always do."

"I hope so." She sounded less confident, but her voice soon picked up. "I see the Homer driveway. Here's goes nothing."

Carolyn Homer answered the door. She was an attractive woman with blond hair and striking eyes.

"May I help you?" Even though she wore a pleasant smile, her voice sounded wary.

"I hope so. My name is Ireland Garrett, and this is my daughter Willow Alexander. You don't know us, but I'm Aunt Purdy's niece." She didn't bother using a last name. Few recognized the woman by anything other than Aunt Purdy.

"Oh, what a sweetheart she is! Please, come right in."

"We don't mean to impose..."

"Not at all! I was making myself a glass of iced tea. Won't you join me?"

"Thank you so much. Tea does sound nice," Ireland admitted as she stepped inside.

"We've admired your home from afar," Willow told their hostess. "It's very lovely. Aunt Purdy assured us it was just as grand on the inside." One peek confirmed it. The entryway led into a huge great room, superbly decorated in upscale rustic design. Very upscale.

"I'll be happy to give you a tour, if you like."

"We'd love that if it's not too much trouble. Again, we don't mean to intrude," Ireland reiterated.

"No trouble at all. I love showing the house off."

"Someone mentioned it was a prototype for a future development? That sounds exciting!" Willow's reply came across as enthusiastic.

"Yes. It's my husband's brainchild, actually. An exclusive, mountain-top gated community. Huge lots, expansive views, magnificent homes, and the amenities of the finest country clubs."

"That sounds almost too good to be true."

"Oh, but it is true," Carolyn assured her. "My husband is a brilliant businessman. He already has investors lined up, begging to be part of his latest project."

Willow felt a tingle at the base of her spine. *Investors.* Why did the word make her so uncomfortable?

Ireland saw the look that crossed her daughter's face. Willow was on to something.

"Oooh, that sounds exciting. Tell me more," Ireland gushed, shifting the conversation her way.

Willow listened with half an ear. Carolyn was obviously proud of her husband, but something in her words sounded too rehearsed. Willow should know; she had once been the same with Marcus. She spouted accolades for his business acumen more times than she cared to admit, all for the sake of bolstering his image. She sensed it was the same with Carolyn. She was trained to make her husband look good.

She felt empathy for their hostess, but that wasn't what concerned her. Willow was concerned about this growing sense of unease. Something about this beautiful home felt off. It felt toxic.

As crazy as it seemed, was the danger she felt earlier coming from within these walls?

She managed to keep a thin thread on the small talk, murmured a reply in all the right places. When needed, she would offer an interested nod or a smile of approval. As a brilliant conversationalist, Ireland covered for her lack of concentration.

"Would you like to see the house now?" Carolyn offered. She had forgotten they had come for a different matter, but neither of her guests corrected the oversight. The less they said about themselves, the better.

"This is the downstairs guest suite," Carolyn said, sweeping her arm to show off the oversized accommodations.

Like Aunt Purdy said, everything in the home was over the top. Did overnights guests really need their own sitting parlor? Or a walk-in closet of that scale? The en suite bathroom was sumptuous, but almost the size of Willow's bedroom. Another bath almost as large opened off the hallway. Carolyn referred to it as the powder roon.

"The sitting room is on this wing," she said as they crossed the great room, "along with a small office for me and, of course, my husband's den and much larger office."

Willow wondered why she said 'of course.' The sitting room was for Carolyn's entertainment needs, while her husband greeted his friends and business acquaintances in the den.

They made a brief round through the rooms on the left side of the wing. While keeping within the home's rustic theme, the sitting room and Carolyn's office had a much more feminine feel to them.

"The solarium is at the end of this corridor. You simply must see the orchids! They're so lovely this year," Carolyn said.

The doors on the right had to be Nathaniel Homer's domain. One was ajar, offering a glimpse of a huge oak desk.

"Oh, I love this oil painting," Willow said, feigning interest in a piece of original artwork. It depicted a rustic mountain setting, dotted with grazing sheep among the jagged, staggering slopes. They looked a lot like the ones just outside these doors.

"We picked that up at an art auction in Springfield. A fundraiser for one of Nathaniel's friends running for office." She tossed her hand like it hadn't cost a fortune. Willow was familiar with the artist and knew a piece that large had a price tag to match.

"You two go on," Willow encouraged. "I'll catch up. I want to enjoy these brush techniques for a moment."

"Oh, you paint?" Carolyn asked.

"I took a few classes in college, but I never could master this particular style or the way he blends his colors so effortlessly." Willow turned back to the painting, peering closer.

The moment they opened the solarium door, Willow slipped into Nathaniel Homer's office. She wasn't sure what she hoped to find, but she couldn't resist the urge to snoop. Something in that office drew her in. The lure was almost tangible.

On one wall was a huge plat drawing, enclosed in an ornate frame like it was a treasured piece of art. Stepping closer, she saw the elaborate plans for the Scrimshaw Project. Plans like that called for *big* money. Talking people into investing on that scale was an art form within itself.

She continued down the wall, reading plaques and accolades for *HardWood International*. There was a picture of a dark-skinned man, presumably Homer, outside a swanky restaurant. The woman at his side wasn't his wife. Was that the man she remembered from long ago? The one she met with Marcus? Something about him looked very familiar, so it was possible.

The same man appeared again, at a ribbon cutting for a shopping center bearing the HardWood name, and again beside the grand-champion steer at a youth livestock show. He held a buyer's plaque in his hand, with the company's banner behind him. And there the man was on a golf course, posing with his wife and two... *daughters?* Surely not!

Willow didn't bother squelching her gasp. That picture couldn't be right. There had to be a logical explanation. Just because they wore matching tennis outfits, monogrammed with a fancy *H,* didn't mean they were family. They were on the same golf team, perhaps. Or maybe *H* signified the name of the golf club.

There had to be some other explanation for the Homers posing beside Sharika and the woman introduced to her as Maude. The linked arms and smiling faces meant nothing.

Or did they? Willow peered closer. Maude—or was it Moon?—shared the same blond hair and striking eyes as Carolyn Homer. Earlier, Willow couldn't decide if their hostess had blue eyes or green. In this photo, they looked decisively green. And Sharika had some of Nathaniel Homer's features. The flat nose, the dark eyes, the shape of his ears.

No.

Just, no.

This couldn't be.

A voice spoke from behind her. Though said quietly, there was a hidden threat in the way the words were said. "I have a lovely family, don't I?"

Willow whirled around and found herself face to face with Nathaniel Homer.

And suddenly, she remembered why he looked so familiar.

28

He kept a smile on his face, but there was nothing friendly about it. "I'm sorry," he lied smoothly. "Did you not hear me? Perhaps I should come closer."

"No." Willow put an unsteady hand out to stop him. "No, I did hear you." She took a tiny step backward. "And—And yes. It's a lovely family."

She managed to answer, even though her thoughts were spinning. Nathaniel Homer's face—this face—was the same as the one she had seen in the video. Yet, that made no sense. It couldn't be the same one. Nathaniel then and Nathaniel now looked the same age. How could the boys' killer not age over the span of twenty-five years?

"I believe you may know my daughters? This is Sharika." He touched his finger to the glass. He was much too close by now, edging Willow into the corner. "And this is Moon. Although, I believe she may have been introduced to you as Maude." He chuckled softly, if one could call it that. To Willow, it sounded evil. "That's my mother's name, you know. In Haitian, it's pronounced *Maud*." He formed his lips to make somewhat of a 'u' sound, like a drawn-out 'mud.'

"Your—Your mother is Haitian?"

"Yes. Sharika gets her coloring from her, don't you think?" It was ludicrous, the way he stood here having what sounded like a perfectly normal conversation. "Although to be fair, both of my parents are originally from Haiti. People tell me I look exactly like my father."

His father!

That was it. That was the explanation. Nathaniel Homer hadn't killed Benny, Josh, and Terrell. His father had.

Not, she realized, that it made her situation any less dangerous. Nathaniel was fully aware that she knew the truth. His father was a murderer. And from the look in his eyes, he could very well be one, too.

"Why are you in my office, Mrs. Alexander?" he asked.

He knew who she was? Her surprise quickly faded. Of course he did.

He knew she had met his daughters. He knew Moon had been introduced to her as Maude. He knew she was looking for Gideon.

He knew everything. She could see it in his eyes.

"I was looking for the bathroom," Willow lied. She was nervous and began to babble. "Then I noticed this plat, and I couldn't help but have a closer look. The frame, itself, is gorgeous, but look at those plans!" She tried to edge behind his desk, pretending to work her way back to the framed plat. "They are exquisite. You've come up with a brilliant design, Mr. Homer.

Just brilliant." She was almost around the massive oak desk. "Imagine! An exclusive subdivision, right here on Scrimshaw Mountain. Brilliant."

His eyes glistened like black granite. Hard, cold, and unyielding. "You know what's not brilliant? You, Mrs. Alexander. Did you really think you could outsmart me? Did you really think you could just come in and take everything away from me?"

"I—I don't even know you. And I don't know what you're talking about."

With a huge rush of relief, Willow saw her mother and Carolyn at the doorway.

"Oh, there you are! I wondered where we had lost you." Carolyn smiled. She showed Ireland into the room, seemingly oblivious to the tension radiating there. "I see you've met my husband. Nathaniel, these ladies are Ireland and Willow. They stopped by for tea. Ireland, this is my husband, Nathaniel Homer."

"Carolyn!"

Just one sharply spoken word, and her face fell. It was hardly the first time she had heard that harsh voice. Carolyn tucked her head and stared down at her feet.

"Carolyn, please leave your guests here so that we may visit. Wait in the den." His voice was more civil, but just as cold.

She looked confused. "But—"

"Close the door behind you." When still she hesitated, he raised his voice. "I said to leave!" He picked up a paperweight from his desk and flung it across the room. She left just in time. It crashed against the door as his wife pulled it closed.

"Sit," he instructed sharply. "Both of you."

Ireland's eyes assessed her daughter. Satisfied that Willow wasn't hurt in any way, she did as the crazed man demanded. Purdy had told her about his temper, but she didn't quite understand the dynamics of the situation yet. The only thing she was certain of was the danger they were in.

"Why are you here?" he demanded.

Ireland lifted her chin like an aristocrat. "Like your wife said. We came for tea."

"You did no such thing. You didn't know Carolyn until today."

"Once we introduced ourselves, she invited us in for tea," Willow argued. "Almost the same thing."

"*Not* the same thing," he told her. "Why did you come?"

"We've always admired your home from the road. We were hoping for a tour of the inside, and Carolyn was nice enough to show us around."

"Shut. Up." He was losing his patience. He looked back to Ireland and demanded, "Tell me the truth. Why are you here?"

"We were trying to identify someone, but I think we already have."

"Let me guess. My father?" he sneered. "You were trying to identify my father?"

"We didn't realize he was your father until now," Willow explained.

"Did I say you could speak?"

"No, I don't believe you did. Did he, Mother?" Willow turned her head to Ireland and mouthed the word, "Run."

"Do not make me mad, Mrs. Alexander," he

warned. "You will regret it."

Willow cut her eyes to her mother, willing her to do as she asked. *Run!* she silently beseeched.

Ireland ignored her.

Nathaniel Homer perched against his desk, stretching his legs out and crossing them at the ankles. His manner was almost leisurely.

"My father," he began, "was a self-made man."

Willow interrupted to bring her mother up to speed. "His father was from Haiti. So was his wife. Her name was *Maud*." She pronounced it the way he had.

"May I go on?" he asked his guest.

"Be my guest," Willow said sweetly. "Oh, wait. There's more." She turned back to Ireland. "Nathaniel and Carolyn have two daughters. Moon, and Sharika. Sharika takes after the Haitian side of the family. Moon looks like her mother."

Ireland's eyes widened. "Moon?"

"Bone bracelets and all," Willow confirmed.

"*Now* may I finish?" Nathaniel was being ridiculously polite. This calm demeanor was more frightening than his display of temper. His mood shifts made him all the more dangerous.

"By all means."

"As I was saying, my parents came here from Haiti. They arrived with the equivalent of three dollars and fifty-three cents in their pockets. My father was a hard worker. He worked for a logging company in Tennessee, and he learned all he could about the business. He worked his way to Arkansas and earned a promotion. It wasn't enough for a young family, but we survived. Then, one day, my father hit gold." He paused for effect.

Gold. Just as they had suspected. It was all about gold.

"Your father," Willow said defiantly, "is a murderer. He killed three innocent young men for the sake of gold."

He moved much faster than she would have imagined. He backhanded her so hard, her head snapped to one side. "They were in his way," he said coldly. "Do you know what it was like for him, to grow up dirt-poor? What it was like for *me?* Some nights, we went to bed hungry. My father vowed it would never happen again. He heard about the hidden gold, and he was determined to find it."

"It was real?" Ireland whispered. She couldn't believe it! People said it was nothing but a legend.

"Real enough to make him a rich man. Real enough that we never had to go hungry again."

"But he murdered those boys," Willow protested. "Doesn't that bother you, knowing he took their lives for the sake of greed?"

"They stood in his way. The same way old man McMurray stood in mine."

"You?" Ireland spat. "*You* killed Gus?"

"Look at that wall," he told them, flinging his arm to the framed plat. "I invested millions in this deal. *Millions.* I wasn't about to let one old man stand in my way."

Willow wiped a trickle of blood from her lip. Her cheek was stinging, but it was nothing compared to her heart. "He was an old man. You didn't have to kill him."

"What was I supposed to do? He refused to sell

me his land!" If he could rationalize a senseless murder of an old man in such a way, Willow knew he wouldn't hesitate to kill the two of them.

"Did you kill his son, too?"

"Just his dog," he said with a shrug. That explained the dog bowl and the dark stain on the porch. "Gideon is alive and well, and completely oblivious to the world around him. Moon has seen to that."

"And Sharika? What was her part in all this?"

His sigh of frustration sounded sincere. "Sharika may look like my side of the family, but she's weak like her mother. Too kindhearted. I tried to bring her into the family business. All she had to do was get close to the son, so he would convince his father to sell. She even messed that up," he said in disgust. "Moon had to step in. The only useful thing Sharika did was find out about the recorder. Apparently, the boys filmed their own deaths. Now *that*," he smiled wickedly, "would have made a block-buster movie."

"I'll be sure to tell the Marshal Service. They have the memory card."

"You're lying."

He sounded confident, but she saw the flicker of fear in his eyes.

Hoping to draw his mind away from the marshals, Ireland changed the subject. "What about the sheriff?"

"What about him?"

"What was his part in all this?"

"His *part*? He's too weak to have a part in this. No stomach for murder."

"At least there's that," Willow muttered.

"And *his* father?" Ireland asked. "Hank Mathers was the sheriff when those boys were killed. Was he protecting your father? Is that why those bodies were never found?"

"He was protecting himself. He and my father were partners. He didn't kill those boys, but he knew, and he said nothing. That made him just as guilty. And just as rich."

"So, you threatened his son, saying you would destroy his late father's stellar reputation," Willow guessed. "You bribed him not to investigate Gus' murder."

"Let's just say I made a healthy donation to his re-election campaign. And I put in a good word to a few of my very wealthy, very influential friends."

Willow raked her scornful gaze over him. "Wealth means a lot to you, doesn't it?"

He put his arms out, indicating the elaborate house and trappings of wealth all around him. "What else is there?" he asked with a malicious smile.

"Honor? Love? Dignity? I'm sure those concepts are foreign to you, but not everyone is as cold and greedy as you."

"You fool yourself, Mrs. Alexander. Everyone is greedy."

The door burst open, and Moon all but fell into the room. Her mother crowded behind her.

"Moon! What are you doing here?" her father demanded.

"Mother called me. She told me to hurry." She noticed the other two women. "What are they doing here?"

"Poking their noses in where they don't belong. Again."

Moon glared at Willow. "You're determined, aren't you? I tried to warn you, but you wouldn't listen."

"That was you?" Willow cried. "*You* bombed my car?"

"I was doing you a favor. I was trying to scare you off. You don't stand a chance against my father. Cross him, and you'll regret it until the day you die."

"I have a feeling that won't be too much longer." It was amazing how calm she sounded, when inside, her mind was racing. She had to find a way out of this mess.

"Nathaniel!" Carolyn gasped. "What have you done?"

"Shut up and go back to the den," he told his wife.

For once, the graceful blonde wasn't so easily dismissed. "Tell me!" she insisted. "What's going on?"

"I'm ensuring our future," he informed her coldly. "These women thought they could stand in my way. They thought they could destroy me. I'm not about to let that happen!"

"We didn't even know you were involved!" Willow snapped. "Gus hired us to find the camcorder and prove who killed those college boys. When we did find it, the film was missing. We didn't even know who you were."

"You snooped around and found the bones. You had the case re-opened."

"But not because of you. We thought the sheriff had done it."

"Done what?" Carolyn wanted to know. When no one spoke, she stomped her foot in frustration. "Someone tell me what's going on!"

"Go back to the den, Carolyn. I'll deal with you later."

"Not this time. For once, you're going to tell me the truth."

"Mother, go back to the den." Moon's voice was weary.

Ireland reached out and took Carolyn's arm. Her voice was gentle, the kind used when explaining something difficult to a child. "They won't tell you the truth, but I will. Twenty-five years ago, your father-in-law killed three innocent young men. All because of a hidden fortune in gold. Everything you have, everything you own, was paid for by those boys' blood."

Carolyn gasped. With her other hand, she covered her mouth. She stared at her husband with horror. "You knew? You knew about this?"

"Your husband is as evil as his father," Ireland continued. "He put millions of dollars into the Scrimshaw Project, but he didn't know that a single old man would stand in the way of his vision. So he killed him. Your husband killed Gus McMurray. And now he plans to kill us because we know too much."

"No! No, I don't believe you! Tell them, Nathaniel. Tell them none of this is true." She begged her husband to deny their claims, but he said nothing. He just stared at her with pity.

"Moon?" she whispered, transferring her horror-stricken eyes to her daughter. She begged her to contradict Ireland's words.

"What do you want me to say, Mom?" the woman asked. The bits and pieces of bone circling her neck jangled when she tossed her hair. "Not every cave has hidden gold inside. Life is expensive. This house. Your diamonds. All the trips you take. All Dad's golf clubs and business expenses. The beach house in Malibu. It takes money, Mom."

When Carolyn would have crumpled to the ground, Ireland held steadfast to her arm. She stood by her side and willed her to have courage.

"Are you going to take this, Carolyn?" she asked. "How long has your husband been silencing you? How long has he been sending you away? How long has he been lying to you?" She gently squeezed the other woman's arm, her voice steady. "Are you going to let him keep doing this? He's corrupting your daughters. He's teaching them to be the same evil person he is. Is that really what you want?"

"I-I—" She was at a loss for words. Her heart was shattered.

"You can stop him. You can stand up to him. You can stand up for yourself and for your daughters." She gave her arm a final squeeze. "You can do this, Carolyn."

"She can't do a thing." Nathaniel laughed. "She doesn't have the nerve. She'll do what I tell her to do. And you're wrong about our daughters. Sharika is as useless as her mother."

The years of verbal and emotional abuse had taken their toll on Carolyn. Rage built inside her. Her husband was a monster, and he was turning their daughter into one, too. What kind of mother could stand by and allow that to happen? What example was she setting for her girls if she continued to be belittled and lied to? She was tired of being treated like a child. Tired of being told what to do. Nathaniel thought he had her under his thumb, but no more.

With a warrior's yell, Carolyn Homer charged her husband.

She was small, but she was fueled by rage. Carolyn flew into him, catching him off guard. She pounded her fists into his chest, and into his head. He ducked and tried to avoid her angry punches, but she was relentless.

Willow sprang into action and tackled Moon. They went down with a crash.

"Get off me!" Moon cried. "Dad, do something!"

"He's busy." Willow struggled to keep the younger woman down. She looked back at her mother. "A little help here?"

Ireland pulled a set of handcuffs from her designer purse. "Allow me."

Willow managed to get Moon's hands behind her back, and Ireland clipped the cold metal bands into place. She heard one of Moon's bracelets crack, as tiny hand-carved skulls rolled onto the floor.

"Sit here and keep your mouth shut," Willow ordered, pushing her down onto the seat. She used Ireland's silk scarf to tie one of Moon's legs to the chair. She used her own set of cuffs to secure her to the chair. Moon wasn't going anywhere without the bulky accessory.

While they subdued Moon, Carolyn took years of anger out on her husband. To his credit, he didn't fight back. He allowed her to rant, calling him endless names and listing the many wrongs he had committed over the years. Her fists didn't hurt that much, but her sudden flare of independence did.

Ireland pulled her phone from her purse. "Keep an eye on blondie." She nodded toward Moon. "I'm stepping out where it's quieter." Between Moon's bellow of anger and Carolyn's lengthy tirade, it was too noisy to make a call. "I'm not calling his buddy. I'm calling Marshal Jennings."

Over the racket of the two wailing women, Nathaniel's commanding voice silenced them all. "Stop!"

Ireland turned around in surprise. He finally had enough of his wife's outburst. He had flipped her around, her back to his chest, and had her in a chokehold. His arm was tight across her throat.

"You're not calling anyone," he ordered. "Toss your phone over here."

"And if I don't?" Ireland challenged.

He pulled a long, pointed letter opener from somewhere on his desk. He held it above his wife's head. "Do you really want to find out?" His voice was deadly calm.

"N—Nathaniel!" Carolyn whimpered. "You— You wouldn't!"

"Shut up. I've heard enough out of you." He tightened the pressure on her neck.

She clawed at his arm as she coughed and sputtered. "I'm sorry. I'm sorry I disobeyed you. Please, let me go," she begged. "It won't happen again."

"I said to shut up!"

From behind Moon, Willow demanded, "Let her go. You know you wouldn't hurt your own wife."

"Wouldn't I?" The look in his eyes was terrifying. The man was ruthless and perfectly capable of killing the mother of his children. "Take the cuffs off my daughter."

"I can't do that. And you can't hold Carolyn hostage forever. The law is on their way."

"You're lying. The old broad never dialed the phone. Now do as I say. Turn my daughter free."

"Turn your wife free," Willow countered.

Carolyn's eyes were wide and filled with terror. She kept tugging on her husband's arm, trying to lessen the pressure against her throat. The more she struggled, the harder he squeezed.

"Carolyn." Ireland's melodious voice drew the woman's eyes to her. "You can do this, Carolyn. Look at me. You're stronger than him. You're better than him. You're a survivor. Don't give up." She couldn't use her gift of touch to convince the other woman, but she had her voice. She moved closer, while still out of his reach. "Keep your eyes on me, Carolyn. Listen to my voice. You will get through this."

Nathaniel raised the letter opener, poised to plunge. "I'll do it. I swear I will. Turn my daughter loose. Do you want her blood on your hands?"

"Do you want her blood on yours?" Willow raised her arm to reveal the gun she held on Moon.

"I'll snap her neck," Nathaniel threatened. "I'll stab her in the eye."

Willow met his challenge. She hoped he didn't notice the way her hand quivered as she bravely bluffed, "I'll shoot her in the head."

"You wouldn't."

She turned his words back on him. "Do you

really want to find out?"

They were in a standoff. Carolyn whimpered, and Moon demanded that her father do something. Ireland kept talking in her steady, hypnotizing voice. As long as Carolyn kept her eyes on hers, Ireland could persuade her to stay strong. If she gave up now, Ireland had no doubt her husband would squeeze the life from her.

Facing the huge floor-to-ceiling windows, Ireland knew something the others didn't. The marshals had already arrived, accompanied by a host of other agencies. They had their lights and sirens off. This was a silent assent.

"This will all be over soon, Carolyn, and your husband will be locked away forever," she told the other woman. "He won't be able to hurt you anymore. He won't be able to push you, or choke you, or order you to shut up. He won't be able to control you, or to corrupt Sharika. Stay strong. You can do this."

Lane Jennings' strong voice spoke from behind Ireland. "United States Marshal Service. Put your weapon down and turn the woman loose. It's over, Homer. You are under arrest for the murder of Gus McMurray. More charges are sure to follow."

Willow sagged in relief. She lowered her gun as Marshal Deats pulled Moon to her feet. He looked surprised when the chair came with her.

Willow weakly defended their makeshift holdings. "Hey, it worked."

A hint of a smile tickled the corners of his mouth. "This isn't half bad, Mrs. Alexander."

It was the closest thing to a compliment she was likely to get.

As Deats loosened the silk scarf from Moon's leg and hustled her out to the police car, Nathaniel continued to use his wife as a human shield.

"What will it be, Homer?" Marshal Jennings demanded. "This is your last chance. Turn her loose, or we'll fire. Your choice."

"You wouldn't take the chance."

"Look around the room. There's a half-dozen pistols aimed at you. And there's a sharpshooter standing outside your window, with an AR -10 pointed at your head. You're the one taking a chance."

Homer half-turned to look out the window. He loosened his grip just enough for Carolyn to slip free. She ran to Ireland, who quickly whisked her out of the line of fire.

Nathaniel Homer knew when he was outnumbered. He dropped the letter opener and surrendered.

As two members of the state police rushed him and put him in cuffs, Marshal Jennings found Willow's eyes.

"Nice work, Mrs. Alexander."

<h1 style="text-align:center">29</h1>

"Mom! Landee!" Everleigh enveloped them in a ferocious hug the moment they stepped through the front door. It was still difficult for Willow to use the back parking lot. Without her little Corolla, it looked so empty.

"Are you okay?" Everleigh pulled back to survey them. "Mom, what happened to your face?"

Willow gingerly touched her bruised cheek, offering a crooked smile. The edge of her bottom lip was busted, making one side of her mouth more swollen than the other.

"Can we sit down first, sweetheart? I'm exhausted, and I know Landee is." Her mother's normally pristine clothes and hair were dirty and mussed.

"Of course! Here, let me bring your chairs."

"I can walk," Ireland assured her, brushing aside her granddaughter's offer of a steadying arm.

"Here," a man's voice said. "Have a seat right here."

Tobias had pulled two chairs a little closer. Just

enough to save their pride, while still saving them a few weary steps.

"What—What are you doing here?" Willow asked. She waited for her mother to take a seat before she sank into her own.

"Everleigh called me. She got a hit on that facial recognition app. I came as soon as I heard."

"You knew it was Homer?" Willow asked her daughter.

"Yes, but the age didn't make sense. What was that about?"

"It was his father who killed the boys. Nathaniel Homer is the spitting image of him." Willow leaned her head back, willing her face to stop throbbing. "Were you the one to call the police?"

"Certainly not the sheriff's office!" Everleigh scoffed. "Not when we suspected Mathers. I went straight to your friend in the Marshal Service."

Willow didn't bother with raising her head. "Don't start that again. He's a colleague, the same as—" She stopped, suddenly remembering Tobias was in the room. She was much too weary to think of complicated situations. "He's a colleague," she repeated.

"How did you know where to send him?" Ireland asked.

Grinning, Everleigh waved her cell phone. "The Family Circle tracking app. I know you don't like it, but it comes in quite handy at times, don't you think?"

"I think I've just become a huge fan," Ireland agreed. "Stalking and all."

"I, for one," Tobias added, "am glad your granddaughter was stalking your whereabouts."

"I know you're both wiped out, but I'm dying to know what happened. It was Homer all along?"

"Two generations of murderers," Willow confirmed. Eyes closed, she was so still, she almost appeared to be sleeping.

"I'm afraid so," Ireland confirmed. "One killed Benny, Josh, and Terell. One killed Gus."

"The warnings and my car were compliments of his daughter," Willow added. "Moon."

"No. Way." Everleigh's shocked gasp accompanied the words. "You're serious? Moon is his *daughter*?"

"The bad one. Sharika takes after her mother." Worry creased Ireland's forehead. "I do hope Carolyn is all right. She had no idea what a monster her husband was."

"I still can't believe this! Sharika and Moon are his daughters, and Moon was the one to torture us with her threats? What about all that self-improvement jargon she was peddling? That bit about spiritual accord and fulfilling your true purpose in life?" Everleigh hadn't believed in Moon's alternative lifestyle, but she had given the so-called spiritual guru credit for being sincere.

"That's all it was. She was peddling jargon," Ireland said.

"Apparently," Willow said around her swollen lip, "her true purpose in life was to follow in her father's footsteps."

Her eyes flew open when Tobias' voice spoke quietly beside her. "Put this on your cheek," he encouraged, offering her an impromptu ice pack. "It should help."

"Thank you," she whispered. "And thank you for coming."

"Hey," he said with a poignant smile, "I told you I was all in." He couldn't help but add a reprimand. "But you should have called me, you know. I would have gone with you two."

Willow couldn't seem to keep her eyes open, but she could still talk. Barely. "It turned out okay. I guess Karnie's charms really worked. They kept us safe."

"That they did," he agreed.

"Kudos to Karnie," she mumbled sleepily.

It had been a long day. A long three weeks. She had discovered a dead body, found the remains of three others, been threatened and harassed, and lost her faithful old car. There had been dead-end leads and misguided theories, and shadows of warning everywhere she looked. She had been backhanded in the face. Hard. But the worst by far was witnessing what greed could do to a person. How it twisted a person's soul and took root in their heart, poisoning the rest of their mind with darkness. The sum of it all had been exhausting.

"Kudos to *Intuitive Investigations*," Tobis replied.

Willow didn't hear him. She was already fast asleep in the chair.

30

Karnie

Outside, the wind howled as a late freeze swept across the mountain. Bits of frigid rain settled on the ground, dusting the earth with ice crystals. The mercury dipped further in the frosted night air.

Inside the cabin, the old woman was warm and cozy. She was loath to admit it, but that robe Gladys Ridley gave her turned out to be warm and fluffy. Coupled with a pair of warm socks and the house shoes Willow had given her, she was as toasty as could be. An antique quilt added the final layer of warmth and comfort.

Karnie took another swig of muscadine wine. She had warmed it on the stove and added a dab of butter. If anything could warm her on a night like this, it was a fine mug of buttered wine.

She adjusted the light at her side, that fancy LED lantern that lit up her cabin better than a half-dozen oil lamps. She had tucked into a gripping novel two nights ago, and she was eager to find out how it ended.

Kicking back the recliner, she settled in to read. Her new chair was a gift from the professor and Willow. He had noticed how her old one was propped up on a brick, so he brought in a nice new leather one that did a little of everything. She could sit up straight or she could recline. She could rock, and she could swivel. She could even do three of the four at one time.

She hadn't let on when they delivered it, but it was the best present she had ever received. Her old chair had lost its padding, and the threads had become brittle and prickly. At the end of a long day, these new foam cushions and the smooth feel of fine leather were a soothing balm for these old bones.

Her days were getting busier. She needed to finish hoeing the garden for spring crops. As soon as the frost melted away, she needed to put plants in the ground. Beets, cabbage, eggplants, and carrots were the first on her list. Onions, too, and summer peas. She still needed to store the last of the winter potatoes and turnips in a dry corner of the dug-out cellar.

There were always rocks and grass to clear out of her herb garden before the basil, chives, thyme, and dill could go in.

A stray hen had wandered her way, and with it came two baby chicks. If the Mustons didn't come round looking for them in a few days, she would need a new nesting box. She would have to gather dead grass for their bedding.

Later this week, Elroy would bring another

delivery. And one day next week, Willow planned to visit. It was a crowded schedule, but she reckoned she could make time for her friends.

The wind howled, but Karnie was snug in her new chair, nursing her hot drink and lost in the make-believe world of her book.

A contented smile settled on the bone witcher's weathered face.

Life didn't get much better than this.

****

FROM THE AUTHOR

I first had the idea for this book when a friend introduced me to 'bone witching,' often referred to as 'grave witching.' I can't explain it, but it works! I even tried it myself.

The rich tapestry of the Ozark Mountains provided the perfect setting for my new series. Each time we visit, I collect stories from the people I meet. I ask for local points of interest, the folklore and legends surrounding the area, historical landmarks, colorful characters who've left their mark in time, or any interesting tidbit that comes to mind. I've gathered old wives' tales, funny stories, natural remedies, and a deep appreciation for the oral histories and traditions of the Ozarks.

I'm borrowing some of those tales and beliefs to weave into my stories. For this book, I referred to Brandon Weston's "Granny Thornapple's Book of Charms" to shape some of Karnie's methods. Admittedly, some of her 'cures' and charms were figments of my imagination, but others are traditional charms and techniques still used by practicing folk healers.

I hope you've enjoyed reading this story as much as I enjoyed writing it. (Researching in person is always the best part!) Please follow the gals of *Intuitive Investigations* for their next adventure, coming this fall.

If you'd like to learn more about my books or to sign up for my email list, please visit www.beckiwillis.com. I love getting personal notes from readers, so drop in for an e-visit anytime at beckiwillis.ccp@gmail.com. And if you know any interesting tales of your own, please share. They might just wander into one of my books!

On a parting note, I have a favor to ask. Would you please take a moment to write a brief review of The Bone Witcher? Amazon reviews can make or break the success of a book—and it's author. A good word on social media, Amazon, BookBub, Goodreads, and personal recommendations to a friend are greatly appreciated.

Thank you so much for reading my story. And as the old-timers say, "Y'all come back now, ya hear?"

ABOUT THE AUTHOR

Best-selling indie and hybrid author Becki Willis loves crafting stories with believable characters in believable situations. Many of her stories stem from her own personal experiences. (No worries; she's never actually murdered anyone).

When she's not plotting danger and adventure for her imaginary friends, Becki enjoys reading, spending time with her family, unraveling a good mystery (real or imagined), dark chocolate, and a good cup of coffee. A professed history geek, Becki often weaves pieces of the past into her novels. Family is a central theme in her stories and in her life. She and her husband enjoy traveling but believe coming home to their Texas ranch is the best part of any trip.

Becki has won numerous awards—including two Killer Nashville Silver Falchion Awards, a dozen Texas Best's Awards, InD'Tale's coveted RONE, and been named Finalist for two Claymore Awards—but feels the real compliments come from her readers. Drop in for an e-visit anytime at beckiwillis.ccp@gmail.com, or www.beckiwillis.com.